Lying in Mid-Air

'Look, Lauryn, I might as well be honest about this. I came here thinking we'd have a nice long lunch, seduce each other over conversation, maybe play footsie under the table. But, now that you're here, I just don't want to wait that long. Do you know what I mean?'

A small slow smile shaped Lauryn's lips into a bow. Eyes shining, she nodded. 'I'm staying in a kind of rundown hotel,' she said apologetically. 'Nothing to write home about, unless you wanted to depress your parents.'

'Does it have four walls? And a door that locks?'

'Four walls, absolutely. Whether or not the door locks is another matter.'

'That's OK. I don't mind having an audience. As long as the maid's open-minded, it'll be perfect. Anywhere you are will be perfect.'

'You mean that?'

'Oh, you have no idea how much I mean it.'

'OK,' Lauryn said softly, almost in a whisper. 'Let's go.'

Other Cheek titles by the author:

TAMING JEREMY
HEAD-ON HEART

Lying in Mid-Air

Anne Tourney

In real life, always practise safe sex.

First published in 2007 by
Cheek
Thames Wharf Studios
Rainville Road
London W6 9HA

Copyright © Anne Tourney 2007

The right of Anne Tourney to be identified as the Author of the Work has been asserted in accordance with the Copyright, Designs and Patents Act 1988.

A catalogue record for this book is available from the British Library.
www.cheek-books.com

Typeset by SetSystems Ltd, Saffron Walden, Essex

The paper used in this book is a natural, recyclable product made from wood grown in sustainable forests. The manufacturing process conforms to the regulations of the country of origin.

ISBN 978 0 352 34142 6

Distributed in the USA by Holtzbrinck Publishers, LLC, 175 Fifth Avenue, New York, NY 10010, USA

All characters in this publication are fictitious and any resemblance to real persons, living or dead, is purely coincidental.

This book is sold subject to the condition that it shall not, by way of trade or otherwise, be lent, resold, hired out or otherwise circulated without the publisher's prior written consent in any form of binding or cover other than that in which it is published and without a similar condition including this condition being imposed on the subsequent purchaser.

eVerity Personality Profile

Is internet dating starting to feel cheap and sleazy? Meeting too many poseurs and scam artists in your cybersearch for love? Welcome to eVerity, the only online dating site that guarantees absolute sincerity from its members! We're so happy that you've made the decision to settle down with a soulmate. The partnerships that we create are meant to last for eternity, or until you die, whichever comes first (fidelity in case of sexual dysfunction or debilitating injury is not guaranteed). Help us determine your TQ – truth quotient – by completing our in-depth personality profile. Choose the answer that best describes your gut response. Elaborate in the text boxes below each question. And always be ruthlessly honest, because ... *in love we trust!*

Would you date a man who had a history of being less than open in his intimate relationships?

Lauryn: Yes. When you say 'less than open', you're talking about lying, right? I don't think I've ever dated a man who wasn't deceitful in some way. I tend to go for the charming bullshitters. I wouldn't be attracted to anyone who tortured small animals or conned old ladies out of their life savings. But sexy liars? Sure. Why not? Lies are the lube of identity.

Veronica: No. Crazy, yes. Lying, never. Don't lie to me unless you're Pinocchio, and I'm sitting on your face.

Chloe: Maybe. I'm stupid with guys. My last boyfriend lied to me all the time. I think he got a thrill out lying; his stories were so bizarre. Every few weeks, he would tell me that he had to spend a few days visiting his sister in Alaska. She could never come to visit him here in San Francisco because she had a rare genetic disorder that made her skin peel off when it was exposed to sunlight, and she was too embarrassed to go out in public. Eventually I figured out that he didn't even have a sister, and, every time he said he was going to Alaska, he was really screwing another woman who lived in my apartment building. Needless to say, we're not together any more. But I'm still a disaster with guys.

Have you ever lied to make yourself seem more attractive to a member of the opposite sex?

Lauryn: No. Well, occasionally. Reality can be such a grind sometimes; you need a vacation now and then. A little creative embellishment never killed anybody. But, in my heart, I do believe that honesty is the foundation of any meaningful lasting relationship. If I thought I had a chance at finding my soulmate, I'd make an effort to present myself as openly as possible. In return, I'm a warm, accepting, forgiving lover, who doesn't mind if her partner tells a few white lies to improve his public image.

Veronica: No. Why would I lie about myself? I'm young, I'm hot ... and I'm pierced in all the right places. Boys want me. I want boys. End of story.

Chloe: No. I don't believe in lying. I know this sounds lame, but I'm looking for something eternal. Immortal, even. I want to be able to look into my lover's eyes and see his soul – beautiful and clear and pure. Why would he expect anything less from me?

Would you end a relationship if you found out that your partner had lied to you?

Lauryn: No. See above.

Veronica: Yes. Was my first answer not absolutely clear to you, you moronic excuse for a dating service?

Chloe: Maybe. I would hope that it would never get to that point, but, if I loved my partner enough, I'd be willing to work through it with him. I'd at least try couples therapy first. Therapy is good. Lots and lots of therapy.

Chapter One

Three Women, Three Orgasms

The pre-dawn hours were Lauryn's favourite time for sex, while her head was still too fuzzy to worry about the random dislocations of her curly hair, or the fact that her eyes were two different colours – the left blue, the right green – before she put in her tinted hazel contact lenses.

Today, waking up alone, the hair and the eyes were both moot points, but she still felt like indulging in some solitary self-amusement. She wasn't all that horny, but her muscles held a cranky tension that felt like it needed to be soothed before she martialled her body through the day's routine. In eight minutes her alarm would go off. In an hour she'd be heading for the airport in a taxi: another flight, another business trip. Nine hours from now, Lauryn would be advising yet another human resources committee about 'streamlining their workforce' and 'trimming corporate fat', all the while feeling like a blonde android from a TV infomercial about exercise equipment.

Reaching into the drawer of her nightstand, she fumbled for her vibrator. She finally found it wedged between a grove of prescription bottles and a book of inspirational thoughts called *Daily Spiritual Gems For Women Who Are Too Busy To Breathe*. Her fingernail snagged on the spiral-bound edge of a notebook she bought on her last trip; she had filled three pages with resolutions for self-improvement before abandoning the journal to oblivion in her nightstand. Now, ready for takeoff, she lay back among the pillows and parted her thighs.

Lauryn shuffled through her mental File-o-Fantasies, settling on a sweet memory of being tongued to a shimmering orgasm by a guy who washed dishes at Bob's Big Boy where Lauryn's mother worked as a waitress. Ned was his name, or Nico, or was it Nemo? Lauryn couldn't remember, but she knew it started with an N. She dated him for about fifteen minutes while she was at home for Christmas break during her sophomore year in college. A surfer, whose tangled sun-streaked hair was always stiff with salt, he had written Lauryn a love poem on the back of a napkin, and had handed it to her folded up in an iridescent abalone shell. What could she do, after that, but fall into bed with him, fucking him on the Raggedy Ann bedspread that she'd had since she was six years old? In the bedroom of the shabby San Diego duplex where she grew up, with 'Jingle Bell Rock' playing on the radio, Lauryn had had an orgasm that was worthy of a beach in Maui.

Whatever happened to Ned/Nico/Nemo, anyway? He was probably working at a surf shop, or cramming fruit into a blender at a smoothie stand in some mall in San Diego. Or maybe he'd finished his two-year English degree at community college, and was publishing his poems on the internet. She'd have to look him up some day ... if she could remember his last name.

As she flipped the switch on the vibrator with her thumbnail, Lauryn's flesh softened automatically, a conditioned response to a buzzing whose results would be as precise and predictable as a hedge-trimmer.

Nothing.

Her hand plunged back into the drawer, frantically digging through her bedside clutter. But Lauryn, even after four years of college majoring in business with a minor in anthropology, followed by two years in an MBA programme and six years building a career as a consultant, *never* thought far enough ahead to buy batteries for her vibrator.

'Shit,' she said, throwing the useless plastic egg across the room. 'Shit, shit, shit!'

A small head, topped by triangular ears, popped up from the blankets, as Lauryn's cat woke up and leaped after the flying toy. At least one pussy would be entertained this morning, Lauryn thought, as the numbers on her digital clock shifted, and her alarm went off.

But she couldn't stop thinking about Ned, and now she was drenched, her body still waiting for the buzz that had never come. Her index finger felt more like Ned's tongue, anyway, gentle and deft, teasing out the button buried in her lower lips. The memory of that tongue was almost ten years old; like a fine whisky, its burn mellowed and ripened, while its flavour grew richer and more potent. Ned had been a virtuoso lover, instinctively pinpointing the half-centimetre spot on Lauryn's clit – the microscopic summit of a tiny pink Everest – that brought her to a shattering peak in less than four minutes. She opened one eye and looked at the clock: 6:07.

Lauryn sighed as her hand slipped free from the damp clutch of her inner thighs. She'd taken care of her own sexual needs, easing the tension from her mind and body, and she was only seven minutes behind schedule.

Who said she wasn't efficient?

I desperately need more glamour in my life, Veronica thought, staring off the edge of her futon at the rogue Cheeto lying on the floor. Either that, or a better vacuum cleaner. Or a lover who doesn't leave snack-food trails everywhere he goes, like a post-modern Hansel, struggling to find his way through the freaking forest of life.

Devin stirred beside her, mumbling something about World of Warlocks as his hands cupped Veronica's breasts. Her boyfriend was a diehard gamer; he could lose himself in the alternate universe behind a computer monitor for days on end. Veronica was a recovering gaming addict, herself; in fact, she and Devin had met in an online tournament. Veronica had been playing an oversexed witch who cast spells with her magical pussy powers. Devin had been playing an evil dwarf. Veronica had become so intimate with him as the sadistic hunchbacked Machiavolicus that she'd been surprised to meet him as a soft-spoken beanpole named Devin, with baby-blue eyes that looked constantly astonished at finding himself in the 'real' world.

Devin was still gaming; he'd practically made a career of it, opening up a shop online to sell magical objects, power points and weapons to gamers who weren't skilled enough to earn those items for themselves. He didn't earn enough to pay rent for his own apartment, or buy a car, but he was so widely liked among his geeky buddies that he managed to coast through life without a permanent address or any reliable source of transportation.

Devin was a man of many talents; unfortunately for his chequing account, all of them involved either gaming or sex. He was giving Veronica's breasts their morning massage now, milking her nipples in a way that drove her mad. Annoyed as she was by the random Cheeto, Veronica's hips were still doing their usual dance in response to Devin's nimble fingers. He had an intuitive way of knowing when she was pissed off and needed extra fondling; his left hand had given up her breast and had worked its way down to the damp silken folds between her legs.

'Mmm,' she sighed. 'Play that tune a little faster.'

Devin obeyed. He was such a sweet guy, maybe a bit too sweet. Veronica wished he'd get the urge to smack her ass now and then, or pull her hair, but he was eternally respectful, perpetually polite.

'Permission to enter?' he murmured into her ear. He was also an incorrigible nerd.

With an impatient grunt, Veronica parted her legs and thrust her bottom backwards. For once, she wished he'd just take her, raw and crude, without asking for her blessing. Still, he had a beautiful cock, long but not too long, thick but not too thick; whenever he entered her, Veronica felt like a well-fucked Goldilocks. Everything was just right. Devin's fingers had found her trigger button, and he was tickling her lightly as he slid back and forth in time to the rocking of Veronica's hips. His breathing grew harsh, and she heard him stifle a groan. She knew he wouldn't come until he felt her go tense all over, felt her inner muscles do their squeeze-dance around his shaft.

She was almost there, her body tight as a cat about to leap, except for the loose, humming, simmering zone below her waist. Veronica knew an outstanding orgasm when she felt one coming on, and this was going to be a doozy. Devin had gotten so skilled at playing her pussy that he could bring her to a climax in minutes; add to that the rhythmic friction of his thrusting, and Veronica was approaching heaven. Too bad she was an atheist.

A coarse moan burst from Veronica's lips as she toppled over the edge, giving herself over to the waves of pleasure.

'Oh, Vee. I can't live without you,' Devin said into her ear at the critical moment.

Veronica stiffened. Her spasms didn't stop, but her brain suddenly kicked into red alert. *I can't live without you.* What was that supposed to mean? Was Devin going to ask if he could move in permanently? Was he planning to ask her if he could borrow her vehicle, an old hearse that she'd painted pink, to drive to that gaming convention he wanted to attend in Florida?

Or maybe the 'I can't live without you' was just Devin's response to sexual passion, a quirk he hadn't exhibited up until now. They'd only been dating for three months; he could have a whole host of idiosyncrasies that Veronica knew nothing about.

He was launching into his own orgasm now, his hands gripping Veronica's hipbones. After he had panted his way to a finish, Devin plunged into sleep.

Sheesh. That was a close one. Veronica edged away from Devin's unconscious body. He was a sweet guy. A genuinely *nice* guy. He always made her come first; he could mix up a mouth-watering marinara sauce using nothing but tomato paste, water and blind faith; he was polite and considerate and never left the lid up on the toilet seat.

But ... Devin wasn't going anywhere in life. And Veronica was. Her job sucked, but she had plans for something better. Huge plans. She was going to start her own business, involving sex and glamour and absolutely no witches, dwarves or Cheetos.

This thing with Devin, as nice as it was, had a definite expiry date.

Meanwhile, Veronica had to get to the airport, where she worked as a shoeshine slave. She climbed off the futon, gave Devin a swift peck on the cheek, and padded off to the bathroom for a scalding hot shower.

They met at night, long past moonrise, under the cherry tree in the garden behind the house she shared with her husband. All dishonour faded under the white veil of the tree's blossoms, which shifted above her as she gazed past her lover's head. The moon peered down at her, a tender conspirator, giving her a reprieve from her shame. What shame could there be in love like this? Her lover's hands and mouth held nothing but worship; he had unwrapped the sash of her kimono as if he were breaking open the door of a sealed shrine, and it wasn't until he had stroked her body into life that he began to kiss the twin cherries of her nipples.

Her nipples ... they had always been so responsive, rising at a brush with silk, a breath, a glance. Her lover's lips were teasing them now to a point that was almost unbearable. When his mouth began to travel, mothlike, down her belly, she arched her back, feline, her nails digging into his back. She didn't care who saw the raised red tracks she left on his skin; he was hers to mark however she wished.

Later, she would write a poem about their meeting tonight, and have it delivered to him. The first line was already taking shape in her head, even as she gave herself over to the avalanche of her climax...

[I] you find under cherry tree
[You] limp to with weak heart...

The screech of the electric tea kettle almost knocked Chloe off her chair. Talk about weak hearts – her own had shot off like a startled pigeon at the sound of a contemporary appliance. Though her body had just been yanked back to 21st-century San Francisco, her mind was still in tenth-century Japan.

'Limp with weak heart,' she muttered to herself, glancing at the poem she'd been translating. 'So my lover has erectile dysfunction and a heart condition. Nice job!'

As she hopped up to silence the tea kettle, Chloe's big toe caught on the leg of her folding chair, making a gruesome little crunch as it separated from the rest of her foot. Mute with pain, she dropped to the floor, cradling her foot and rocking back and forth to the squeal of the tea kettle.

Chloe's family thought she dwelled in an ongoing fantasy about the past, divorced from the grim realities of modern life. If only they could see her now, suffering the side effects of a graduate student's miserably poor existence: cheap furniture (the old folding chair that she'd found outside by the dumpster) and cheaper shoes (the straw flip-flops that she'd bought in Little Tokyo because they reminded her of Japan, while costing next to nothing). If she had decent furniture, solid footwear and adequate funding from the Department of Asian Studies, she wouldn't be writhing in pain in the middle of a mouldy basement studio apartment.

Her pride smarted along with her toe as Chloe recalled the note her father had included along with the last cheque – just a loan, of course – he had mailed her. *If this poetry thing doesn't work out, sweetheart, I'd be happy to find you a job here at the firm. We can always use translators for our Tokyo clients.*

'This poetry thing', which her wealthy dad could wave away like a horsefly at a picnic, happened to be Chloe's life. She hadn't studied Japanese for eight years so that she could nod and simper and pour tea for her father's Japanese clients. And that's exactly what she'd be doing if she worked at his architectural firm: filling some fake position as a 'translator', while mincing around playing the role of waitress-slash-ass-kisser at company meetings. Chloe couldn't have translated design specs into Japanese to save her life, any more than her father could appreciate the stunning simplicity of a *haiku*.

Chloe dragged herself to her feet and hobbled over to the corner that served as her kitchen. Stupid straw flip-flops. They were probably meant to last for a summer, but she'd been wearing them for four years. She poured hot water over a tea bag, green tea scented with jasmine, and watched the liquid turn amber, the scent of dried flowers rising from the mug.

'Wish I hadn't given up coffee,' Chloe sighed, suddenly longing for a rich black jolt of caffeinated brew. She'd been up for most of the night, trying to finish a set of translations for her poetry seminar, which would start in five hours. She'd been working so intently that she'd started to hallucinate, imagining that she herself was a female poet from courtly Japan, having a tryst with some anonymous nobleman under a flowering cherry tree.

The men Chloe had been meeting lately had been far

less than noble. Most of them were grad students, just as broke as herself, and the dates would end in a wrangle over the bill for dinner, followed by a wrangle for sex.

Chloe didn't want insta-sex. What she craved didn't even exist any more: a long convoluted courtship, spiced with intrigue and flowers and poetry, handwritten on notes, which her lover would tuck into secret places in her apartment for her to find. She imagined something like the doomed love affair between the ninth-century poet Ono No Komachi and her nobleman; the beautiful poet had promised to become his lover, if he would visit her for one hundred nights. The guy had almost succeeded, but he'd caught a cold one night, or something, and didn't make the cut. He'd died of frustrated love and longing.

So beautiful. So tragic. To die for the woman you desired, in a love immortalised through erotic verse: that was the kind of commitment that Chloe wanted. Instead, she got groping, pizza that she always seemed to end up paying for and last-minute dates arranged by Instant Messenger.

No wonder she was staying up till all hours tweaking those ancient love poems, working and reworking each phrase. Chloe wasn't a perfectionist; she was just a garden-variety escapist.

Pressing her mug of tea between her breasts, she limped back to her desk and switched off her lamp. Then she made her way over to the futon that lay on her floor – one advantage of minimalist Japanese decor was that it saved her a lot of money – and lay down to finish her cherry-blossom fantasy. The mug of tea grew cool on the floor beside her bed as Chloe opened up her thighs for her imaginary nobleman and let him do things to her that would never be described in any *tanka* poem. *Tanka* was all about the elliptical image, the sensuous allusion. And really, that was what Chloe wanted, to have a curtain drawn over sex at the hot raging peak, so that she could savour her orgasm in blissful darkness. As she drifted down, it occurred to Chloe that the nobleman in her fantasy looked disturbingly like her therapist, Aidan.

'Holy crap!'

Chloe sat bolt upright on her futon. Heart pounding, she stared through the darkness at the ceiling as a terrible thought occurred to her.

She wasn't going to her translation seminar today. She was supposed to be on a plane in two hours, flying to Chicago to read a paper at a conference given by the Society of Ancient Asian Verse, arranged by her graduate adviser, and paid for by her father, in the hope that this whole 'poetry thing' might someday bring his daughter a little more than a fondness for daydreaming.

Chloe tunnelled into the futon and threw her comforter over her head.

'Humans don't fly. Humans don't fly,' she muttered to herself.

On her desk sat a paperback book entitled *You CAN Overcome Your Worst Nightmares*, along with a prescription bottle containing two Xanax: one for the flight to Chicago, one for the flight back. Now those pills weren't going to do her any good, because, consciously or subconsciously, she had forgotten all about presenting the paper that she'd sweat blood over for the past six months. There was no way she could take a shower, get dressed and snag a taxi in time make her flight.

No way.

Besides, everyone knew that humans weren't built to fly.

Chapter Two

Cruising Altitude

Desire is a disease whose primary symptom is a willingness to lie.

Who used to say that? Lauryn wondered. Probably her college roommate, Cynthia, the philosophy major who never shaved her armpits and renamed herself Snatch. If Snatch had been right, and desire was truly a sickness, then Lauryn should be quarantined.

Flipping through the copy of *Vogue* that she'd bought at the airport newsstand, Lauryn felt dizzy with lust. Lust for a restorative cream that would wipe out wrinkles and flatten her belly, for a titanium bracelet, for a rococo ceiling like the one in the layout of the heiress du jour's Paris apartment. With every business trip, *Vogue* seemed to get fatter, as its advertisers fought for the attention of women like Lauryn, women who wanted too much, but who couldn't afford to buy anything but magazines.

Lauryn's head throbbed. The black velvet headband she was wearing – her attempt to look glamorous in spite of not having been motivated to wash her hair that morning – was blocking the blood flow to her brain. The headache was unpleasant, but not unbearable; it gave her an excuse to ignore the laptop that she'd brought with her for the trip. She should have been reviewing her spreadsheets right now, getting ready to play executioner at the food-processing plant in Oakland that was planning a series of lay-offs. Instead, she hugged her *Vogue* like a teddy bear and leaned her head against the window. Watching the other passengers move down the aisle, she assessed them one by one, trying to predict who her seatmate would be.

Not you, she prayed, looking at the wild-eyed woman wearing the tie-dyed blouse and the PETA button. No one with kids, please. And no hound dogs; Lauryn wasn't in the mood for being hit on today.

The stream of passengers had trickled to a stop. So far, the seat beside Lauryn was still empty. For the first time since she left her apartment that morning, Lauryn let herself exhale. Chicago to San Francisco, with nothing but her phonebook-sized *Vogue*, a few morning cocktails and her own company.

Bliss.

Or it would have been, if Lauryn had been able to stop thinking about the person who should have been sitting next to her. As she watched the flight attendant jadedly perform her semaphores about what to do in an airline disaster, Lauryn wondered what had happened to the missing passenger. Had she/he been hit by a car on the way to the airport? Hooked up at a bar the night before and decided to spend the morning in bed with a new lover? Won the lottery? Been called away to somewhere distant and romantic and glamorous?

Reviewing these possible accidents of fate, it dawned on Lauryn that she spent way too much time dreaming up alternate futures for total strangers, and not nearly enough time planning her own. Here she was on another grim business trip, preparing to justify the lay-offs of over two hundred people. Her apartment was empty of all other life forms; even her cat was on vacation at a friend's house in the suburbs. Lauryn's wardrobe looked like a yoga instructor's cast-offs, though Lauryn herself hadn't done as much as the mountain pose in months. She was a 28-year-old woman clutching a magazine filled with images of lives she'd never have, furniture and clothes she could never hope to buy, paper strips of perfume and packets of lotion that she couldn't possibly afford.

'Excuse me.' Lauryn hailed the flight attendant. 'Could I get a double gin and tonic?'

The long-stemmed brunette turned her fawnlike eyes, slightly widened, on to Lauryn. So graceful, so slim, so lovely. How many exotic cities had those big Bambi eyes seen? Lauryn had wanted to be a flight attendant once, about a hundred years ago, back in the days when they were still called stewardesses.

'We'll be serving drinks after take-off,' the flight attendant said. She obviously hadn't perfected her professional neutrality yet; a hint of reproach seeped into her voice.

'What if we forget about the tonic, and you just bring me a couple of mini-bottles of gin?' Lauryn suggested.

Bambi's eyes grew huge. Lauryn imagined a set of cogs turning in her pretty head as she tried to remember whether pre-flight cocktails were allowed by FAA regulations.

'Oh, forget it,' Lauryn grumbled. 'I can wait.'

She raised her *Vogue* in front of her face like a fencing mask, and pretended to concentrate on an ad for a rejuvenating foot soak. The ad, picturing a model sinking her toes into a basin in which a miniature Garden of Eden was growing, promised that its soaking salts would restore your aching swollen feet to their original pristine condition.

Lauryn found this advertisement reassuring. *Vogue*'s advertisers knew the truth about the magazine's readers; they were not just heiresses, models, creative types or professionals in business suits. They were sales clerks and nurses who worked long shifts on their feet, secretaries who wore pumps that were too narrow. They were women like Lauryn, who humped around airports all across the country, dragging their carry-on luggage behind them in a perpetual race for –

An annoying thump broke into Lauryn's thoughts. So much for having the row to herself; a lumpy leather bag had landed in the seat beside her. The bag's owner stood beside her seat, trying to cram another carry-on item into the overhead compartment. Lauryn stared at the bag. Somehow its battered misshapen appearance offended her. It looked like something that would belong to a person who never had quite as much money as they needed to lead the kind of life they wanted, someone who was perpetually behind the power curve in life, always vaguely off-track.

Someone, in other words, too much like herself to be intriguing.

Lauryn yawned and leaned her head against the window. She closed her eyes and pretended to be asleep. Now, if only she could stay alert enough to catch the rattle and clink of the drinks cart when it trundled by...

'Hey. Mind if I look at your magazine?'

Lauryn opened one eye. The owner of the ugly bag had settled in the seat beside her. The brown beast was now resting on his lap. He cradled it gently with one hand. Was he smuggling a live iguana in that thing?

As Lauryn's one-eyed gaze moved across the bag, she couldn't help noticing that her seatmate was pretty damn attractive. He wore frayed, rumpled khakis, a long-sleeved denim shirt and a pair of glasses that sat crookedly on his nose. His faded shirt made his eyes look searingly blue. His hair was the same colour as his slacks, and almost as rumpled, sticking out in dark-blond tufts around his open, almost-but-not-quite handsome face.

'Did you say you wanted to look at my magazine?' Lauryn repeated.

The owner of the ugly bag smiled. His smile, like the wire frames of his glasses, was off-kilter, but somehow it worked for him. Lauryn felt a lurch in the pit of her belly, where her warmest, darkest feelings came from.

She almost didn't recognise that response at first; it had been so long since she'd felt that instant gut-deep desire.

'I know what you're thinking,' he said. 'You're thinking that either I must be gay, or that I'm straight and I want to spend the flight drooling over the models.'

'Well, no,' Lauryn said, although she *had* been thinking something along those lines. 'You just surprised me. But here. Knock yourself out.'

She handed over the *Vogue* with a sense of disappointment. Now this rumpled, crooked, increasingly attractive stranger would spend the rest of the trip ogling photos of women who were far prettier and thinner than Lauryn.

'Actually, I'm not gay. And I wouldn't be interested in any of these women, unless maybe they gained fifty pounds.'

He took the magazine from Lauryn. The contrast between his long tanned masculine fingers and the magazine's glossy pages made Lauryn's mouth go dry. She loved 'guy' hands – strong capable hands, maybe with the knuckles a bit banged up, and the cuticles ragged, and the nails cut crooked, or chewed.

'I shot the photos for an article in this issue,' he went on.

'Really? I'm impressed.'

'Don't be. They're just a couple of shots from Rome. I wanted to take another look at them; I'm bad that way. Always second-guessing myself after my stuff is in print.'

He straightened his glasses on his nose and squinted at one of the pages, staring at the images with a critical scowl that reminded Lauryn of the way she felt when she looked at her thighs in the mirror. At least she understood the banged-up bag now, and the protective way he held it in his lap. He was flying home from a photo assignment, probably somewhere exotic, and the bag held his cameras and equipment. Ugly battered bags were OK, Lauryn decided, as long as they held expensive toys.

'You're kidding me, right?' Lauryn asked. 'You're a *Vogue* photographer?'

He shook his head, his smile widening. Now that those blue eyes were focused on Lauryn, they looked significantly less critical. In fact, to her amazement, they seemed delighted to be staring at her.

'I'm not a *Vogue* photographer. I'm a freelancer who got lucky. I'm also a jerk. Here I am getting my fingerprints all over your shiny new magazine, and I don't even know what your name is.'

'It's Lauryn. With a "y".'

'Lauryn with a why,' he repeated. Then he grinned. 'With a woman like you, no one would ever ask why.'

Coming from any other male stranger, that remark would have made Lauryn feel like she'd been splattered with slime. But the curve of his mouth and the light in his blue eyes made it clear that he didn't take himself that seriously. He'd just tossed a shimmering ball in the air, and was waiting to see if Lauryn wanted to join his game.

'So what's your name?' she asked. Brilliant counterplay.

'Joel. With a, um, J.' He scratched his head. 'I guess there aren't too many ways to spell 'Joel', or I might have tried to be more original.'

Lauryn laughed. 'Being original isn't always a good thing. I changed my name to add the 'y' when I was in college. I thought it would make me seem more sophisticated.'

'Has it worked for you so far?'

'Sure.' Lauryn shrugged. 'The only problem is, I have to spell it for everyone to make sure they know how sophisticated I am.'

'So tell me about yourself, Lauryn.'

'What do you want to know?'

'Tell me about college. Tell me about high school. Hell, tell me about kindergarten – this is a long flight.'

Joel let the pages of *Vogue* fall shut, a shimmering cascade of unattainable images. He crossed one long leg over the other, no small feat in such a cramped space, and leaned back in his seat as if there was nothing he'd rather do than sit next to Lauryn on this plane, listening to her talk about herself.

Poor Joel. From the clothes he was wearing, and the beat-up camera bag, Lauryn would have said he was an idealist, a knee-jerk liberal, a firm believer in full disclosure from the very first moments of any relationship, especially a relationship that might involve nudity, tongue-kissing and sweaty groping in the near future. There he sat waiting for her story, with those frank blue eyes and that self-deprecating grin that made the back of Lauryn's neck prickle. He probably assumed that whatever came out of Lauryn's mouth would be the Truth, with a capital T.

Little did he know...

As soon as an airplane reached cruising altitude, Lauryn was in a truth-free zone. Up here, thousands of feet from the ground, she could be anyone she wanted. Lying, for Lauryn, was like a hot-oil massage for the imagination, complete with aromatherapy, ambient music playing in the background and the occasional sip of warm brandy.

The things she made up about herself, the stories she created, weren't *really* lies anyway; they were aspects of her identity that hadn't been realised yet. Putting it that way, Lauryn's casual embellishments sounded like a New Age self-improvement project, a profound exploration of self and soul. Not at all like the typical bullshit you might tell a stranger on a plane, just to make yourself seem a little more glamorous, feel a little less drab.

Lauryn smiled. She was glad she'd put on lip gloss that morning. 'Well, I got my bachelor's in business administration from UCLA. I got my MBA from Yale.'

'Yale? Wow. An Ivy-League girl.'

'Yes,' Lauryn sighed. 'It was rough, going to college in California, having grown up in Massachusetts. That's why I went back East for my MBA. My family has a house on Cape Cod. They've been there for ages and ages. One of those crazy, sprawling families, you know? My dad's a lawyer, one of those straight-up, classic honest guys. My mother was a famous beauty, that was her claim to fame. That and her seven kids.'

'Seven?'

Lauryn rolled her eyes at the thought of her fictional family. 'Yes. Can you believe it? I grew up with six brothers and sisters. Talk about competition! But you know, that's what helped me succeed. Growing up with all that love ... and all that talent around me. My brothers and sisters are amazing – every single one of them is an overachiever in one way or another. I had to be constantly on point to keep up, but I always knew that no matter what I did, I'd find unconditional acceptance in that crazy house.'

That crazy house. That crazy childhood. Yes, it had been crazy, all right, growing up in a two-bedroom apartment with a single mother who worked as a waitress at Bob's Big Boy. But Joel didn't need to know that. Lauryn felt a pang of guilt as she watched his face change in response to the twists and turns of her fake family history. She imagined a poster of herself, a mug shot hanging in the post office, with a notice for her arrest: DAUGHTER OF SINGLE MOTHER, FATHER UNKNOWN, COMMUNITY-COLLEGE GRAD: SOUGHT FOR IMPERSONATING THE SUCCESSFUL IVY-LEAGUE-EDUCATED OFFSPRING OF A PROSPEROUS NUCLEAR FAMILY.

But what were the chances that Joel would go to that hypothetical post office and find out who Lauryn really was? They'd never see each other after the flight. When the plane landed, they would go their separate ways, or maybe, if Lauryn were unusually lucky, they'd end up having too many cocktails together and fall into a bed somewhere later. Either way, the life Lauryn had invented would dissolve in Joel's memory like a sugar-free breath mint, its fakeness sweet, fleeting and entirely unreal.

'So what are you doing now?' Joel asked. 'With a background like that, you must have an awesome career.'

Lauryn hadn't intended to go any further than the fictional family, but here was Joel, holding the door open for her with a flourish. How could she resist an opening like that?

'Well, as a matter of fact, my life *is* pretty amazing. I owe it all to my family. They were so supportive of me going into international finance. I audit businesses all over the world on a contract basis. I spent the last three months in Paris; now I'm on my way to corporate headquarters in San Francisco. My next trip will be to Belgium. I'll be in Bruges all winter. Have you ever been there?'

'The closest I've been to Belgium was the bottom of a chocolate box,' he said. 'But it's at the top of my list. I always wanted to go – just never found the right excuse. Why don't you tell me all about it?'

And like an Amtrak derailing into the rosy clouds of Lauryn's imagination, she hurtled into space, inventing a job, a social life and repertoire of sensual experiences that were far, far better than her own.

Life on airplanes seemed to be in a perpetual state of shrinkage. Shrinking leg room; shrinking bags of peanuts (now almost universally replaced by pretzels); shrinking meal service, reduced to bone-dry sandwiches that you had to pay for. Even the pillows and blankets felt thinner these days. Joel used to love flying, but lately it felt less like an adventure and more like an exercise in endurance.

Until today. Sitting next to Lauryn, listening to her talk about her jobs in Paris, Geneva, Tokyo, Joel felt the world grow large again. Life didn't have to feel like the inside of a shoebox, he suddenly remembered – there was a whole panorama of colours and tastes and smells out there, waiting to be savoured, *needing* to be savoured. Because, as much as we need pleasure, Joel believed, pleasure needs us, too.

He'd had that lesson pounded into his brain on his last assignment, at a monastery in Tibet. Photographing the monastery – the ancient structures, the monks going about their daily routines, the glorious mountains – was the toughest challenge he'd taken on to date. Joel had spent six weeks not only capturing that simple rarified world, but also following the monks' routines: waking, working, sleeping.

Joel had even tried to learn to meditate, but, whenever he sat still, his mind kept drifting to sex. The more he tried not to think about the smell and taste and texture of the lovers he'd left behind, the more alarmingly vivid his fantasies became, until the images of female flesh took on a hallucinatory life of their own. All of the details of the world around him, from the lush green curves of the mountains to the pure fragrance of the high-altitude air to the juices of the fruit he ate for breakfast, reminded him of sex, hitting his senses with a sharpness that left him reeling. Out of all the hours he'd spent attempting to release his thoughts and bring his mind back into focus, he'd experienced maybe thirty seconds of uneroticised clarity. Maybe. It was probably more like fifteen.

But, during all those long quiet days that he spent obsessing over sex, Joel had also done a lot of thinking about his life. The silence of the monastery tended to make you contemplative, whether you wanted to be or not. By the time his six-week stay was over, Joel had realised three important things: he was a horny pleasure-addicted bastard; he was unenlightened and probably unenlightenable; and he desperately needed a vacation. Not a vacation from work, because Joel hadn't exactly been deluged with assignments lately, but from the constant grinding stress and instability of being a freelancer. He wanted to settle down for a while into something semi-permanent, maybe pick up a gig at an architectural firm or a studio, and enjoy the ease of a predictable cash flow. But, first, he wanted to play. He wanted to take long aimless walks with his Nikon; meet fascinating women; get rip-roaring drunk and watch baseball; stuff himself on fattening food. If you wanted to do all that, you couldn't do better than San Francisco.

'This restaurant had an exhaustive wine list,' Lauryn was saying. 'It was like reading an epic poem; I didn't know where to start! We finally settled on a pinot grigio, to go with the lobster ravioli.'

Joel nodded and smiled, trying to keep his eyes fixed on Lauryn's. It was hard, though, because the animated motions of her hands kept drawing his attention to her breasts. She was wearing a black leotard with no bra, and – he would love to believe – no panties. Over the leotard she wore loose cotton pants, in a shade of natural hemp. When he first saw her, her hair was heavily disciplined with a strip of black cloth. She had since taken the band off, complaining of a headache, and the adorable mess of her blonde curls made Joel wonder why she ever thought the band was a good idea to begin with.

'I love fine dining, don't you?' she rhapsodised.

'Most definitely.' Joel couldn't remember the last time he'd eaten at a place where your meal wasn't assigned a number.

'I'm probably obsessed with food, but eating is such a

sensual experience, so all-consuming. Think about it. We're not only engaging all of our senses when we have a meal, we're taking matter into our bodies, making it part of who we are. Who wouldn't take all that seriously?'

'It's a lot to deal with,' Joel agreed.

Clearly, this was a woman who preferred what Joel thought of as 'real stuff' – no McAnything for Lauryn. The rings on her fingers had to be pure silver, and her clothes had not even a thread of polyester (even her lint was 100 per cent natural, he assumed). She drank high-end wines and dined at the best restaurants and the only kind of peanut butter in her kitchen would be that natural salt-free kind, with chunks.

Intense. She was an intense girl – woman, he corrected himself internally, no *person* – pursuing life at full throttle, always reaching for the best, the richest, the fullest.

Which meant that Joel would probably strike out. He was an average guy, clad in polyester-blend khakis, and he had bought the frames for his glasses from an optometrist at SaveMart. But all his deficiencies only made him want her more. Didn't every man, at one point in his life, fall for a woman who was higher up on the food chain than he was? Didn't the mating dance demand the occasional lunge for something better?

'God, how embarrassing.' Lauryn laughed, shovelling handfuls of curls off her face. Her high cheekbones were stained with pink. 'I've been talking about myself through this whole flight! Non-stop Lauryn, from Chicago to San Francisco. You must be bored senseless.'

'Not at all. Your life is fascinating. Way more so than mine.'

'Oh, I can't believe that. You being a freelance photographer and all, getting paid to run around the world having adventures.'

'I only get paid for the pictures,' Joel admitted. 'Not for the running-around part. And any adventures I have are usually accidental.'

Lauryn laughed, a smoky purr that seemed to vibrate in the pit of Joel's belly. As she leaned over to sip her cocktail, Joel let himself have one quick look at her cleavage. Her breasts were smallish, firm, round, with stubborn little nipples that seemed to be doing their best to burst through her leotard. Her rib cage was narrow, her waist even narrower, and the baggy pants couldn't hide the lean grace of her legs. In short, she was built like a dancer.

Joel loved dancers – or women who were built like them, or even women who *wished* they were built like them. He wasn't really all that picky. He craved women in general; in fact, he was beginning to suspect he was addicted.

But he met a few women, here and there, who rose above the rest of the female population. Watching Lauryn, sneaking stealthy glances at her body, reminded him of a trip to the Serengeti five years ago. As he photographed the lionesses, sheer gold swimming through tall brown grass, Joel felt a longing that was equal parts lust and envy. Crouched down with his camera, hiding behind the telephoto lens, he wished he could be an animal, too, so he could capture one of those female cats and mate with her in the African sun...

'I wish I could take better pictures,' Lauryn remarked. 'Mine always come out blurry, or crooked, with people's heads cut off. I've decapitated most of my friends and relatives. Even the relatively decent ones are, well, boring. I don't have much of an eye.'

'It takes time and practice,' Joel said vaguely, hoping he sounded like a seasoned pro, and not just some guy on a plane regurgitating the same advice you could get from your high-school art teacher. The truth was, time and practice didn't cut it for every amateur photographer. Sometimes what was needed was not only a new pair of eyes, but a whole new head.

'That's my problem. I don't have the time,' Lauryn said. 'I'm always working. Even when I'm in a foreign country, I hardly ever take pictures. I'd rather just remember my experiences, so I can bore total strangers to death talking about them.'

'Nothing wrong with that,' Joel reassured her. He was relieved that she hadn't brought up modelling. The only thing worse than meeting a woman who wanted tips on photography was meeting an aspiring model hoping to snag some free shots for her portfolio. 'You tell a great story.'

An odd expression fluttered across Lauryn's face; for a split second, her composure slid away like a mask in an old horror movie, and underneath was – what? Fear? Shame? Joel couldn't tell but, through years of watching people's faces move, he'd learned to make a note of changes like that. He couldn't figure out what caused the change; all he knew was that he had tripped a nerve.

'Thanks,' Lauryn said, smiling. Instantly, the mask was back in place, the face of a woman with perfect cheekbones and a taste for Real Stuff. 'So tell me who you are, Joel. I'm tired of hearing myself talk about myself.'

Joel ruffled his hair with his fingers, shifted his legs around. As the reality of the airplane settled around him, he felt way too big for the little seat, the tiny tray table. The plane had been built for Lilliputians, and he was a massive clumsy Gulliver, trying to patch together an identity in fifteen seconds or less.

Joel imagined how that identity would come across to the sophisticated blonde sitting next to him. Struggling freelancer, making his financial ends meet with a few studio jobs here and there: weddings, holiday portraits, stuff like that. Perpetually single, always falling in love, never finding the 'right' woman (or, more accurately, finding too many of the right women and never managing to hang on to them). A few bursts of social activity here and there, a bit of travel, a one-room apartment in Chicago that doubled as a studio-slash-darkroom.

'Well, I guess you could say I'm a globetrotting shutterbug,' Joel said. 'Chicago is my hometown, and now it's my home base, too. Of course, I try to avoid the place as much as possible.'

'I know exactly what you mean.' Lauryn took a gulp of her drink. 'What was your latest greatest assignment?'

'Italy. Wasn't really an "assignment", though; I mostly knocked around Rome and Florence, catching up on all the culture I missed as a partying art-school delinquent. Hit the museums, the cathedrals, all that good stuff, but, frankly, the thing I liked best was the food.'

Lauryn laughed again. Sexiest laugh ever, bar none. 'What about a love life? Anyone waiting for you back in Chicago?'

'My roommate is a golden Labrador Retriever named Scott; he's the greatest roommate a guy could ask for. Loves sports, drinks leftover beer, doesn't chew the furniture when I'm out of town.'

'No time for a real love life, in other words.'

Joel rolled his eyes. 'No time whatsoever. But that hasn't stopped me yet.'

'So tell me about her.'

'*Her*? I wish it were that simple.'

'There's more than one woman, in other words. A girl in every country?'

'Not necessarily. On my last assignment, I was at a monastery in Tibet. Six weeks of staggeringly beautiful scenery and staggeringly boring celibacy. It just about killed me. I tried to learn how to meditate, but all I could think about when I closed my eyes was sex. By the time it was over, I'd made a vow that I'd never go without getting laid for more than three days until I'm too old to make love any more.'

Lauryn laughed. 'Think you'll ever settle down?'

'Maybe. Who knows? For now, I'm having too much fun.'

Lauryn raised her plastic cocktail glass, ice cubes clinking in her G&T. 'Me too. Here's to not settling down. Because, really, who wants to?'

'Not me.'

Joel lifted his can of tomato juice, and they sealed the toast. They polished off their drinks, in a silence that could either be companionable or awkward; Joel wasn't sure which. Lauryn stared down at her hands, fidgeting with her rings. Joel watched her out of the corner of his eye. She had that funny look on her face again; a hint of a pout, a dissatisfied twist to her mouth. Joel wondered, for a flash of an instant, if she was one of his tribe: a born bullshit artist. With all her class, her sleek edges, her natural-fibre clothes, she could still be feeding him a truckload of, well, fiction.

Whatever she was, whoever she was, Joel suddenly wanted more than anything to take her somewhere for a drink, so he could spend the rest of the afternoon – and maybe the night, and maybe the following morning over pancakes – finding out.

He hadn't thought about where he would take her. An airport bar wouldn't be good enough; she'd want to go somewhere sleek and upscale and hip. He couldn't take her to the bar at his hotel; that would look presumptuous, and, besides, since he's got reservations at a Sleep-A-Ways Inn in the Tenderloin, the closest thing to a bar would be the soft-drink machine in the lobby.

Time stopped for a beat or two, the way it does when you're about to dive out of an airplane with nothing between you and the earth below but a parachute, while his mouth hung open, waiting to speak the words that his mind was preparing.

As usual, Joel's body was way ahead of his brain.

Chapter Three

Grow Your Own Wings! It's Cheap and Easy!

What's wrong with me? Chloe asked herself for the millionth time that morning. How could I have missed that freaking flight?

She gnawed her fingernails and stared blankly at the issue of *Buddhism Today* that lay open in her lap. All the magazines in her therapist's office had something to do with Eastern spirituality, whole foods or wellness. Once she had found a local newsletter for S/M enthusiasts tucked inside an issue of *Yoga Journal*, but she had to assume it had been left by another client.

Chloe's therapist, Aidan, would never advocate any form of sexual power exchange. He was far too focused on what he called the 'birth of love through the equal ebb and flow of inner light, nourished by the sensual interaction of bodies'. He had even published a book about it, which was selling at a decent clip in New Age bookstores. Chloe owned a copy herself, with Aidan's elliptical signature on the inside cover. The book lay on the floor beside her futon; she had read it three times, trying to figure out if it contained a key to Aidan's secret sexual desires. So far, Chloe hadn't managed to decipher her therapist's hidden passions, but she hadn't given up hope.

Today, Chloe wasn't here to talk about her usual gripes – her lack of a relationship, her grad-school anxieties, the massive block of mental concrete that lay between herself and her dream of leading an exotic life in Japan. Today Chloe had called Aidan for an emergency session to discuss airplanes, more specifically, why her heart stopped at the mere thought of boarding one.

The door of Aidan's office opened. A tall devastatingly gorgeous woman with olive skin and the raven ringlets of a gypsy fortune teller stepped out, enveloped in a purple kaftan and a cloud of patchouli. She held a handful of Kleenex to her nose with one hand, and was carrying the tissue box with the other. Aidan followed her, looking haggard in her wake.

Oh, great, Chloe thought. I get to follow The Queen of a Thousand Sighs again.

It wasn't Chloe's fault that she knew all about Dawna, a struggling actress who went through lovers as quickly as she did Kleenexes. Dawna's rich throaty voice penetrated Aidan's door, allowing Chloe to overhear every angst-ridden detail of her life. Chloe figured that Dawna must need an obscene amount of therapy, since she always seemed to be sweeping out of Aidan's office whenever Chloe came in.

'Chloe. How good to see you. Come on in.'

Aidan's greeting sounded sincere but anaemic. Dawna had drained him again. Now he'd spend Chloe's session staring out of the window, imagining Dawna intertwined in some ornate position from the *Kama Sutra* with yet another uncaring lover, while he listened to Chloe whining about how she'd 'forgotten' to board an airplane that morning.

Still limping on her bruised foot, Chloe shuffled across the floor. She tried to hide her battered pink Hello Kitty backpack – a comfort fetish, which she carried in times of extreme mental stress – from Dawna's arch gaze, but it was too late. Dawna glanced at Chloe with a mixture of distaste and curiosity, as if she were a beetle crawling across the wall, before floating off on a wave of musk.

'How's your poetry going?' Aidan asked, ushering

Chloe into his office. 'Any new inspiration since we last met?'

Chloe perched on the edge of a straight-backed bamboo chair across from the low table that Aidan used as a desk. She usually collapsed into one of the beanbags on his floor, but she wanted to convey that this wasn't just one of her usual daddy-funded bitch sessions.

'This isn't about the usual stuff,' Chloe said.

'It's not?'

'Nope. For once I'm not going to whine about my sexual frustration, or school. Well, it's kind of about school. And maybe about sexual frustration, too.'

'Really? What are we talking about today?'

In a flash of interest that almost seemed more personal than professional, Aidan perked up. He leaned over and turned down the volume on his stereo, which was playing a CD of ambient flute music.

Half Japanese and half Irish-American, Aidan was a babe. It wasn't his glossy black hair, pulled into a ponytail, that got Chloe going, or the muscles toned by yoga and martial arts. It was his eyes: deep-brown almond-shaped eyes that turned black when his interest was piqued, while his eyebrows rose winglike across his pale forehead. She was ashamed to admit it, but she had told a few whopping lies about her sex life just to watch Aidan's pupils dilate and his brows do that wing trick.

Then there were his hands – long ivory fingers, smooth knuckles, clean transparent nails. They looked like the hands of a cellist or a sculptor, form flowing perfectly from function. At the moment, his fingertips were pressed together in a steeple. Maybe he was praying for Chloe to reveal that she was lusting after him.

More likely, he wasn't.

He was a bit too New-Agey to be a full-blown transference crush, but those dark eyes and fine fingers set off a fire in Chloe's belly that had nothing to do with a passion for therapeutic exchange.

'I missed a flight this morning,' Chloe began. 'Not on purpose. Not because I was late. I missed it because I'm chicken about flying.'

'This is something new. Tell me about it.'

'It's new to you, but not to me. I've never been on an airplane. Ever. And it's ruining my life!' Her voice rose to a wail.

'How so?' Aidan's dark eyes flashed.

'The flight I missed this morning was supposed to take me to a conference that could have made my career. I was going to present a paper there. I'm supposed to be standing at the lectern right now, reading it, as a matter of fact. Instead, I'm falling apart in my therapist's office.'

Aidan pulled a fresh box of Kleenex off his bookshelf, tore open the tab and handed the box to Chloe. 'You're not falling apart. Tell me why you missed the flight.'

'I overslept. Well, no. That's not really true. I wasn't sleeping; I was *falling* asleep. I'd been up all night working on some translations, and, uh –' masturbating, Chloe thought '– just doing nothing in particular. I made some tea, stubbed my toe and lay down. Then, all of a sudden, I woke up out of nowhere and remembered that I was supposed to be boarding a flight in Oakland in less than two hours.'

'Berkeley isn't all that far from the airport,' Aidan pointed out. 'Hypothetically speaking, you could have gotten there, made it through security and gotten on the plane. Or you could have called the airline to reschedule. But you didn't. Why?'

'I hate airplanes! That's the truth. The idea of flying makes me want to throw up. I can't think of any practical reason why airplanes should work. What holds them up? What makes them stay in the air? Why can't I just take a boat to Japan; that's been my dream my whole life, and I can't do it because of this stupid phobia!'

'So the problem's not with you, really. It's with flying

in general. You don't have any faith in aerodynamics. Is that what I'm hearing?' Aidan asked.

'No. Not really,' Chloe admitted. 'That's just what I tell myself to make myself feel better. I know I have aviophobia; I know it's not entirely rational. I even had my doctor give me a prescription for Xanax, just so I could get on this plane today. The problem, the *real* problem, is that I'm terrified. Not just of airplanes, but of everything. Flying. Sex. Life.'

Aidan sat back in his chair and folded his hands in his lap. Chloe heard the breath flow gently out of him, the way it did when he thought he'd helped her to a crisis point.

Hah. If he only knew! They were barely getting started – the crisis was way down the road somewhere, looming large and ugly.

The conference and the dreamed-of trip to Japan were just the beginning. They hadn't even started to talk about orgasms.

'I think what we need to do,' Aidan said, 'is help you grow a pair of wings.'

Chloe stared. Had he gone nuts? Good luck, she thought; if I ever fly, it's not going to be using my own equipment.

Aidan's eyes shifted to the wall clock above Chloe's head. 'We've made a promising beginning,' he said. 'Should we pick this up again later in the week? Or do you need to come in tomorrow?'

'Later this week will be fine,' Chloe said, not wanting to seem as needy as she felt. Maybe she really was getting the hots for Aidan. She thought about him way more than she'd ever thought about any of her other therapists. She'd had a crush of one kind or another on all of them, even the prune-lipped anti-Freudian named Barb, who suggested that she buy a vibrator and give up on finding the right man, because a 'life among books' was really much more satisfying than anything a penis could offer.

Had Chloe been imagining things, or had Aidan's mouth twisted just a little when he looked at the clock and saw that their session was over, as if he were actually disappointed?

'I'll put you down for Friday,' Aidan said. 'How about two thirty? That'll give you time to grab something to eat and get over here from campus. You have a seminar from eleven to one, right?'

'How do you remember all that stuff?' Chloe asked. 'Do you know everything about all your clients' schedules, or do you just know mine because I'm here bugging you all the time?'

Aidan lifted his head. His eyes met hers. 'You never bug me, Chloe. Ever. I'm your therapist, remember? This is my job.'

'Right. OK. See you Friday at two thirty.'

His answer, especially the words 'this is my job', left Chloe feeling small and silly and disappointed. But what was he supposed to say? *Yes, I know everything about you because I want to make mad love to you, and I've been stalking you since the day you walked into my office.*

To steal one of Aidan's favourite phrases, that would have been a promising beginning.

'Chloe?'

'Huh?' Chloe wheeled around, hoping to glimpse a last-minute flash of lust crossing Aidan's face. She saw nothing but a wry look of amusement.

'I love your backpack. Very kitschy. Very cool.'

'Um, thanks.'

She clutched Hello Kitty to her chest, curling her arms around the bag, which she'd had since junior high, and scuttled out of Aidan's office before he could catch her blushing.

Aidan liked, no *loved*, her backpack. It was a beginning, a promising one. Maybe.

'Listen, Lauryn. Let's say, hypothetically, that everything I've told you is a lie. The trendy career, the relationship rap sheet, the cool Labrador Retriever – everything. Would you still have a drink with me after we land?' Joel asked.

Joel propped his elbows on the armrest that barely separated his body from Lauryn's. On the intercom, the pilot announced that they were starting the descent into San Francisco. How could anyone hate flying? Landing was the only part that sucked. In mid-air you could be anyone you wanted to be, sitting next to a stranger with shaggy khaki-coloured hair, eyes as blue as a morning sky at cruising altitude and a crooked Charlie Brown smile that made her willing to believe just about any tale he told her, the wilder the better.

'Well, first I'd want to know if *anything* you told me was true,' Lauryn said. 'Then I'd know if it was safe to consume booze with you.'

Joel rubbed his chin as he pondered the question. His fingers made a sandpaper sound against the stubble. Lauryn felt dizzy, imagining how that stubble would feel grating her inner thighs.

'The only thing I said that you can be sure of is that you're the hottest woman I've seen since I left Florence.'

A neon flash of jealousy, totally unexpected, eclipsed Lauryn's view of Joel's face. 'Who's in Florence?'

Joel upped the volume on his smile, turning it into an amped-up grin. 'Some chick I met hanging out in the Uffizi,' he replied. 'Botticelli's Venus.'

Lauryn stared at him, swallowed and exploded into giggles that would have done a junior-high cheerleader proud. She couldn't help it; the come-on was so absurd that the laughter hit her like an unexpected orgasm.

Joel sat there through the whole attack, grinning like a Cheshire cat as he watched Lauryn try to get a grip on herself. It took her a few minutes to catch her breath. Her stomach muscles ached and her skin tingled, the way it did when she'd just stepped out of a hot shower.

'So what do you think? Want to risk having a drink with me?' Joel repeated. His eyes twinkled behind his glasses and his lips formed a smug smile that she found irresistible. She might have acted on her impulse to kiss him if the flight attendant's slender arm hadn't descended at that moment to pick up their plastic cups.

'The pilot is preparing for landing. Please return your tray tables to their upright cocked position,' the flight attendant reminded them.

Joel and Lauryn looked at each other. Lauryn felt laughter bubbling to the surface again. 'Do you think she knows she said "cocked"?' Lauryn asked under her breath, as the brunette floated on down the aisle.

'I think that's probably the way she practises it in front of the mirror at night: "Is that a cocked tray table, or are you just happy to see me?"' Joel cooed.

'Hey, if it works, don't knock it,' Lauryn said. 'The flight attendant probably gets more action than I do.'

Joel leaned closer. With most people who were almost but not quite strangers, Lauryn would have instinctively backed away, but Joel's size, the warmth of his body, made her want to lean in, too. He was so close that she could catch a clean scent coming off his skin – no swanky aftershave, she thought gratefully, just the scent of soap.

'I'd love to change that,' Joel said. His offer sent a flurry of electric shocks up and down Lauryn's arms. 'Just say the word.'

Joel's eyes met Lauryn's, up close. She'd remembered to put in her tinted lenses that morning. But, for once she didn't really care about her mismatched eyes, and she got the feeling that Joel wouldn't care much either.

'The word,' she said.

'Which hotel are you staying in?' Joel asked, as they walked up the jetway together and into the waiting area.

Standing in the airport, Joel was even taller than Lauryn had realised, tall and rangy and suntanned, with enough bulk on his bones to make him well worth holding. A businessman, cursing into a cell phone and dragging a carry-on bag that looked like a coffin on wheels, bumped into Lauryn from behind, sending her reeling into Joel's chest.

'Oh!' Lauryn gasped as her body collided with Joel's wide firm chest. His flesh felt big and solid, comforting and arousing at the same time, but his clothes were surprisingly soft, as if they'd been laundered a million times. His smell reminded her of sunlight on clean sheets. For a moment, as he caught her, his arms surrounded Lauryn, and the wave of lust that went through her body almost sent her to her knees. The guy she was currently kind-of-sort-of involved with, another business consultant with her firm, was short and wiry and filled with a nervous sweaty energy. Joel felt huge by comparison – big as a bear, strong and calmly capable.

'Sorry about that,' she managed to say, as he helped her catch her balance.

'No problem.' He chuckled. 'It was my pleasure.'

Lauryn felt the seconds tick by as she tried to come up with an answer to the question he'd originally asked. She didn't want Joel to know that she was staying at a rundown dump in the city. He probably thought that a professional woman with a high-powered career would stay someplace elegant, like the Nikko.

'Um, you know what? I don't even remember,' she

said, with a flip of her hand and a stiff little laugh. 'Too many cities, in too many months. I'd have to check my Palm Pilot to see what the company booked for me.'

Joel nodded, as if this were completely plausible. 'I know how it goes. Sometimes you don't know if you're coming or going. So where would you like to go?'

Lauryn thought she saw a flicker of something like relief in his sea-blue eyes, then decided that she must have imagined it. Now that it had come down to the moment of truth – God, was there anything more painful than a moment of truth? – Lauryn suggested that they go to the most generic part of the city she could think of, an area where she could hide among the other tourists.

From the airport, Lauryn and Joel took a taxi to Fisherman's Wharf. They found a bar that strove for elegance on a street lined with tacky souvenir stores and restaurants offering clam chowder in sourdough bread bowls. The place was neutral ground, the type of place where a couple of strangers from different cities might buy each other a few drinks before slinking away for some anonymous sex.

'What'll it be, kids?' the bartender asked. A flute-thin gentleman with a greying pompadour and red bow tie, he looked like he should be conducting a brass band in the middle of Mayberry, not serving up drinks in the middle of the afternoon.

'Bloody Mary,' Joel said. 'Hold the blood. Just give me a double vodka tonic with a stick of celery in it.'

Lauryn laughed. 'What do you call that? An Anaemic Mary?'

'Got to get my fibre somewhere,' Joel said with a grin.

We do look like tourists, Lauryn thought, glancing at the reflection of Joel and herself in the mirror behind the bar. What was it about modern life that made you feel like you were always travelling, even when you were at home? Or was that just Lauryn's life? She thought about the apartment she'd left back in Chicago, not really a home, just a space surrounded by four walls, where she kept her stuff while she was on her business trips. Joel's life must be similar: always packing up his gear to fly to one location or another, looking for images that he could sell.

At least he got to go to exotic places, Lauryn thought enviously, sneaking glances at Joel out of the corner of her eye as she sipped her drink. He looked so carefree, stirring his drink, his camera bag lying beside him on the ground. His broad shoulders sloped forwards at a relaxed angle; his blue eyes gazed calmly into his cocktail, as if he had nothing more pressing to do than stir the ice cubes and watch them spin. She couldn't stop thinking about the accidental hug they'd shared at the airport.

As if he'd felt Lauryn staring, Joel looked up and gazed at her instead. She felt her face getting hot. Joel didn't look at her the way other men did. The typical male stare, in Lauryn's experience, was either an outright elevator leer or an expression of fake sincerity hiding an assessment of her curves. Joel was watching her as if she were a bird, or a tree, something with a life of its own.

'What are you looking at?' she asked.

'A woman with a lot on her mind. A woman who just came off a long flight and probably could use a massage.'

'Let me guess. Massage just happens to be your hobby.'

'Ah, but I didn't say that.' Joel's smile was mysterious. 'I was going to suggest a little place I know in Chinatown. The women who work there have hands of steel; their massage kung-fu is very strong.'

'Hmmm. How *Emmanuelle in Bangkok*.' Lauryn managed to keep her tone offhand and dry, but several pulse points were throbbing, like stars, in the most sensitive spots in her body.

'And I wasn't going to suggest that we go together, or lie naked on tables side by side, staring into each other's eyes as we confessed our kinky sexual experiences.'

'You weren't?'

Lauryn's mouth was dry. Kinky sexual experiences? If only she had a few to confess. Joel probably had lovers all over the world, a whole rainbow made of silken skin and lips and nipples, all in different shades of cream and almond and ebony, pink and violet and crimson.

'Not unless you wanted to.'

I want to! I want to! Lauryn's mind filled with images of Joel's broad upper back being kneaded by a pair of skilful female hands, ploughing up and down the skin that lead to his waist, his butt, the backs of his thighs. She hadn't even touched her gin and tonic; she was already drunk on a fantasy worthy of a porno movie from the 70s.

'I always loved those *Emmanuelle* movies,' Joel mused, a misty look in his eyes. 'The whole concept just got to me. Here's a couple that agrees that they can each have sex with as many people as they want, as long as they only truly love each other. Then they make this pact to tell each other about everyone they fuck –'

'Hold on. If we're going to tell each other fairytales, I'd prefer Cinderella.'

'Why? Are you missing a shoe or something?'

'Something. I'm not sure what it is, but it's not a lover who wants to nail everything in sight.'

Lauryn scowled into her cocktail. She plucked out the lime wedge and sucked on it viciously. She didn't want to talk about *Emmanuelle* any more, or about lovers who fuelled their libidos with anyone and everyone.

'Hey. We don't have to talk about cheesy porn flicks any more,' Joel said softly. He covered Lauryn's wrist with the warm solid weight of his hand. Lauryn gulped. She was just grasping the reality that Joel was touching her, *really* touching her, when something started gnawing its way through her pocket like a furious man-eating insect.

'Damn,' she sighed, pulling out her cell phone and

glancing at the display. 'It's my boss back in Chicago. I have to take this.'

'No problem.' Joel stood up and stretched. 'I need to see a man about a horse anyway.'

Lauryn gave Joel's back a hungry once-over as he ambled off to the men's room, raking his khaki-coloured hair with his fingers.

'Lauryn, where the hell are you?' Stanley Kramer's voice, perpetually harried and annoyed, cut through time and space like an electric drill.

'On my way to Oakland,' Lauryn said. It wasn't exactly a lie; she was *planning* to go to Oakland. She just happened to be sitting in a tourist bar in the meantime, drinking cocktails with a photographer who was trying to tempt her into an illicit Chinatown massage.

'The Client's just called,' Stanley said, giving the word 'client' an ominous capital C. 'They thought you'd be at the headquarters by now.'

'My plane was delayed. Seriously delayed. We almost ran out of fuel in mid-air,' Lauryn improvised.

'Really?'

'Yes. It was terrifying. I saw my life pass before my eyes.'

Lauryn heard Stanley cringe over the airwaves. 'God, I knew there was a reason I don't fly. Well, listen, I smoothed things over for you, but you need to go and show your face at Corporate. I bought you a couple of hours – try to get there by three.'

'OK. Whenever.'

'No, *not* "whenever". Get. Moving. *Now.*'

When he was trying to act tough, Stanley liked to bark orders in gruff monosyllables, separated by periods. He thought it made him sound like Tony Soprano, though he actually sounded more like Homer Simpson with a head cold.

'Yes, boss.' Lauryn held the sleek sliver of a phone

away from her face so she could flip off the mouthpiece. 'May I be excused?'

'Yeah.' Stanley chewed and swallowed something, probably either an antacid tablet or a breath mint. He had an eye on a succulent blonde temporary admin assistant in the office, and he was constantly trying to tame his dragon breath. 'And, Lauryn?'

'What?'

'You could be in Switzerland right now. Think about it.'

Lauryn flipped the cell phone shut without saying goodbye. That son-of-a-bitch, he couldn't let her go without taking that final dig, reminding her of the repulsive 'deal' he'd tried to negotiate with her. A six-week job in Geneva – finally! – if she'd spend an afternoon with him at the Downtown Hilton. She'd said no – *hell no!* – and had been sent to Oakland instead.

Yuck. Just thinking about Stanley laid out naked on a hotel bed, his pasty body spreading across the sheets as a smarmy grin spread across his face, made Lauryn feel like a million ants were scuttling across her skin. Stanley was a sleaze ball, but he was a proud sleaze ball, with a sense of self-righteous machismo that had been wounded by Lauryn's rejection. He never missed an opportunity to turn the knife by reminding her of the opportunities she'd lost when she refused to screw him.

A firm weight fell on to Lauryn's shoulders. Palms pressed against her tight muscles, fingertips rubbing the hollows under her clavicles. Joel stood behind her barstool. There was something so intimate about the way he had just walked up and started rubbing her, as if they were longtime lovers, not near-strangers who had accidentally sat together on a plane only a few hours ago.

'Ugly phone call, huh?' he said, moving around her to resume his place on his barstool.

'You could say that.' Lauryn closed her eyes. She wished she could sit with Joel in this bar forever, at least until it was time for them to move to a horizontal position.

'Personally, I don't carry a cell phone. I used to have one, but I accidentally flushed it down a toilet in London. Never had it replaced. I hate being interrupted when something important is happening.'

'Me too,' Lauryn agreed. 'But it's kind of a necessity, in my line of work.'

'Yeah, well. You're a high-flying executive contractor. I'm a sporadically employed freelancer. We're from different worlds, baby.'

Not as different as you might think, Lauryn said to herself. She had a sudden impulse to tell Joel all about what she really did – flying around the United States to one boring technical complex or factory after another, analysing corporate data to justify lining up employees on the chopping block – but dragging out the truth at this point would be like pulling a moth-eaten wool coat out of the closet and throwing it on over her sexy carefree travel clothes.

Joel hooked his index finger under Lauryn's chin and lifted her face, tilting her jaw at a slight angle. He examined her features carefully, as if she were a Ming vase. Somehow, his inspection didn't make her feel objectified; it made her feel desirable. She found herself thinking about how he would look at her as he was removing her clothes – he would take his time, peeling things off one at a time, caressing her with his fingers and his eyes at the same time.

'You have to go, don't you?' he asked.

Lauryn nodded. 'I'm sorry. But I do.'

'That's OK.' His voice was soft, slightly husky with disappointment. 'What are you doing for dinner?'

You, Lauryn wanted to say, but actually said, 'Can I call you?'

'No phone. Remember?'

'Give me the name of your hotel. I'll leave a message.'

Joel's eyes skirted hers. 'Um, I'm not sure yet. Want to meet somewhere?'

Lauryn pulled a pen out of her purse and scribbled down the name and cross streets of her favourite restaurant in Chinatown. 'My plans are still up in the air for tonight; I might have to go out with the client. How about we meet here tomorrow at eleven? For dim sum?'

Joel took the napkin, folded it and slipped it into the pocket of his denim shirt. Then he smiled that juvenile-delinquent smile, and wrapped his arms around Lauryn in a hug that took her breath away and filled her head with images of hard male muscle and sweat-slick skin. Salt under her tongue ... firm flesh filling all of her empty spaces ... mingled scents of musk and sweat and soap. Her lips accidentally grazed Joel's neck as he let her go, leaving her with a hint of his taste in her mouth. She wanted to bite him, hang on to him with her teeth. Instead, she busied herself with her Palm Pilot and her cell phone and her pager, all the toys that supposedly kept her connected to the world, while keeping her apart from the one person she would have liked to spend the day with.

'Tomorrow at eleven,' Joel said, with a dramatic sigh. 'It's gonna be a long night.'

'Not too long, I hope. Have a good one,' Lauryn said. She walked out briskly, aware that she had an audience in Joel and the bartender, hoping she looked successful and independent. Hoping she looked like something other than what she was.

Did everyone want to be something else, or was it just Lauryn? Waiting to hail a cab, she watched two middle-aged women walking down the Wharf, loaded down with bags from SF MOMA and F.A.O. Schwartz and Nordstrom's, stopping at the storefront of a tacky souvenir shop and staring inside, mouths sagging at the corners, as if they were already disappointed with the city that was supposed to relieve them of the routines of their lives back home. Instead, they were strolling through San Francisco on a weekday afternoon, doing what they would be doing anywhere on earth: shopping.

Lauryn breathed a sigh of relief when a cab pulled up to take her away from Fisherman's Wharf.

'So how's your day going?' asked the cabbie. He was a heavyset guy with his arm slung over the back of the seat, offering Lauryn a whiff of his garlicky body odour.

'Well, I met the hottest guy I've met in ages on a plane this morning. Had a drink with him. Made a date with him for tomorrow, but you know how that goes; I'll probably never see him again. But other than that, hey, it's going great! Can you take me over the Bay Bridge? I have to be in Oakland by three.'

The cabbie shook his head regretfully, jowls a-quiver. 'From love to Oakland,' he said. 'Could it get any worse?'

'Let's hope not.'

As the taxi drove over the bridge, she pulled out her Palm to review the agenda that she'd planned for this afternoon. The figures on the grey digital display made her eyes glaze over. She tossed the evil mechanism into her bag, took out her pen and a pocket-size notebook, and soon found herself doing something that always soothed her.

God, what would she do if she couldn't make lists? Resort to smoking pot, probably, or maybe crack. The world seemed so much more manageable when you could reduce it to a series of neat even lines.

Firsts of my 'Love Life', by Lauryn Baxter

- First love – Connor O'Halloran. Fifth grade. Kissing only, no tongue action (neither of us knew about tongue involvement yet).
- First date – Melinda Johnson. Eighth grade. I didn't know it was a date ... until she tried to french-kiss

me at the movies. To her credit, I don't think she knew she was going to do it either.

- First full-blown fuck – Bill Bartleby. Water-polo coach, freshman year in college. Kind of an accident. Crush gone wild.

- First engagement – Steve Castignola. Twenty-two years old. Engaged for a full 37 hours before he cheated on me. Realised this was going to become a pattern, dumped him.

- First airplane-inspired sexual encounter – 23 years old. Flight from Chicago to Salt Lake City. Met older businessman-type-guy, very attractive, realised he would be much more attracted to me if I had a different life. So I made one up.

Here Lauryn stopped writing. She always stopped her lists when they started to feel like the lists were interrogating *her*. Twirling the pen in her hand like a miniature baton, she thought about all the men she'd met on airplanes, how her stories had changed and expanded over the years. At first she had thought of it as self-promotion, no different than what advertising executives did. You never knew when you might be seated next to someone influential on a flight, someone who could pull a few strings to get you a new job. It was networking, really.

Eventually, after sexual encounters with the grey-haired businessman, an aspiring rock producer, an amateur rugby player and a couple of attorneys (not on the same flight, of course), Lauryn had been pushed to the glum realisation that she was a woman who lied to get laid. She rarely lied on the ground, only when she was airborne, and the fudging that she did to prolong her stories only counted as necessary maintenance. Once she'd create the illusion of a wealthy family, a brilliant job, a life of travel, she had to do a certain amount of juggling to keep all those balls in the air.

So there had been a lot of post-flight cocktails, followed by post-flight kisses and post-flight sex. The sex had an intensity that Lauryn never seemed to find with the men she met on solid ground. Charged by visions of success and power, Lauryn became a jaguar in bed, hungry and predatory. Her lovers were usually awestruck and grateful, though often guilty.

Some of them had girlfriends, after all. And wives and kids. The married ones were the worst. At least Lauryn had learned to recognise the moist milky imprint that a freshly removed wedding ring left on a guy's finger.

'Hard to believe a classy lady like you is still single,' said the cab driver. He'd been breaking into Lauryn's thoughts with the occasional attempt at conversation, but she'd fended him off so far.

'Classy?' Lauryn repeated, with a cynical snort. 'I didn't think anyone used that word to describe women any more.'

'They don't. Because there ain't a lot of class left in the world.'

'What makes you think I'm classy?' Lauryn asked curiously. 'You saw me for the first time forty minutes ago. We've hardly said three words to each other.'

The cabbie shrugged his meaty shoulders. 'Being classy, in a woman, is a lot like being crazy. You don't know how to describe it, but you know it when you see it.'

'How do you tell the difference? Between classy and crazy?'

'Aw, that's no problem. Two totally different things.'

'I'm not so sure I believe you.'

'Maybe that's why you're single. You gotta put more trust in people. Men especially.'

Right, Lauryn thought. When I can fly from Chicago to San Francisco by flapping my arms and wishing on a star, I'll start trusting men. She thought about Joel, and wondered if he was still sitting at the bar nursing his Anaemic Mary. Or had he already moved on, seeking out someone more sophisticated, more beautiful, more intriguing?

'He'll be there to meet you tomorrow,' the cabbie said. 'Don't worry.'

Lauryn looked up, startled, and met the driver's oyster-grey eyes in the rearview mirror. 'How did you know what I was thinking? Do you read minds or something?'

He smiled. His front tooth twinkled – gold. 'It's all over your face, lady. You got one of those see-through faces. Bet you couldn't tell a lie if you tried.'

Chapter Four

Shinegrrl

Working at the airport was the best thing that had ever happened to Veronica. Each morning, as she drove up the ramp to the parking garage, she caught a second-hand rush from the streams of travellers coming and going, the airplanes lofting purposefully into the blue sky. Sailing on the borrowed excitement of other people's journeys, Veronica spent her days with a perpetual buzz. Then there was the never-ending sideshow of humanity inside the airport: men and women zipping by in business attire, tired parents trailing flocks of toddlers, glamorous gazelle-like beauties who looked like they were jetting off to Italy or Greece for a modelling gig. Veronica never got tired of watching the parade.

But she did get tired of the popular misconception that any form of footwear needed and deserved to be lovingly shined.

Veronica stared at the battered scuffed hiking boots, still caked with reddish mud, propped up on her shoeshine stand and tried not to show her dismay. What did people think she was doing here, using the job as an excuse to get high on shoe polish? How was she supposed to clean up a pair of clodhoppers like that, with a sandblaster?

'Um, you know, I don't know that there's much I can do with these,' she said, peering up at the lanky man who sat in the chair. He had a glum hatchet-face, half hidden by a scruffy beard. With his knobbly hands propped on the arm rests, he reminded her of Abe Lincoln.

'I know,' he said with such dejection that she knew she was going to cave and clean his boots anyway. With only two words, he managed to convey to her the fact that his whole life was a series of impossible requests, unfulfilled hopes. Abraham Lincoln had suffered from depression, too, if she remembered correctly. Maybe this guy was distantly related.

'OK. We'll see what we can do.'

Veronica pursed her lips into a tight professional knot as she dug through her kit, looking for a stiff bristle brush. She'd have to knock off some of that mud before she could even begin to attack the boots themselves, which were actually made of good-quality leather. Feeling like she was on some kind of archaeological dig, she began to hammer at the lumps of dried dirt that rimmed the soles. By the time she was done, she was going to be thoroughly covered with dust.

'What have you been doing, anyway?' she asked her customer. 'Climbing mountains?'

He shook his long head. 'Digging graves. That's what I do for a living.'

'Nice work, if you can get it,' Veronica said. 'So what brings you to San Francisco?'

'Funeral. My aunt died. My mother won't let me in the house with all this mud on my shoes. Probably wouldn't even let me in her car.'

'Don't you have another pair?'

'Nope. This is it.'

Veronica wished she hadn't asked. You could learn a lot by getting a close-up view of people's shoes. But Veronica wasn't sure that, in her eight months of shining shoes at the airport, she'd learned anything she couldn't have lived without.

Except for one thing. And that one secret was going to make her the stinking-rich envy of the entire alternative community of San Francisco.

But most of what she'd learned was much more mundane. First of all, not many people wore good leather on their feet any more, at least not when they travelled. Veronica had had all kinds of footwear presented to her, from crêpe-soled Hush Puppies to Nikes to dominatrix boots with six-inch heels (that lady, who regally asked Veronica to call her Mistress P, had left Veronica one of her best tips ever), but she rarely got a customer with anything on his feet worth polishing. She'd learned very quickly that, for her average client, shoes with mirror-clean toes weren't the objective. A visit to the throne where Veronica slaved away with her rags and tubes and bottles was far more likely to be a matter of erotic curiosity than one of grooming.

The world was full of people who wanted a hottie with Bettie Page bangs to slave away at their feet for fifteen minutes. Simple as that. Which was OK with Veronica, because she found kinky sex a lot more interesting than polishing shoes. She even played it up by wearing her black jeans a little tighter, cutting off her T-shirts at the midriff and wearing rows of silver bracelets that clinked musically – slave-girl style – as she rubbed away with her chamois cloth. The guys loved to watch her bottom wiggle as she crouched over their cheap shoes, and Veronica loved to be watched doing just about anything.

Veronica's butt wasn't providing much of a distraction for Abe Lincoln. Her customer was sunk so deep in his gloom that he didn't even notice when she stood up and flashed him the Celtic-knot tattoo that surrounded her belly button. He must have really loved that aunt of his to be so depressed that he didn't even glance at her navel piercing. Straight, gay or any variation thereof, men *always* looked at Veronica's belly. She had tight abs and a lean waistline that dipped like a ski slope down to her hips and butt.

According to everyone but Veronica, her ass was her best feature. A 'ghetto booty', her roommates called it, perched round and high as a beach ball above her sturdy thighs. Though she was perfectly willing to use whatever assets she had to further herself in life, Veronica didn't care much for what she called 'my fat ass'. No matter how hard she worked out, how many sets of stairs she climbed, how many squats she did at the gym, her ass maintained its florid dimensions. Unless, of course, she happened to eat an extra brownie, or forget to request skim milk in her latte, in which case the extra calories would be converted instantly to ass-flesh.

Veronica had to catch her breath as she brushed the red dust off her jeans. Cleaning Abe's boots had given her a workout. Staring down at his toes, he looked sceptical.

'Your boots look *so* much better,' she reassured her bearded customer. 'Almost like a new pair. You'll be a knockout at the funeral.'

'You really think so?' he asked.

'Absolutely. You're a new man.'

Go for it, Abe! Get out there and grab life by the balls! Veronica had to restrain herself from launching into a motivational speech; the guy was so morose that his mood was beginning to get her down, too. She was relieved when he finally heaved a sigh, rose from the chair and paid her. He didn't give her a tip, but, with some customers, leaving was all the tip she needed. As soon as he was gone, Veronica hung up the gold velvet rope in front of the chair to indicate that no shoes would be shined for the next fifteen minutes, then went to Starbucks for her break.

'Well, I just burned two hundred calories and half an hour of my life,' she grumbled to the girl behind the counter. With her fuchsia hair tied in pigtails at the top of her head, magenta lipstick and silver-studded features, she looked like a china doll gone bad. Imogene was one of the 'skanks', as Veronica affectionately called them, who shared her loft apartment. She had twice as many piercings as Veronica, and most of them were in her face. Eyebrows, lower lip, tongue, nose, clit – you name it, Imogene had a hole through it.

'Who was that guy?' Imogene asked, scrunching up her pretty face. She had already started preparing Veronica's skinny latte. 'He looked like some old president or something. Who's the president on the dollar bill?'

'Abraham Lincoln,' Veronica sighed. Some days she could swear that Imogene's cultural literacy was leaking out of all the extra holes in her body.

'So how's The Plan going? Any progress?'

'Not today, unfortunately. But it's only two o'clock. Some big investor could still come up to the shoeshine stand and offer to finance NaughtyChix.'

'Really? You really think that could happen?' Imogene's face lit up like a pink Christmas-tree light.

'Sure. Why not? Someone could always come along and drop a million dollars in my lap for no particular reason.'

'You never know. It could happen.' Imogene hunched her shoulders, as if to ward off the acid splash of Veronica's sarcasm.

'Listen, kiddo, nothing's going to happen unless we make it happen. Santa Claus isn't going to stroll by and give us a sack of cash so we can start a goth-girl whorehouse. Face it, we're going to have to start in the mud and claw our way up the hill.'

'I thought you said we were going to have an escort service, not a *whorehouse*,' Imogene squeaked. 'We're not going to have a bunch of creepy guys come over and pick us out of a line, are we?'

'Shhh. Don't talk so loud.' Veronica jerked her head to the left. A tall blonde woman in a business suit was standing at the counter, stirring Nutrasweet into her americano. Ever since she'd come up with the idea of starting an escort service catering to people who had a fetish for alternative girls, Veronica had become a bit paranoid. She still wasn't sure that the enterprise was entirely legal, or that the Russian mafia didn't already have a monopoly on the escort business. But, most of all, she was terrified that someone was going to steal her idea and corner the goth-girl meat market.

'Buzzsaw still wants to take our portfolio shots for us,' Imogene said, lowering her voice. 'He'll do it for free.'

'I bet he will,' Veronica muttered. The last thing she wanted was to let one of Imogene's bed-buddies take the portfolio shots of the girls, unless he happened to have some actual photography experience. Buzzsaw had none. He had recently bought a digital camera (or, more likely, stolen it) and suddenly believed he was Helmut Newton, with a vast amount of talent and a calling to photograph nude women all over the city.

'But he's good,' Imogene whined. 'He took some pictures of me last night. Wanna see them? I have my laptop with me; I could pull them up for you –'

'Later. Starbucks isn't the best place to look at amateur nudie pics,' Veronica reminded her. 'And I think it would be better for us to work with someone who doesn't have personal ties to any of us. Know what I'm saying?'

Imogene pouted. 'I've only known Buzzsaw for three weeks.' Three weeks was an eternity in Imogene's love life.

'I'll take a look at his photos tonight,' Veronica said more kindly.

'Well, we need to get *someone* to take our pictures, so we can get some exposure.' Imogene handed Veronica her latte. 'I don't want to be pumping coffee at the airport forever.'

'I know you don't. Any more than I want to be shining shoes.'

Imogene was right. Photos were a key part of The Plan, and Veronica was going to need a lot of them. Out of all the guys that they knew as a collective, there were probably at least three – other than Buzzsaw – who could have put together a decent portfolio. But Veronica wanted something better than 'decent'. She wanted photographs that were not only at least semi-professional, but artistically compelling, provocative and breathtaking. She wanted photos that promised not only a night of company with a sexy, quirky, tattooed and multiply pierced woman, but a full-blown erotic escape. She wanted photos that wouldn't simply advertise NaughtyChix, but would also tell a story about each one of her escorts.

And she wanted photos that would tell any potential creeps out there that *her* girls were valued, loved. There wouldn't be any flesh-burgers served up in Veronica's escort service. She was going to take care of her girls.

After Lauryn left the bar, whisked off in a cab like some kind of corporate Cinderella, a leaden grey feeling came over Joel. Not exactly loneliness – he was used to living and travelling alone, and he liked his own company – or disappointment, just a sense that something bright and colourful had flown out of his grasp.

'Your girlfriend's a knockout. You must have a way with the ladies,' commented the bartender. With his spiffy hair and bow tie, he looked like a retired ladies' man himself.

'You could say that.' Joel finished his drink and began to crunch on the celery stick. 'Not my girlfriend, though. I met her on an airplane this morning.'

The bartender gave Joel an appraising look, taking in his mussed hair, rumpled shirt, battered camera bag sitting beside him on the bar. 'Well, you must have something going for you, kid. I've never met a woman like that on a plane, much less picked her up and taken her out for drinks. Maybe I should do more travelling.'

'I've never met a woman like that on a plane, either,' Joel admitted. 'Probably never will.'

'Think you'll see her again?'

Joel shrugged. 'That's up to her.'

The bartender grinned. 'That's how it goes these days. Always up to the woman. Let me guess – she's the one with the cell phone and the pager and all the other gadgets. You just wait around for her to contact you with one of them.'

Joel tried to smile back, but his mouth wasn't into it. 'You know the drill.'

He pushed his glass aside and peeled a few bills out of his wallet to pay for his drink. The old guy had a bit too much insight for Joel's taste. Lauryn hadn't given him her cell-phone number or the name of the hotel. All he had was the napkin with the name of a Chinese restaurant written on it and a tentative date for tomorrow at eleven.

Most of the time, Joel liked the way he'd put his life together. He found himself reaching for the same phrases over and over again to describe his philosophy of dating: 'let's leave it up in the air', 'we'll play it by ear', 'just roll with it'. Every now and then, those phrases seemed stale, like the tired old drinking songs that he used to sing with his buddies in college.

The bartender pushed Joel's money back. 'This one's on the house,' he said. 'Save your money for the blonde. She looks high-maintenance.'

'Thanks.' Joel took his money back, leaving a couple of dollars as a tip. The bartender probably thought he was broke – which was reasonable – and felt sorry for him – which wasn't. Joel had a damn good life, the kind of life that guys who read *Playboy* and *Maxim* drooled over. Cool career, plenty of travel and an all-you-can-eat buffet of women who didn't expect anything from him, other than a night of live music and cocktails, followed by sex that could be soulfully intense or insanely kinky, depending on what the lady wanted.

For the most part, Joel had given Lauryn an accurate version of his freelancing bachelor existence. He did feel a nudge of guilt about telling her that he had a pet. Scott, the golden Labrador Retriever, belonged to a neighbour from Joel's building. Joel had taken Scott to the park a few times when the neighbour had to work late. Ever since Joel had given Scott a workout with the tennis ball, throwing it over and over again for Scott to retrieve it, the dog always greeted Joel with a fervent canine adoration. As far as Scott was concerned, he *was* Joel's dog, if only by proxy.

Even though he'd been burned plenty of times in the past, Joel was optimistic about Lauryn. There had to be at least a dozen Imperial Palaces in San Francisco. Maybe Lauryn would be waiting at the one she'd specified; maybe she'd just written down a name at random to give Joel a bone to chase. Either way, Joel would be at the Imperial Palace at eleven: rolling with it, playing it by ear, keeping his plans up in the air.

After leaving the bar, the first order of business was to get the hell away from Fisherman's Wharf. The wharf made Joel feel like a tourist, awkward and out of place. He thought about taking a taxi to the Tenderloin to check in at the hotel, then remembered what the bartender said about saving his money for 'the blonde', and he hopped a bus instead. At the Sleep-A-Ways Inn on Fillmore, he took a shower, then put on clean underwear and a fresh white shirt. The shirt wasn't any less rumpled than the one he'd been wearing on the plane, but at least it smelled like detergent rather than sweat. Joel didn't mind being rumpled, but he drew the line at reeking.

Back on the street, Joel took a few random shots of architectural features on the buildings in the Tenderloin. To the casual tourist, those old buildings looked like grimy rundown wrecks that should be torn down and replaced with a Gap or a Blockbuster. To Joel, they held all kinds of hidden secrets: vaulted windows, ornate doorways, scrolls and cornices and even the occasional gargoyle.

Searching for gargoyles, Joel's eye alighted on a cluster of goth chicks drinking coffee at a table outside a cafe. Sitting in the shadows of an awning outside a coffee house was probably their version of sunbathing. With their chalky skin, inky hair, fishnet stockings and hardcore makeup, the girls looked like a gaggle of witches meeting for their weekly *kaffeeklatsch*. Joel's fingers twitched on his camera, but he resisted the impulse to take their picture. One woman in particular held his attention, a sultry smoking siren wearing dark shades and a razorblade sneer. Her full breasts emerged like the top of an alabaster valentine from a black leather bustier, over which she wore a bottle-green velvet jacket that set off her long auburn hair.

But Joel didn't photograph women, not if he could help it. Too many complications. Buildings were much safer – buildings and landscapes, monasteries and mountains, outdoor structures that carried no baggage of sexual attraction or romantic expectation. He forced himself to walk by the coffee house without taking another look at the auburn vampire's cleavage.

Stay out of trouble, stay out of trouble, Joel chanted to himself. San Francisco was overrun with fascinating women, in all colours and sizes and shapes. If he stopped to chat up all of them, or even paused for a leer, he'd be stuck on this block for the rest of the afternoon.

Struck by the seafood craving that always came over him when he was anywhere near the Pacific, Joel stopped at a sushi bar to get a bite to eat. As soon as he walked into the place, he knew it was the real deal. He could always tell when he was in an authentic Japanese establishment, because he immediately felt like he was dwarfing everything around him: the dimensions of the room, the furniture, the eating utensils. A petite smiling butterfly of a woman led him over to the sushi bar, where he draped his limbs on a stool that teetered under his weight. Behind the bar, a grim-looking man was slicing a ruby-red salmon fillet with alarming precision.

'So what's good here?' Joel asked the girl sitting next to him. He couldn't see much of her, under the cape of wheat-brown hair that fell over her profile. She was reading a book in Japanese, and a notebook lay open on the narrow wooden ledge in front of her. A pink backpack sat beside her on the floor.

'Hmmm?'

'What's the specialty of the house?'

The girl looked up at Joel, apparently noticing his presence for the first time. Her grey eyes had a distant fogged-over look and were rimmed with puffy skin the same colour as her backpack.

'I have no idea,' she said in a vaguely surprised tone that implied that she'd stepped out of a spaceship and awoken to find herself in a sushi bar.

'I only asked because it looks like you spend a lot of time here,' Joel said, nodding at the notebook.

'I do. I always come here after I see my therapist.'

'Great. That's great.'

Joel turned to the cup of steaming green tea that the butterfly hostess had set down in front of him. He clearly wasn't going to get any insider information from the zoned-out woman sitting beside him. Oh, well. When in doubt, he always ordered a California roll. You couldn't go wrong with crab and avocado rolled up in rice and seaweed.

All of a sudden, a pale slim hand floated into his field of vision.

'I'm Chloe,' said the girl. 'I'm sorry, I'm kind of out of it today. Xanax always does that to me. The *nigiri-ika* is great, if you like squid.'

It took Joel a moment to realise that the girl wanted to shake his hand. He obliged, noting that her skin was smooth and cool, her fingers long and pliable.

'I'm Joel,' he said. 'Squid and Xanax. Is that some kind of new diet? Or is it just the specialty of the house?'

The girl's mouth – a very lush and moist one, he noticed – puckered as if she might be about to cry. Instead, her lips curved into a wan smile, then parted as she laughed. 'The Xanax was for a flight I was supposed to take this morning,' she said, brushing a strand of hair away from her face with an irresistibly delicate motion. 'I should be in Chicago right now, at a conference. Instead, I'm here, consoling myself with love poems and sushi. The pill was just an afterthought.'

'Hey, if it's consolation you need, you could do a lot worse than poetry and sushi. Funny, I flew in from Chicago today. I guess we should have switched cities by now. But, frankly, I'm glad you decided to stay in this one.'

Joel was, he realised, very glad that Chloe was in San Francisco right now. She wasn't the type of woman who would knock his head off its axis, but the more he studied her face, the more he wanted to look. No makeup, no artifice, nothing but clear skin, clean hair and open grey eyes. And that mouth – full, ripe, kissable – hinted at a sensuality that she probably saved for seafood and poets.

'It wasn't a conscious decision,' Chloe admitted. She picked up one of her chopsticks and began to pry off a sliver of wood with her thumbnail. 'I'm phobic about flying. I thought I could do it this time; the trip meant so much to me. But, in the end, I missed the plane. Sure, I can tell myself that I just forgot to go to the airport. But people who are terrified of airplanes don't forget when they're supposed to be on one.'

'No, they don't,' Joel agreed. 'No more than people who are scared of sharks forget when they're supposed to meet their friends at the beach.'

The waitress came to take his order. Joel asked for the

assorted sashimi platter, which included the *nigiri-ika*. He wasn't really into squid; he would give his portion to Chloe. In fact, he'd probably be willing to give her a whole lot more than squid, he thought, feeling like a perv as he surreptitiously checked out her figure. Under her T-shirt and jeans, she had a slim, supple body – small breasts, wasp waist, slender hips. All that gorgeous glossy hair filled his imagination with fantasies of her riding him, the long strands tickling his chest as she bent down to kiss his nipples.

Chloe would be the kind of lover who could appreciate the fact that men liked to have their nipples kissed, too. And Joel could tell by the way her mouth pursed with pleasure as she ate her spicy tuna roll that she'd bring a subtly sensual appetite to the whole kissing process, no matter what part of his body those luscious lips were addressing. Everywhere he looked, he saw sweet, tentative, tender spots in Chloe: her fear of planes, her book of love poems, her beaten-up pink backpack. She brought out an absurd Neanderthal urge in him to protect her – so politically incorrect that Joel was embarrassed to admit it to himself – by grabbing a handful of that sexy hair and dragging her off to a cave.

'I don't know what's going to happen now,' Chloe said mournfully, as she arranged translucent pink slices of pickled ginger on top of her sushi. 'Missing that flight could do a lot of damage to my career. Such as it is.'

'What do you mean?'

Chloe fixed Joel with a sad rain-coloured gaze, as if he couldn't possibly understand her plight. 'Finding a position as an Asian Studies professor isn't like getting a job designing databases. There just aren't that many jobs out there for people like me. I'm an anomaly in the modern world. Look at me, I'm a poetry geek who has fantasies about being a geisha girl. My dad keeps trying to get me to work for his company as a translator, but I can't stand the idea of translating technical stuff. I hate technology, especially if it flies, and I carry a Hello Kitty backpack. Look at me! I'm a mess!'

Seeing that she was about to sob into her dish of soy sauce, Joel couldn't resist wrapping his arms around Chloe and pulling her against his chest. Hugging a woman in distress was just the right thing to do. Getting aroused by the pressure of her long smooth torso against his, on the other hand, felt downright sleazy. When she tucked her face in the hollow of his shoulder and sighed, the warmth of her breath and the subtle shift of her breasts made Joel so hard that he almost groaned out loud. Why hadn't he just suggested that she set up a few extra appointments with her therapist?

Dude, you really need to stop hugging strangers. At least the female ones, Joel reproached himself. He'd made the same mistake with Lauryn only an hour earlier, pulling her against him and squeezing her like a python. Women usually thought of Joel as the big-brother type, too goofy and cuddly to pose a direct sexual threat, but, if they could get a visual of the inside of Joel's head when he held them tight, they'd probably need a support group to get over the psychological trauma.

Then they'd have him thrown in prison forever.

'I need to go home, before I totally humiliate myself.' Chloe sniffled.

'You're not humiliating yourself,' Joel reassured her, though in fact everyone in the restaurant was watching their display of emotion with fascinated horror.

'Yeah. I am. I can't lose my rep here; they make the best sushi in the city.'

She pulled away from Joel and wiped her nose with the back of her hand. In a lot of people, that faux pas of basic hygiene would have been just plain gross. In Chloe, for some reason, it was charming. And sexy. Of course, everything was sexy to a male who'd been living in a monastery for six weeks, at least if he were a healthy agnostic like Joel. Now that Chloe and Joel had broken their messy embrace, the waitress padded up to the sushi bar to serve Joel's lunch.

'Sure you don't want to stay and help me eat this?' Joel motioned at the gorgeous collage of fish and rice. Horny as he was, he hadn't eaten anything all day but a bag of airplane peanuts and a celery stick marinated in vodka. His empty belly was starting to rumble in protest.

'Why don't you get that to go, and come back to my place?' Chloe suggested. 'I live just up the hill. And I make a mean pot of green tea.'

Joel froze, his chopsticks poised over a piece of salmon sashimi. He'd been all set to watch Chloe drift off into the golden sunlight of a San Francisco afternoon, while he ate his sushi and reflected on her charms. Was this shy self-effacing poetry geek, who'd been about to dissolve into tears only moments ago, making a pass at him now? Or was his male ego simply warping an innocent invitation for tea into a full-blown come-on? He had figured that he'd finish his lunch, maybe catch a movie, then head back to the hotel and watch some TV before crashing for the night.

'But you hardly know me.' Joel laughed. 'You know my first name. And you know I love raw fish. I could be a dangerous sushi-loving psychopath.'

'So could I. What makes you think that only men are dangerous?'

Chloe narrowed her grey eyes and tilted her head. A sheaf of hair dipped across her face. On a tougher woman, that look would have been a threat. On Chloe, it was damn cute. 'Cute' was enough to convince Joel that he should take Chloe up on her offer, in spite of the fact that signs of mental instability had cropped up throughout their conversation like buttercups in a spring meadow.

What the hell. Joel was a journalist – to have any kind of glory, you had to take risks. You had to be flexible.

The waitress was already on her way to the bar with a Styrofoam container, leaving Joel no choice but to follow the sad sexy delicious Chloe back to her lair for some hot green tea.

Chapter Five

Logging On, Taking Off

'Hey, gorgeous. Whatcha looking at? Indulging in a little porn break?'

Lauryn slammed her laptop shut. She wheeled around to see a familiar male face leaning over her, his lips poised to nuzzle the back of her neck. This wasn't the first time that Barry's smouldering Mediterranean eyes had stared down into Lauryn's, but, on the prior occasions, there'd been cocktails and karaoke involved, followed by fondling, nudity and mutual embarrassment at the conference they had attended together the next day.

'Hi, Barry,' Lauryn said weakly. 'When did you get into town?'

She was sitting in the break room at B&M Associates, checking her online dating profiles on her wireless laptop. It figured that Barry would saunter up behind her while she was ogling a half-naked guy with washboard abs ('Dave, 27 years old, enjoys rugby, playing the ukulele, and lip-synching to Nina Simone') on MatchMeat.

'I landed in Oakland about an hour ago. Came straight over.' Barry set down his paper cup of coffee so he could straighten his tie and brush invisible dust off his steam-pressed trousers. As always, he looked impeccable, even after the flight. Anal-retentive little suck-up, Lauryn thought meanly. Barry was irresistibly hot, with his gym-toned muscles and honey skin, but he had an unbelievable Napoleon complex.

'Not me.' She yawned. 'I stopped for drinks in the city before I even thought about crossing the Bay Bridge.'

'That's why you'll never get out of this gig,' Barry gloated. 'Did I tell you that Stanley tapped me for the job in Brussels next month?'

Lauryn sat up straight. '*What*? He promised he'd consider *me* for Brussels!'

'He *did* consider you, blondie. Then he picked me.'

Rage and frustration welled up in Lauryn's throat, almost choking her. The job in Brussels, auditing a diamond importer, would not only have fulfilled Lauryn's dream of working internationally, it also would have taken her out of the human resources loop and elevated her into the realm of pure financial analysis. The job had everything Lauryn longed for – glamour, travel and lots of meaty number-crunching.

She knew why she hadn't gotten the job. It wasn't because she was burned out, or because she wasn't qualified, or because she hadn't been working her tail off the past few years. It was because she'd dragged her feet about doing a lap dance for Stanley.

'One of these days, I'm going to file a sexual-harassment suit against that fat jerk,' she muttered. 'If anyone ever needed a subpoena suppository, it's Stanley.'

'Aw, don't be bitter. There's a job in Paris coming up in September. Maybe you'll be more qualified with a little more experience under your belt.'

Lauryn snorted. 'Barry, it's not the *experience* under my belt that Stanley's interested in. Believe me. The guy's made it extremely clear that he won't send me out of the country unless I polish his knob for him. It's sexual harassment, plain and simple. Good old-fashioned quid pro quo.'

'So do something about it. Hey, I agree with you, the guy's a sleaze ball. Don't quote me on that, though. I wouldn't want to risk losing Brussels.'

'That's my problem, too,' Lauryn sighed. 'I don't want

to risk what little I already have. Or the possibility of having more someday.'

'I gotta tell you, it's not going to happen with Stanley. You'll never get what you want if you don't take a few risks here and there.'

'I know. Believe me, I know.'

'It could be worse. You could be working for a place like this. Lifetime B&M flunky, with your head on the chopping block. Twenty years of working for the man, and you're about to be downsized.'

Lauryn looked around at the dismal break room, with its cinderblock walls, rows of vending machines and bulletin boards bristling with OSHA posters and flyers advertising company picnics. Barry was right – painfully right. With her background, Lauryn could have easily ended up working for a place like B&M, standing in a factory line for eight hours a day, punching out widgets or whatever these people did. If she hadn't won a scholarship to a state university after two years of struggling through community college while working full-time as a waitress, she could very well be right here.

Of course, Barry didn't know all that. Like all of Lauryn's lovers, even the on-again, off-again ones, Barry had only received the heavily revised version of Lauryn's history, complete with the WASP nuclear family and the Ivy-League degree.

'Hey, there's nobody in here,' Barry said in a bedroom *sotto voce*.

Still standing over Lauryn, he leaned over and wrapped his arms around her from behind, cradling the undersides of her breasts in his palms as he crooned into her ear. Lauryn felt her body responding to him – nipples hardening, inner thighs softening, backbone arching – but she resisted. She and Barry had discovered that they shared a scorching-hot sexual chemistry and a taste for public sex. But, through the lust that fogged her vision when Barry touched her, Lauryn could see that the sparks between them were ignited more by competition and mutual hostility than by any actual desire.

'I'll take a rain check,' she said, squirming out of Barry's arms. Lauryn was a closet exhibitionist and, on any other day, it would have been an illicit thrill to lie on the Formica tabletop with her legs wrapped around Barry's shoulders as he peeled off her panties with his sturdy white teeth. But now that she knew she'd lost Brussels, Lauryn knew that sex with Barry would leave her with a bitter slimy aftertaste.

'Suit yourself,' Barry said with a shrug. Never one to take a blow to his ego over sexual rejection, he strutted out of the break room, smoothing his hair with one hand.

As soon as Barry was safely out of snooping range, Lauryn opened her laptop, and went back to the alternate reality of MatchMeat. She didn't consider her encounters with the men she met online to be 'dating'. She thought of them as social research. She wasn't looking for love, or a mate for eternity, or even one of the ubiquitous 'fuck buddies' who were constantly offering themselves through the spam she found in her bulk mailbox. All she wanted was a way to while away an hour or two, on the client's nickel, when she should have been crunching their numbers.

As part of her ongoing research project, Lauryn occasionally followed up on some of the offers she received. When one of the guys who responded to her online profiles aroused her curiosity – or just plain aroused her – she'd agree to meet them for dinner or a movie, or maybe a company picnic.

But Lauryn's 'research' had taken a shady turn when she started lurking on MatchMeat, a San Francisco-based dating site for gay males. About a month ago, when Lauryn was starting to feel a bit burned out on the heterosexual internet dating scene, she had started toying with the idea of pretending to be a man online.

There was hardly anything new about gender-swapping on the internet, but having a cyber-penis was a revolutionary discovery to Lauryn.

So was the sheer volume of mouth-watering males that she might have been able to choose from, if only she'd been an outgoing witty gay man instead of a bored, lonely single heterosexual female.

Surprisingly enough, it wasn't hard for Lauryn to convince the men on MatchMeat that she was a buff, charming 25-year-old bartender named Lou, who practised martial arts in his spare time and was saving up his tips to get a degree in soundtrack composition at the University of Southern California.

Lou, who had a suspicious resemblance to a black-haired blue-eyed male model in an Aer Lingus advertisement Lauryn had found in a magazine on one of her flights, had no trouble finding potential partners on MatchMeat. From the first time he sauntered into one of the chat rooms (called the 'Sausage-Smoker's Lounge'), Lou had knocked the other guys out of their tight whities. He was sexy, charming, debonair; an expert on single-malt whiskies; expert martini mixer; runner; practitioner of the gentle warrior arts; and, most of all, a movie buff, who could rattle off random facts about the score to just about any film you could name, from the very first talkies to the latest blockbuster action flick.

With the help of her scanner, Google and the Internet Movie Database, Lauryn was able to invent a male alter-ego who was so desirable that it almost scared her. Dozens of men, then *hundreds*, wanted to hook up with Lou, for everything from cocktails to just plain cock. When it came to his male endowments, Lou modestly admitted that he was hung like a marble stallion. He was even willing to email photos of his 'hidden talent' (thanks, *Playgirl* 1986!) to men whose offers of love or devotion or fucking or funding piqued his interest.

Then Lou met Matt, and Lauryn's gender-bending fantasy turned into Frankenstein's monster. Or Frankenstein's crush, as the case might be. Matt was a dreamy achingly sensitive college senior who was making his first tentative splash into the shark pool of online love. He tried to bluster his way into Lou's heart with suggestions of rough sex, but, even if Lou couldn't recognise a faker, Lauryn could. Lauryn made sure that Lou, who could be a bit of a player, was careful with Matt's emotions when they chatted online. When Matt's friendly flirty emails began to sprout wings and fly off into the realms of romance, Lauryn reluctantly decided that this tender new relationship – and Lou himself – had to be euthanised.

Matt was crushed when he found out that Lou was really Lauryn. His disappointment almost made Lauryn consider the whole fabrication thing; she had always thought of her inventions as embroidery, a little harmless embellishment that made the ragged edges of her life look prettier. But she had to admit, not only to Matt but to herself, that she'd stepped over the line with Lou. Lou wasn't just a prettified version of her own back story; he was an alternate identity, who had taken on a love life of his own. Lauryn apologised to Matt via every form of communication technology available to her – by email, instant messenger, text messenger, even over the phone. She offered to make up for his pain in any way he could think of; sex was probably out of the question, since she didn't have Lou's endowments, but she'd do absolutely anything else. Anything.

'OK. I want you to start telling the truth,' Matt had said, with a earnestness that made Lauryn feel like she had the moral stature of a cockroach. 'Stop lying to people. But, most of all, you need to start being honest with yourself.'

Telling the truth, the ruthlessly unadorned truth, seemed so bleak, so ... boring. Being honest, at this stage in her life, would be like trying to clean out the closet where she'd been stashing all her boxes of old photos and high-school yearbooks and tax forms. Lauryn simply wouldn't know where to start rebuilding her identity – which parts to keep, which parts to throw away. Would she have to toss the contact lenses that made her mismatched eyes the same shade of smoky hazel? What about the sexy ash-blonde streaks in her hair, would she have to relinquish those, and let the whole world see that her natural hair colour was unadulterated dishwater? And what about the tanning salon – would she have to give that up, too?

You could start with the fake degree from Yale, said a sly voice in Lauryn's head. *Why don't you just admit that you got your MBA at a state school in Southern California? Why are you so ashamed of who you are?*

'Shut up! I'm not ashamed. I just have an image to maintain,' Lauryn muttered. There was nothing wrong with having a working-class background; the world loved a Cinderella story. But after Cinderella moved into the castle with Prince Charming, she couldn't have run around reminding the nobility about her scullery-maid origins. She'd never have maintained her princess cred, if she hadn't discarded her past.

A plump silvery-haired woman who had come into the break room to browse the vending machines gave Lauryn a curious look. Lauryn managed to produce an apologetic laugh – *oh, silly me, talking to myself again!* – and the woman turned back to the array of candy bars. That woman, with her polyester stretch pants and natural grey hair, probably told the truth about herself every day of her life. She woke up in the morning, put on unflattering clothes that did nothing to hide her weight, eschewed any form of makeup and walked out to her car to drive to a job that she was thoroughly proud of.

All bipeds were liars, in one way or another, Lauryn believed, even those who didn't diet, dye their hair or frequent tanning salons. Lying was part of the human condition. What was the point in having an imagination, if you couldn't use it to brighten the dark dusty corners of your life?

'So why Japan?' Joel was standing in the middle of Chloe's apartment, hands in his pockets, checking out her décor: the bookshelves overloaded with texts in Japanese and Chinese, the tatami mats on the floor, her futon, her shamefully extensive collection of manga and anime, contrasting with the lavishly erotic hentai prints on her walls. What was going through his head? Chloe wondered. Did he think she was smart, exotic, intriguing? Or just a geek with too many books and a few lewd posters?

'Why not?' Chloe replied. She meant to sound offhand and breezy, but the words came out sounding prickly.

'Hey. I'm just trying to get to know you better,' Joel said softly.

He accepted the steaming mug that Chloe handed him, but, instead of sipping the tea, he set the mug down on her computer desk and lifted a strand of hair off her shoulder. He rubbed her hair between his thumb and forefinger, an almost unconscious gesture that she found both touching and sexy. Joel reminded her of a big brother, not her own, fortunately, but someone else's. Inviting him back to her place had been scary, but Chloe was in the mood for doing something scary today, something bold and outrageous that would reassure her that she wasn't the world's biggest chicken because she'd missed her plane that morning.

Bringing Joel home had seemed like a good idea. So did taking his face in her hands and pulling him down for a hard sudden kiss.

Kissing Joel hadn't been part of Chloe's agenda, at least not so soon. She had imagined them drinking their tea, talking about books and movies, getting to know each other in all the polite conventional ways. But, when Joel touched Chloe's hair, tugging ever so gently at the strand as he fondled its silky length, she felt an urge to kiss him and, for once, Chloe obeyed one of her urges instead of letting it fizzle out and die. She felt a tremor of shock run through his body, and he stiffened at first, as if he weren't sure where the kiss was going. But it didn't take long for him to figure that part out, and soon the liplock had deepened into tongue play.

You don't even know this man! shrieked an inner voice that sounded suspiciously like Chloe's mother. There was only one way to stifle those shrill protests – Chloe would have to get to know Joel better, and the natural next step seemed to be wrapping her arms around his waist and pulling his large strong torso against hers. He felt so good, like a big athletic bear, that Chloe couldn't keep her hands from roving across his back and shoulders, then down to his waist and finally to his firm butt. For a man who was being groped all over, Joel was remarkably restrained at first, letting Chloe take the lead and touch him where and how she pleased. She wasn't used to seizing that kind of control in a makeout session; usually she was the one who held back, letting her lover caress and manipulate her while her body hesitantly opened under his touch.

Today, Chloe was hungry. There was something about Joel that woke her sleeping appetites, making her want to not only kiss him, but to devour him; not only hold him, but squeeze and grasp and tease and tempt him. While most tall men intimidated her, Joel's size made her feel safe enough to do whatever she wanted. French-kissing him. Grinding her hips against his. Running her fingers through his hair, which felt as soft as goose down and smelled of Johnson's Baby Shampoo.

Chloe only wished she could get past the nagging thought that she was trying to kiss and clutch her way past Aidan. The realisation that she was thinking about her therapist while making out with another man was disturbing at the very least. Images of Aidan's deft hands and gorgeous eyes kept swimming to the top of her consciousness, even as she rubbed against the planes of Joel's chest and abdomen like a cat in heat. And when Joel groaned, drawing her hips against his body so that his hardness came in direct contact with her pubic bone, Chloe had the strangest feeling that, in some bizarre way, she was being *unfaithful* to Aidan.

How could you be unfaithful to a guy you weren't romantically involved with? Especially if the nature of your professional relationship killed the possibility of romantic involvement, anyway? Chloe squeezed her eyes shut, as if closing her eyes would have any effect on her inner visions of a man with gleaming black hair and a supple feline body. When Joel lifted her off her feet, scooping her up as if she were no heavier than a Ming vase, and carried her over to the futon, Chloe had a moment of panic.

Why don't you just admit that Aidan is the Japanese nobleman in every one of your tawdry erotic fantasies? she asked herself. *Be honest with yourself. Be honest with him. You need to find another therapist. And you need to stop brooding over Aidan when you're about to be ravished by the most attractive guy you've met in months.*

'Chloe? Earth to Chloe. Are you OK?'

Joel leaned over Chloe, whom he'd arranged on her back on the futon. His blue eyes – such a clear pure blue – searched hers with a worried look. The skin between his eyebrows wrinkled in an incredibly cute way.

'I'm fine. Peachy,' she said. She reached up to pull him down on top of her, but he resisted.

'I don't want to do this if you don't really want to. I'm so turned on right now that I'm about to explode, but I have this sneaking feeling that you're not really with me. Is there something on your mind? I've got a condom, if that's what you're worried about. I always play safe.'

Chloe smiled. She traced the edges of Joel's lips with her fingertip. His mouth was moist, bitten red from their kissing. She could feel the ridge of his hard-on pressing against her upper thigh, and the thud of his heart under her palm when she stroked his chest, yet here he was asking what was on *her* mind.

'There *was* something on my mind,' she admitted. 'But I'm not thinking about him – I mean, it – any more. I promise.'

'Are you sure? Because I know this is all happening really fast. Faster than I'm used to myself. The last thing I expected when I woke up this morning was that I'd end the afternoon on a futon with a sexy woman.' Joel laughed, and his cheeks flushed like an embarrassed teenager's.

'You think I'm sexy? Are you joking?' Now it was Chloe's turn to blush.

'It should be fairly obvious that I think you're sexy. I'm lying on top of you, hard as steel, using my superpowers to fight the desire to tear your clothes off.'

'Well, you can stop fighting. In fact, I'll help you.'

Chloe yanked her T-shirt over her head and wriggled out of her bra, while Joel unbuttoned her jeans and pulled them down. Soon she was naked, except for her underpants, and Joel was hurriedly stripping off his own shirt and khaki trousers. He slowed down for a moment, and with gentle deliberation peeled off her panties, gazing not at her pussy, but into her eyes.

'You're not just sexy, Chloe,' he said. 'You're gorgeous.'

'So are you,' she replied, and she meant it. From his sincere blue eyes to his long tanned torso to the thick arch of his cock and his muscular thighs, Joel was a gorgeous man. She hadn't really seen that until now; when she first met him, he had struck her more like an easy-going, rumpled best-buddy type, the kind of man that Chloe would refer to as a 'cutie' rather than a 'hottie'.

Sans clothes and glasses, his naked body was charged with erotic energy. When he parted Chloe's thighs, she thought he was going to put on his condom and enter her right away. Instead, he slid downwards, off the edge of the futon, and spread her lower lips with his fingers so that he could lick the inner shell of her pussy. His tongue wove through the folds slowly, as if he were savouring the taste of that tender flesh. Then he began to lick more insistently, nibbling and biting at her fleshy outer lips, before his tongue began to flick at her clit.

Chloe groaned – a husky unladylike growl. Ordinarily she wasn't a big fan of oral sex; she always worried about how she smelled and tasted, and whether her lover's tongue was getting tired. But Joel was eating her with such hunger, moaning himself as he lapped at her swollen bud, that she just gave in and enjoyed it. She couldn't remember the last time that any man had made her feel so selfishly good. Spreading her legs wide, she wove her fingers through Joel's hair, guiding the motions of his mouth, showing him which parts of her pussy needed attention. He was an eager student, quickly finding her most sensitive areas – the underside and very tip of her clitoris, and the warm pink grooves alongside the button.

A warm tingling self-awareness was melting Chloe's lower body. Her skin seemed to vibrate, as if her body were purring with anticipation. Her hips moved involuntarily, finding a rhythm that matched the motions of Joel's mouth, and, as the first waves of her orgasm rolled through her, she wrapped her legs around his neck and squeezed him with her thighs. Her toes curled, her legs stiffened. The climax had a life of its own, swelling and surging and peaking, taking over her consciousness, turning her into a banshee. It didn't even occur to her, until her pulse subsided to its usual tempo and she was struggling to catch her breath, that she might have suffocated Joel in the process.

'Oh, no. I'm sorry. I didn't mean ... I could have ...' she babbled. 'Are you OK? Did I get too crazy? It's just been such a long time.'

Joel looked up at her with an expression that could

only be described as a classic 'pussy-eating grin'. Smug, self-satisfied and utterly content, he didn't seem to mind that she'd lapsed into a moment of raving sexual mania.

'You can't get too crazy when you're coming,' he said. 'Don't ever apologise for enjoying yourself in bed. Or on a futon, or on the floor, or on the bathroom sink.'

He pulled himself up so that he was lying on top of Chloe, arms braced on either side of her body, and then he entered her, just barely, with the head of his erect cock, teasing her outer lips before he drove himself all the way into her. It was a long shivery slide, and her wetness made her more than ready for it. Joel's blue eyes fluttered shut as he started to thrust – seven times, eight, then all of his muscles stiffened, and he was shouting out in pleasure. Chloe just held on to his shoulders and watched him. She loved watching a lover's face when he was coming; she would never get used to that sense of pride and surprise that came from knowing she'd triggered that intense explosion.

'Now it's my turn to apologise,' Joel gasped, collapsing on to his elbows. 'It's been a long time for me, too.'

Chloe could feel his heart hammering in his chest, its vibrations thundering through to her own. His face was damp, face flushed brick-red. Chloe placed her palm against his cheek; his skin felt almost feverish.

'You were perfect,' she said. 'This was perfect. You were exactly what I needed to make up for this morning.'

Joel laughed, still breathing raggedly. 'Glad I could be of service.'

He rolled over on to the futon, face-down, and promptly passed out. So much for perfect, Chloe thought, but she couldn't really say she was disappointed. She'd been impulsive, she'd been sexually assertive and she'd been given the best orgasm that she'd had in recent memory. What did it matter if she couldn't fly in airplanes, as long as she could *fly*?

Bootybuddies:
Try our Sexuality Survey!

Thanks for choosing BootyBuddies as your hot new online hookup spot. Find the booty you've always wanted (but probably couldn't afford) right here in our raging assortment of hot 'n' horny singles! Tired of being rejected by dating services that assume you're looking for a soulmate? Want to bond for a night, not for eternity? You've COME to the right site! Satisfaction – sexual, at least – is 100% guaranteed. Answer the questions below to let us know what kind of lover you are. Sweet and shy? Wild and crazy? Hey, it doesn't matter to us, as long as you get off! Be honest, or not. At BootyBuddies, you'll be anonymous unless you request otherwise. Live a little, live a lot – what the hell!

Have you ever masturbated on an airplane?

Lauryn: Absolutely. Well, not really.

I want all that – the freedom and lack of gravity, et cetera – I really do. I think about sexual freedom a lot, about being uninhibited enough to make myself come on a plane. You'd think with all my frequent-flier miles, I'd become a frequent airplane masturbator, too. I did do it once, not with a vibrator, but with my, um, pager. And it wasn't on purpose; it was more like an accident. I dropped my pager in my lap, and it worked its way under my skirt and went off in mid-air. I guess you could say I went off, too. It wasn't anything special. It lacked, I don't know, intimacy. I took my pager out for cocktails after the flight. We talked, and we both agreed we'd be better off staying friends.

Veronica: Hey, if I had the money to fly, I'd diddle myself on a plane. Why not? It would be more fun than watching a lame movie. As it is, I take a Greyhound if I have to go anywhere. I can't even afford a car right now. But, if you really want to know something pervy about me, I do like to watch people in the airport and make up sexual fantasies about them. When I'm having a slow day, sometimes I'll sit down and find somebody hot to look at – guy, girl, makes no difference to me, as long as they're sexy. And I'll start imagining undressing them, kissing them, fondling their ass or their tits. There's been a couple of times I've made myself come that way. Not so anyone would know ... I've got this way of masturbating in public so no one could ever figure out that I'm getting off. Wish I could tell you my secret method, but I'm thinking about having it patented someday.

Chloe: Masturbate? On a plane? With other *people* on it? No. Not me. Never. Actually, to tell you the truth, I don't even fly. It's not that I don't want to – fly, I mean. I'm just terrified of being so high in the air, with no wires or anything to hold me up. Sex scares me. Orgasms scare me. It's all part of the same problem, you know? I just can't stand the idea of being so high ... with no wires or anything to hold me up.

Chapter Six

Frequent Fliers

Veronica's inbox was overflowing again. Feeling monumentally bored, she scrolled through the pages of emails from men (and women) who were responding to the profiles she'd set up on various online dating sites. Winks, nudges, outright solicitations for no-strings sex ... none of the offers was remotely appealing. It never ceased to amaze Veronica that the more bitchy she was in her profiles, the harder she worked to come across as a tough-as-nails punk, the more hotly she was pursued.

'OMG UR SO HOTT!!' exploded one of her admirers, whose username on BootyBuddies.com was Dinkyboy.

What woman in her right mind would want to date a guy named Dinkyboy? Veronica wondered. She cackled to herself as she hit the delete button and watched his message vanish into the cybervoid.

Veronica had originally started surfing the dating sites to get ideas for her escort service; she wanted to know what people looked for, when they threw themselves out in the world in a quest for sex, love, companionship, eternal commitment. The answer, she found, was a frustrating paradox: not enough, and too much. Either their expectations were so high that you could get a nosebleed just reading about them ('I am seeking nothing less than my perfect match. Beauty, intelligence, financial and mental stability are must-haves for any woman who would aspire to date me'), or so low that they could send you into a major depressive tailspin ('I am lonely. I need someone. Please').

Somewhere between those extremes there had to be a middle ground, but it was obvious to Veronica that the denizens of the internet-dating world were having a hard time finding it. The problem was, she believed, that they relied too heavily on their own resources, which were pretty damn skimpy to begin with. You couldn't just pop up online, post a few photos of yourself, record an earnest list of your likes and dislikes, and expect to be flooded with offers of eternal devotion. Even the search for hot tempestuous sex required more ingenuity than that. You couldn't find mind-blowing sex sitting in front of a computer monitor; you needed to hold your nose and dive into the real world. And, if you weren't brave enough to take that plunge on your own, you needed someone to hold your hand and jump with you.

That's where Veronica, with her little stable of NaughtyChix, would come in. Her mission: helping wealthy horny men hook up with gorgeous intriguing women who would introduce them to all kinds of deviant adventures. At prices ranging from three hundred dollars for a night on the town to five thousand dollars for an exotic weekend getaway, who needed online dating?

Well, maybe geeks who didn't have any money. But Veronica wasn't worried about them. The only men she cared about were the attorneys, doctors, software giants and other major-league players who could afford her escorts.

The NaughtyChix light bulb had gone on over Veronica's head about six months earlier, when she was surfing the web for modelling sites. One of her clients at the shoeshine stand had told Veronica that her look was in these days at a lot of modelling agencies; goth chicks, pierced and tattooed, were selling everything from beer to diapers, right along with the traditional long-stemmed blonde supermodels. More out of curiosity than anything else, Veronica had gone online to check out the opportunities. She'd found a couple of agencies, but, more importantly, she'd discovered the escorts. Page after page of sleek glamour girls, many of them boasting advanced degrees along with a superabundance of charm and erotic talent, charging prices for their time that blew Veronica's mind.

Baffled, Veronica showed some of the sites to her roommate Odessa. The auburn-haired Odessa was the worldliest of her friends, as cynical as she was stunning.

'Can you believe the prices these girls are charging?' Veronica had asked. 'What do you have to have to charge five hundred bucks for two hours? A platinum pussy? And, if these guys have enough money to pay those kinds of prices, why don't they just find some hot gold-digging girlfriend?'

'Veronica, darling,' Odessa had said, 'you're missing the point here. The point isn't what you're paying for; it's the fact that you're paying at all. Sure, the girls are yummy. But, at that price, they're not just candy; they're a commodity. Men like to pay for expensive toys; spending money inflates their egos. Finding a gold-digger girlfriend would be an option, sure, but the problem with girlfriends is that they don't go away when the meter's up.'

'Wow!' was all Veronica could say, her mind reeling at Odessa's crazily mixed metaphors. She thought she knew all there was to know about sex, but this whole escort business was virgin territory (so to speak) to Veronica.

Veronica had thought it might be fun to put up a spoof of those websites, featuring her eclectic collection of roommates charging outrageous prices for dinner and drinks. They'd all get shit-faced together and use Imogene's digital camera to take pictures of themselves, then they'd post them online and advertise their 'services' at nosebleed rates.

Then it dawned on her ... why should it be a joke? Veronica's roommates were exotic, offbeat, a totally different breed from the feline beauties who were selling their services online. Men who had a craving for something a bit more spicy, a bit more quirky, might be inclined to shell out a few hundred bucks for a taste of strange. Veronica thought her roommates might be offended by the suggestion that they charge money for their time, but they were titillated, excited, thrilled by the idea.

'I love it!' Imogene had squealed, looking like a pierced chipmunk as her face scrunched with glee. 'I'm gonna be a hooker!'

'You won't be hookers,' Veronica had told her roommate sternly. 'I don't want to ever hear that word around here. You won't be hookers, whores or call girls, or any variation of the term. You'll be *escorts*. Big difference. If you choose to give your date a party favour after he takes you out to dinner, that's your business, but any money you make in that case will be a gift, not a fee. Got it?'

The girls got it.

They still loved it.

Thus, NaughtyChix – Odessa complained that the name of the service sounded like a breakfast cereal for perverts, but Veronica refused to change it – was born. The service hadn't gotten off the ground yet, but NaughtyChix was definitely prowling the runway. All they needed was someone to handle the financial end of things, and a decent photographer who was willing to do stunning work at bargain-basement rates.

Blowing air through her pursed lips, Veronica closed her email and went back to the project she'd been working on, writing the copy for a series of profiles for NaughtyChix:

Imogene: She's the girl next door gone wrong – gorgeously wrong! Imagine Imogene sipping champagne in your limo, giggling at all your jokes, shocking your straitlaced colleagues with her pink hair, piercings and tattoos. Let this wild-child lead you on a reckless ride through the city's hottest underground clubs, or whisk her away for a lost weekend in the wine country. Her supple young body will tantalise you; her carefree spirit will delight you. Life is short – party hard!

Odessa: This glamorous auburn-haired vixen has the body of a gothic goddess and an IQ of 152. She'll engage your mind with her intellect while seducing your senses with her beauty. Odessa's elegant beauty, razor-sharp wit and extensive collection of evening wear make her the perfect companion for nights on the town, fundraising benefits or private weekends in San Francisco's elite hotels. Indulge yourself in a heady combination of brains and beauty with this seductive siren!

Dawl: Let the city's sexiest tomboy show you *all* her favourite plays! She's cute, tight and can talk baseball with you all night. In or out of the bedroom, sports are her passion. Need a fun hot companion for your Superbowl party or company softball tournament? From hiking to horse-racing to major-league football, Dawl knows the score, and she'll keep you on top of your game!

Mandy: Jayne Mansfield rides again in this 21st-century version of the classic platinum-blonde sex goddess! With her knockout hourglass figure (42–30–38) and her lusciously pouting lips, Mandy will bring a taste of Hollywood style to any public event. Heads will turn everywhere you go when you have this stunner draped on your arm. This blue-eyed darling has a voice like honey and a personality to match – she'll turn any night or weekend into a blissfully sensual experience.

OK, enough of that tripe. Veronica was satisfied with her copy, but words didn't mean much without pictures.

What NaughtyChix needed was a scrapbook; men were too visually oriented to be satisfied with staring at black-and-white words.

Besides, Veronica herself was getting horny. Writing about fantasy sex made her feel like indulging in a little exotic role-play, too. Why should her girls have all the fun? Veronica punched Devin's number into her cell phone. His roommate Bob answered, his 'Hello' sounding distinctly stoned.

'Is Devin there?' Veronica asked, wondering what kind of apathetic dweeb started hitting the bong at nine thirty in the morning.

'Uhhhh ... I think so. He's somewhere around here –' Bob hesitated, as if it were possible to lose your roommate in a two-bedroom apartment.

'He's not stoned, too, is he?'

'Hell, no. I'm not sharing my bud with Devbo.'

Thank God for small favours. 'Good. I'm coming over. Don't let him go anywhere.'

'You wanna talk to him?'

'No. And don't let him know I'm on the way.'

Veronica snapped her cell phone shut and turned off her computer. Imogene had left early that morning – today was her day to open at Starbucks – and her closet yawned open, spilling an array of colourful scanty skirts, tops and dresses, thong panties and sheer stockings on to the floor. Imogene was a slob, but that made it a lot easier to borrow her clothes. She'd never know in a million years that Veronica had raided her closet for some appropriate seduction attire.

Devin seemed to need a lot of extra stimulation these days. Maybe he was smoking too much ganja, or spending too many hours lost in Warlock World, but Veronica could barely get his attention any more. As she rifled through Imogene's heaps of nylon and lace and Lycra and spandex, searching for something that could drag his eyes away from his 24-inch monitor, Veronica considered her relationship. Their erotic pilot light was definitely sputtering out; each time they got together, it seemed to take more energy, more sexual fuel to reignite it. Sex shouldn't be that way, Veronica thought. Not after three months.

Imogene's clothes were all so ... *ho-ish*. Veronica couldn't think of a more tactful way to describe the dozens of stretchy little bra-tops and micro-minis, fishnet this and fishnet that. All this stuff looked hot on Imogene, with her skinny little body and pert tiny tits, but any one of these outfits would make Veronica's hefty bottom look like a couple of sandbags bound in elastic.

Ah. Now this was more like it. Reaching deep into the chaos of the closet, Veronica found a flared black-watch plaid skirt and white blouse with a prim Peter Pan collar. What was this getup? An old uniform from Imogene's days at Sacred Heart, or a Halloween costume? Whatever it was, Veronica liked it. And the plaid number was probably the only skirt in Chloe's wardrobe that would fit over her broad bum.

She stripped off the sweatpants and grubby T-shirt she'd been wearing and slipped into the uniform. The skirt was a bit snug around her waist, but that didn't matter; she'd be out of it soon enough. The buttons on the white blouse strained over her full breasts. Twirling around in front of Imogene's full-length mirror, she pushed her full lips into a sulky pout. Once she tied up her hair in pigtails and donned her geekiest pair of glasses, she would look like the world's sexiest schoolgirl.

Poor Devin. Veronica almost felt sorry for him. He was about to be dragged out of his online universe and right into one of her oldest secret fantasies.

Devin shared a basement apartment in the Mission District with his roommate Bob, another sporadically employed programmer. As Veronica skipped through the Mission, swinging a boxy, black little-old-lady purse that she'd bought at an estate sale, she couldn't help revelling in all the stares she was gathering from passers-by standing in front of taco stands and walking out of used-record stores. The world must be full of people with twisted minds, she thought, or maybe that was just San Francisco. There wasn't anything especially kinky about her attire, it was just the appeal of a twenty-something woman strutting her stuff in pigtails and plaid that seemed to turn everybody on.

Everybody except Bob, that is. When he opened the door of the apartment, squinting into the daylight from the cavernous depths, Bob just looked confused. 'Are you trying to convert people?' he asked, blinking at Veronica's Catholic-schoolgirl garb. 'I'm kind of an atheist.'

Veronica ripped off her geeky glasses and scowled at her boyfriend's roommate. 'It's *me*, Bob. It's Veronica. Get a clue.'

Bob shrugged and stepped back, letting Veronica stomp inside. 'Whatever' was his only comment. 'Devbo was in his room, last time I checked. But that was sometime last week.'

Bob wandered back to his computer desk, where a homemade soda-can bong spun out the last skunky smoke of some pricey greenbud. Veronica had no idea how Bob could afford such expensive marijuana, when he seemed to work only about six days out of the year. She figured he had to be dealing, which implied that 'Devbo' was probably in on this little enterprise, too.

'You guys need to quit doing drugs and grow up.'

Veronica didn't really care what Bob did with his life, but she couldn't resist throwing that remark his way as she walked towards Devin's bedroom.

'OK,' Bob replied amiably, pressing the can to his lips for another hit.

Hopeless. These guys were hopeless. Veronica didn't know why she bothered. She opened Devin's door without knocking, and found him predictably installed in front of his 24-inch monitor, in the midst of an intense battle involving monsters and skeletons.

'Hi, Devin,' she simpered, sweet as fresh apple pie. 'Why dontcha turn around and look at me?'

Veronica posed behind Devin's ergonomic office chair, waiting for him to finish his slaughter so he could turn around and notice her sexy outfit. She sucked the tip of her index finger, twirled a pigtail, flicked her hips back and forth to feel the pleated skirt whisk her bare thighs.

'Hnnnngh.' The noise that emerged from Devin's slack mouth seemed to signify something between 'hello' and 'leave me alone'.

'Devin!' Veronica grabbed the back of her boyfriend's chair and wheeled him around to face her. 'Leave that freaking game alone for ten seconds. Look. At. Me.'

Devin's eyes accommodated to the shift in perspective, from staring at a virtual 3D battlefield to staring at the lush body of his girlfriend, poured into tight white cotton and plaid. That was more like it, Veronica thought, as his agile hands instinctively reached for her hips and pulled her closer. Veronica straddled his thighs, giving him a clear view of the sweet milky-white inner skin.

'So what do you think? Do you like my uniform? I was late for school today. I'm a bad girl.'

His hands were already reaching under the skirt, roving for the hem of her white panties. They were the only pair of white cotton underpants that Veronica owned, and she'd chosen them with care. She wanted to look innocent, fresh, untainted – as different from her usual self as possible.

'Gosh, Vee,' he sputtered, 'you are so freakin' hot.'

She tilted her head, batted her eyes, sucked her fingertip again. 'Do you think I'm pretty, Devin? 'Cause sometimes I just don't know.'

'You're delicious, sweetheart. You look good enough to eat.'

'So do you.'

'Well, what are we waiting for, then?'

Devin grinned and pulled Veronica down on to his lap. She could feel the ridge of his hard-on nudging its way into the groove between her thighs, and she subtly ground her pussy against it, as if she weren't aware of the havoc she was wreaking on Devin's libido. On the flat-panel display, the battle was burning its way to a catastrophic conclusion in Devin's game; his dwarf army was being demolished.

He's mine now, Veronica thought. You warlocks and monsters can all go to hell. She wrapped her arms around Devin's shoulders, running her fingers along his shoulder blades, her nails down the back of his neck, lightly scratching the hair at the base of his thick ponytail. Devin's body always felt so good – sinewy, but not too thin, his muscles holding a latent strength that belied all the hours he spent sitting in front of his computer. Veronica loved the way his body responded to her, the way his hips rose to meet hers, drawing her so close that she could feel the drumbeat of the pulse in his erection. He groaned as her hands made their familiar circuit from the nape of his neck to the front of his throat, then down the planes of his chest to his pebbled nipples, which she circled with her palms.

Veronica caught herself. She didn't want to take control this time; today she was in the mood for a new game. Lifting her hands off of Devin's chest, she ran her finger along her lower lip in mock hesitation.

'I don't know about this,' she said, in her best imitation of a naive teenager. 'What do we do next?'

'Huh?' Devin's mouth drooped in a puzzled pout.

'I mean, I've never even kissed a boy before. Can you show me what to do?'

Light dawned in Devin's eyes, telling her that he was catching on. 'Sure, honey,' he said softly. 'Kissing is easy. It's as easy as rolling out of bed, only a whole lot more fun. It goes like this.'

He took Veronica's face in both hands and pulled her tenderly towards his mouth. The trip seemed to last forever as she looked into his clear blue eyes, which shone with expectation. His respectful touch, which often left her frustrated and longing for something rough and hard, fit this scenario perfectly; she was going to be his tender young ingénue, and he was playing the perfect teacher.

And what a teacher Devin was turning out to be! His lips met Veronica's lightly, almost tentatively, with just the faintest hint of tongue shifting behind his full lips. But Devin didn't shove his tongue into Veronica's mouth, or grind his lips against hers with such gusto that she felt his teeth. In reality, Veronica's first kiss had been a gnashing nightmare of braces, slobber and a tongue as thick and salty as a slab of corned beef. Thirteen years old at the time, she remembered thinking that, if the kiss ever ended, she would never suck face with another boy again for the rest of her life.

Devin was kissing her delicately now, his lips pressing hers with just enough urgency to send a ripple of electricity up her spine. She longed to kiss him back, hard and heavy, the way they usually did, but she forced herself to stay in her shy virginal role. Devin's hands were on the small of her back, moving her body back in forth in a rocking-horse rhythm that was suggestive without being lewd. She knew he was getting harder as her lush weight bore down on his groin; she could hear a moan rumbling deep in his chest, swallowed by her mouth as he continued to kiss her.

Veronica broke away and looked into Devin's eyes again. They were unfocused, blurred by bliss.

'Am I doing it right?' she asked, feigning uncertainty. 'The kissing, I mean?'

'You can kiss me a little harder,' he said. 'And use your tongue. Flick it around inside my mouth, like this.'

Their mouths met again, this time with more force.

Devin parted her lips with his tongue and swirled the tip around the soft inner membranes, making Veronica tremble from the tantalising sensation. Meanwhile, his hands had moved up her rib cage and were resting at the very edge of the swell of her breasts. When he began to rub the soft flesh there, her nipples hardened and, when he pressed the balls of his thumbs against the tight peaks, she thought she'd jump out of her skin. If he kept this up, she was going to revert to her usual man-hungry self, tear his clothes off and ride him into the sunset, or into her orgasm, whichever came first.

'Slow down,' she whined. 'I'm still a virgin.'

Devin choked back a laugh, but he managed to stay in character. 'I'm sorry, baby. I didn't mean to be disrespectful. Just tell me when to stop, and I'll stop. Is it OK if I touch you here?'

His hands returned to a respectable distance from her breasts, settling on her waist just above the curve of her hips.

'What I really want,' Veronica said, 'is for you to touch me between my legs. I feel all sticky and funny down there.'

Devin's hand slid into the warm damp crevice between Veronica's thighs, his fingers edging their way towards her pussy lips. When his fingertips made contact with her succulent flesh, his eyes closed and a harsh sigh came from his mouth.

'See what I mean?' Veronica asked. 'I don't know why I get like that sometimes.'

'That's just what happens to girls when they get the horn – I mean, when they're excited. It's natural, baby. And it's very, very good. How does this feel?'

His index finger pried her moist lips apart, searching through her softness until he found the swollen button inside the folds.

'It feels really, really nice,' Veronica moaned. Then her

moan turned into a guttural growl. 'Oh, fuck, it feels *great.*'

'Where did a nice girl like you learn a dirty word like that?' Devin grinned. 'I oughta give you a spanking. In fact...'

Before she knew what was happening, Devin had whirled Veronica's body around so that she was lying across his lap, staring into the forest of his fungus-green shag carpet. Her ass suddenly felt several degrees cooler as Devin flipped up her pleated skirt and tugged down her white cotton panties, then much, much warmer when he began to pepper her cheeks with sharp slaps.

'Ow!' she shouted, all indignation now. 'What the hell do you think you're doing?'

'You talk more like a sailor than a schoolgirl. You know, the more you swear, the harder I'm going to have to spank you.'

'It hurts! Stop it!'

'Not until you promise never to swear again,' Devin replied, slapping her bottom with even more relish.

He was getting into this spanking and, as his hard palm generated a furious tingle in her flesh, Veronica got into it, too. This was what she'd always longed for him to do – take control, get rough, give her a taste of pain. And his roughness was as arousing as she'd always known it would be, making her feel like she could explode into a climax at any moment.

But she didn't. The burning in her bottom kept her hovering on a razor-sharp edge between pain and pleasure; Veronica was aching to come, but Devin's swats kept her orgasm at bay. All she could do was gasp out her shock and delight each time her boyfriend's hand struck her butt, driving her mound into his upper thigh.

'Learned your lesson?' he asked, after what seemed like an endless infliction of agony.

In the aftermath, the fiery pain in Veronica's cheeks

subsided into a delicious tingling that made her hornier than ever.

'I'll never swear again,' Veronica said, almost sobbing in her relief and her need to come.

'Promise?'

'I promise, damnit!'

She turned her head to glare up into Devin's face, which wore an expression of mingled excitement and satisfaction. He'd probably been wanting to do this to Veronica since the first day they met, for every time she'd ever called him a 'pothead' or demanded to know when he was going to separate his ass from the computer chair and join the real world again.

But Devin had taken pity on her now. Instead of whacking her butt, he stroked her smooth cheeks, massaged them, soothing the stinging flesh and refreshing the burn at the same time. His fingers slid down the cleft between her cheeks, coming to rest in the folds between her thighs.

'My, my,' he said. 'You are a naughty girl, aren't you? You *liked* being spanked!'

'I hated it,' Veronica moaned.

'That's not what your pussy's telling me. I don't think you've ever been so wet. Get up here.'

Veronica clambered off Devin's lap, her head spinning from the upside-down spanking. He was already working at the buttons of his jeans. His hands trembled with excitement, and Veronica could tell that the game wasn't going to last much longer. Devin's cock, released from his fly, stood at full attention, long and thick and coral pink, its crown swollen and glistening. Veronica didn't want to play the innocent any more; she just wanted to slide down that gorgeous shaft and fuck her beautiful boyfriend.

Veronica stood up, straddling Devin again with her thighs braced against his, her hands gripping his shoulders. Looking into his eyes, watching his expression shift into a tense mask of lust, she lowered herself down until her lower lips were just barely resting against the head of his hard-on. Hands shaking more than ever, Devin worked frantically at the buttons on her white blouse. His whole body was taut with urgency; Veronica could feel his shoulder muscles bunching under her fingers as he tore at the white blouse, then at her bra. Fortunately, she'd had enough foresight to choose a bra that fastened in the front – a 'frontloader', Devin called it – and within a few seconds her breasts bounced free, ripe for Devin's lips and teeth to lick and nip and suckle.

Meanwhile, Veronica continued her slow inch-by-inch glide down Devin's cock. Her inner muscles tightened around his shaft, swallowing him in warm wet gulps. His whole body was quivering like a tight piano wire as he sucked and nibbled her breasts; Veronica knew he wasn't going to hold out much longer, and neither was she. She could already feel her clit thrumming, her pussy clenching, nipples aching – all the warning signs that she was about to hit a shattering climax. She and Devin hardly ever spent this long pleasuring each other; sex between them was sweet but swift. This long tantalising makeout session, combined with the total surprise of the spanking, was driving Veronica wild.

She sank her full weight on to Devin's erection, gasping as she felt his full length. Then she rode him, hot and crazy, bucking her hips and grinding against him at the same time. Still clutching his shoulders, she gritted her teeth and dug in hard, driving her heels into the floor to push him even deeper inside her and intensify the friction even more.

It was a contest now – seeing which one of them would come first. Veronica thought for sure she could take Devin over the top when she started to rotate her hips in deep circles. She was so wet that her flesh was making juicy sounds against Devin's velvety cock skin; how could he last this long?

Then Devin bit down on her nipple, his teeth delivering some serious pain to the stiff tender bud, and the shock sent Veronica over the edge. Her orgasm was a rough wrenching ride; she shuddered from head to toe, rocking with pleasure, and the sounds she made sounded so savage and guttural that she didn't recognise them as her own. Though Veronica had beaten him to the finish, Devin was right on her tail, fingers digging into the curves of her hips as he hit his own peak. Teeth clenched, throat flushed, eyes glittering, he thrust up into her, each spasm bringing a groan of joy from his lips.

They clung to each other, exchanging shaky sighs and whimpers, as their pulses settled back to normal and they remembered how to breathe again.

'You're a good teacher,' Veronica mumbled into Devin's neck. 'You should consider giving private lessons.'

Devin's cock was softening, sliding reluctantly out of her body. Veronica hated to feel him go. Sex was so good with him, whether it was playful and cosy, deliciously deviant or just hot and hard and intense. But, as soon as their flesh parted ways, she seemed to find flaws in him wherever she looked: his chronic unemployment, his gaming addiction, his refusal to trim the split ends off his long hair. If you truly loved someone, Veronica believed, you accepted them with all their chinks and dings and random stains. You didn't scrutinise every detail of their appearance; you saw a complete complex being, someone you loved in their entirety.

Devin laughed at Veronica's suggestion. 'I'd never make a living giving sex lessons,' he said. 'The only student I'd ever want is you, and you're too broke to pay me.'

Veronica sighed, giving Devin's split-ended ponytail an affectionate tug. Damn the game-obsessed, pot-smoking geek. Why did the lover with the most flaws also have to be the only one who was loyal?

Chapter Seven

The Horny Woman's Guide to Imaginary Travel

I might be promiscuous, but at least I'm punctual, Joel thought, glumly stirring sugar into his third cup of tea. The pot had grown cold, and the cute waitress was starting to give him the hairy eyeball. He'd been sitting at the Imperial Palace for over twenty minutes – 24 minutes and 37 seconds, if anyone was counting – waiting for Lauryn and trying to keep his eyes off the waitress's sleek hips. Every time she walked away from his table, before returning every few minutes with her cart of steaming dumplings to see if he was ready to eat, Joel's eyes were drawn like magnets to her butt, twitching like a cat's under her red satin cheongsam dress.

The Imperial's management should know better than to let their staff dress like that. The golden-brown tidbits of dim sum, as fragrantly mouth-watering as they were, offered no match for a provocative bod like that.

Lauryn's lateness was a mixed blessing. Joel had started out the day feeling like a dog, waking up with a raging erection at memories of the unexpected surprise of making love with Chloe. Now that it looked like he was going to be stood up, he was feeling like less of a dog, but he still felt slightly doggish. Blame it on Tibet – without those weeks of forced celibacy, he might have been able to concentrate on pursuing one woman at a time. Instead, he was prowling the city with a roaring appetite for female flesh; the way his hormones were going, he'd be better off in jail.

Or maybe not. Joel had never really been curious about how it would feel to hold hands with muscle-bound inmates named Rock or Shitbrick.

Sweet Chloe – what a treat she'd been, a delectable morsel for any man, much less a starving guy like Joel. Mid-afternoon pickups obviously weren't part of her typical routine; under her boldness, she'd been shy and nervous and terrified of seeming gauche or clumsy. After they'd put their clothes back on, after Chloe had made a fresh pot of tea for them to share, Chloe had asked if she would see him again. Joel had had to think about it for a second, but, in that second, he saw hurt blossoming in Chloe's grey eyes. Feeling like a heel, he'd given her his cell-phone number, knowing even as he wrote the number in her little pink address book – was the woman *addicted* to Hello Kitty? – that he'd probably regret it.

'Hey, there. Sorry I'm late. I got dragged into a meeting this morning. Fortunately they let me do it by conference call, or I might have had to flake on you.'

Joel looked up from his tea, and there stood Lauryn, all windblown blonde-streaked curls and lightly tanned skin. She leaned over and kissed his cheek, her lips a whisk of velvet against his skin. Through the fabric of her sheer blouse, he caught a whiff of fruity body spray, a scent he couldn't identify and didn't need to, judging by the sudden swelling in his groin.

Lauryn sat down, brushing invisible dust off her form-fitting faded jeans. God, she looked good. Her breasts bounced a little as she pushed her chair under the table, nipples slightly erect under the creamy cloth of her shirt. Her throat was so slim and smooth and supple that Joel immediately imagined kissing its lean lines, tasting her skin, sucking slightly, leaving love marks with his teeth. She chewed her lower lip as she scanned the room for the dim-sum cart, taking Joel's fantasies to a totally different level. Once he managed to stop staring at her mouth and visualising those lips moulded around his cock, Joel noticed that her eyes were two different colours – blue and green.

Funny, he could have sworn they were both the same shade of hazel.

'Damn, I wish I hadn't been so late,' she sighed. 'It always gets packed in here after eleven. The cart's never going to come around.'

'You're probably right. Now that you're here, the waitress is going to stop coming by every thirty seconds to see if I'm ready to eat.'

Lauryn flicked out her napkin and spread it on her lap. 'You should have gone ahead without me. I would have called, but you didn't give me a number at your hotel, and you don't have a cell phone.'

'Well, to tell you the truth, I do,' Joel admitted. 'I just don't give the number out very often.'

Lauryn's full mouth drooped. 'You mean you didn't want to give the number to *me*. That's fine. I understand. You meet women all over the world; why would you want hundreds of females having access to you twenty-four hours a day?'

'There aren't *hundreds*, Lauryn. Dozens, maybe, on a good day.'

'That's not funny.'

'I know. And it's not even true. There are only three women on earth I've ever given my cell number to. Two of them won't speak to me any more, and the third has no choice – she's my mom.'

'I thought it was kind of odd that a journalist wouldn't carry a cell phone,' Lauryn said with a haughty sniff, straightening her spine. 'But I don't know why you felt you had to lie about it.'

'I don't know either, sweetheart. Maybe it was wishful thinking. I really never wanted one; the twenty-first century kind of shoved it on me. Honestly, I hate the damn thing. And I really did flush one down the toilet once. It took me a month to replace it. Forgive me? Please?'

'OK. Whatever. We hardly know each other, so it wouldn't make sense for you to give me your private number.' Lauryn waved her hand, flipping away the whole exchange, but her bi-coloured eyes still had a hurt wary look.

How could someone who supposedly made a living through his visual acuity have missed those eyes? Joel wondered. One blue eye, one green; if he'd known she had a mismatched pair of eyes like that, he'd never have let Lauryn get away at the bar yesterday. He was a devout worshipper of female beauty, but it was always the flaws that caught his heart. The bump on a broken nose, the asymmetrical ears ... and now, these magical eyes.

Dangerous stuff. Joel wasn't in any shape to fall in love right now, shiftless and uncertain as he was, but what else would happen to a guy who woke up to a pair of eyes like that several mornings in a row? Besides, Joel didn't understand that kind of love, the conventional one-on-one kind. To him, love was a glorious experience, but generic, almost abstract, like the soaring high in the pit of his belly whenever a plane took off, that heady combination of speed and freedom that intoxicated his body and mind. The flight itself hardly mattered, and the destination mattered even less; it was the exhilaration of take-off that he adored. Love, to Joel, lacked specifics. Love was his fervent response to Women in General, the whole fascinating population of creatures with bigger breasts and hips than his own, with lush openings in their bodies and bizarre hormonal mood swings.

Some men, he knew, *did* fall in love with individual women. They managed to separate a single female from the lovely horde and bond with her for lengths of time that boggled Joel's mind: five years, ten years, sometimes a staggering thirty or forty. Joel had been the best man at more weddings than he could count; all of his college friends, it seemed, had gotten married three years ago and were now either having children or getting divorced. Meanwhile, Joel was flying here, flying there, chasing images the way cats chase toy mice: with passionate determination, but very little biological purpose.

Joel had always been open to the chance he might change one day, that his mental eye might fall on one female form, zoom in on her and never want to break the focus. But, so far, no woman had held his attention for more than a matter of moments, days or hours. He didn't blame the women themselves, not at all. Each, in her own way, was gorgeous and special and irreplaceable. Joel just couldn't narrow his inner lens enough to bring one woman into continuous clarity. If there were a Ritalin for lovers, something that could fix his attention-deficit problem, Joel would have gladly tried it, if only for novelty's sake. But, as it was, emotional commitment was an act that Joel observed with great curiosity and greater caution, as if he were photographing some bizarre mating ritual that involved nudity, knives and fire.

Joel reached across the table and took Lauryn's hand, fondling her fingers. 'I only give my number to business contacts. And to incredibly sexy intriguing women.'

No need to mention that he'd given his 'secret' number to Chloe only hours before. Joel took a black permanent marker out of his shirt pocket, uncapped it and wrote his number on Lauryn's palm. Under the digits, he drew a heart – corny, but the gesture made her blush. Then he turned her hand over again and squeezed it, feeling the tendons and bones go limp under his fingers. Lauryn was looking at him as if she didn't know whether to smile, laugh or run screaming from the Imperial Palace. A gust of intuition told him that she wanted to lean across the table and kiss him, that she *would* have kissed him, if the waitress hadn't chosen that moment to wheel her cart of goodies back to their table.

'You ready now?' the waitress asked, venom in her voice.

Like a couple of guilty teenagers, Joel and Lauryn yanked their hands away from each other. Lauryn's cheeks were a subtle shade of fuchsia as she hurriedly chose a plate of shrimp dumplings, a sesame ball and a pork bun.

Joel grabbed a couple of dishes at random, blind to their contents. He just wanted to get through this meal as fast as possible so he could take Lauryn somewhere private (hell, even semi-private would do) and lick every inch of her fruit-fragrant body. In the hours they'd spent apart, she'd grown sexier than he remembered her being on the plane. It was like meeting up again with the girl you'd lusted after in college – the one who seemed eternally out of reach, who was a few rungs above you socially and sexually and in every other way you could imagine – and realising that, in her own subtle way, she'd been coming on to you back then, and was coming on to you now.

'Hey, slow down!' Lauryn said. 'You're not supposed to gobble dim sum; you're supposed to savour it.' She demonstrated by picking up a pair of chopsticks and breaking them apart, then selecting a dumpling with dainty precision.

'Sorry,' Joel said, mouth full. 'I'm just really not hungry any more.'

'You could have fooled me.' Lauryn laughed. 'You'd think you hadn't eaten in six weeks.'

Ah, if only you knew, Joel thought. He swallowed whatever it was that he was chewing, dimly aware that it tasted good, took a gulp of his tea and leaped.

'Look, Lauryn, I might as well be honest about this. I came here thinking we'd have a nice long lunch, seduce each other over conversation, maybe play footsie under the table. But, now that you're here, I just don't want to wait that long. Do you know what I mean?'

A small slow smile shaped Lauryn's lips into a bow. Eyes shining, she nodded. 'I'm staying in a kind of run-down hotel,' she said apologetically. 'Nothing to write home about, unless you wanted to depress your parents.'

'Does it have four walls? And a door that locks?'

'Four walls, absolutely. Whether or not the door locks is another matter.'

'That's OK. I don't mind having an audience. As long as the maid's open-minded, it'll be perfect. Anywhere you are will be perfect.'

'You mean that?'

'Oh, you have no idea how much I mean it.'

'OK,' Lauryn said softly, almost in a whisper. 'Let's go.'

Joel pulled out his wallet and took out a few bills, more than enough to pay for what they'd eaten. In every experience he'd had at a dim-sum restaurant, it took almost as long for the staff to get around to tallying up your plates and presenting you with a cheque as it took to eat the food. He caught Lauryn giving the morsels a last longing look just before he took her by the arm and pulled her down the plush red carpet of the Imperial Palace. The bas-relief murals of the Chinese countryside and gilded dragons looming from the ceiling were a blur as he guided Lauryn out of the restaurant, making sure that her bottom accidentally collided with his pelvis every few steps.

'We'll order a pizza later,' he promised. 'My treat.'

She glanced back to smile at him, and the she-wolf hunger in her luscious grin told him she'd already forgotten about food.

As they walked through Chinatown on the way back to Lauryn's hotel, she immediately started having second thoughts – and third, and fourth, and fifth thoughts –

about taking Joel back to the Landmark Hotel. She'd already made one bold move that morning by leaving her hazel contacts in their twin plastic dishes; was it wise to open the door even wider by letting him see where she was staying? She couldn't even remember what state she'd left the room in. If her spatial memory served her right, she'd left yesterday's panties lying on the bathroom floor, her hairbrush in the sink, the bed unmade and her suitcase yawning open in the centre of it like a mouth bored with its own contents.

Bored, as Joel would be, undoubtedly, as soon as he found out about Lauryn's bleak lower-middle-class background, her stagnant career, her life's overall deficiency of colour and excitement. Travel? What travel? Lauryn had been out of the country once, on a disastrous trip to Tijuana, Mexico, with her roommates during her junior year in college. All she could remember of Mexico was a tedious wait to cross the border, followed by a raucous blur of street vendors and urchins waving bright bits of cloth and cheap plastic toys in her face. After that, there was a foggy memory of a bar, tequila shots, the carefree peeling off of clothing... then *nada*. All she knew about that lost weekend was what her roommates told her later, much of it obscenely hilarious, at least from their point of view.

'Like I said, this hotel where I'm staying isn't much. I left the room in a mess.'

Lauryn tapped her foot as they waited at a traffic light. Joel's arm was wrapped around her waist, and he held her tight against his body. He felt large, warm, dependable and real.

'Your room really doesn't matter, as long as you're in it. You *are* going to be there, right?'

'Of course! Why wouldn't I?' Lauryn shouted, trying to make herself heard above the din of traffic.

'Well, the way you keep apologising for the state of your hotel, I figured you might want to avoid the place altogether. I thought you might just drop me off and leave me to spend the afternoon making love with one of the housekeepers.'

'You wouldn't! Really?'

'If she had eyes that were two different colours, I'd seriously consider it.'

Lauryn stiffened. He'd noticed. She honestly had wondered if he would. He probably thought she was a freak now. Either that, or he had a fetish for women with mismatched facial features.

'I've always hated my eyes,' she said. She thought her voice had been swallowed up by the street noise.

Then Joel bent down and murmured into her ear, 'I love them. Why do you wear contacts?'

His voice was deep and throaty and intimate, as if they were already lying naked in each other's arms, instead of standing on a street corner in Chinatown with cars and buses and taxis trying to plough down all the pedestrians who were darting across the street against the light.

'Same reason you tell people you don't have a cell phone,' Lauryn retorted.

Her reply came off bitchy, but she didn't feel that way. Joel had a way of wrapping her in a warm safe sphere, she'd noticed, a place where she felt calmly sensuous and desirable, no matter what was going on around them. In the airplane, in the bar on the Wharf, in the restaurant, and now here, in the middle of the street, Joel somehow created the illusion that he and Lauryn were in the middle of a snow globe, glancing out at the chaos occasionally, but always drawn back to each other.

The Landmark Hotel (a landmark of what, Lauryn wasn't sure) was located a few blocks from the grandiose Chinatown Gate on Grant Avenue. Not one of the city's worst neighbourhoods, but certainly not the best. In less than 48 hours she'd been approached by five vagrants asking for change or a free feel, had overheard two bar fights from her open window, and had stepped in several substances on the sidewalk that she didn't want to identify.

Still, she could be doing much, much worse. Lauryn would rather stay in a flophouse in the city than in the generic chain-motel that Stanley's secretary had picked out for her. She would rather pay twice as much, out of pocket, to spend her nights in San Francisco than while away the hours watching television sitcoms in a featureless motel room in the East Bay.

'Here we are,' she said brightly, hoping the cadaverous desk clerk sitting behind the bullet-proof, nicotine-stained window wouldn't give her a hard time for taking a man up to her room. No such luck. The clerk had to see Lauryn's driver's licence, and Joel's, before buzzing them in.

'He your boyfriend?' the clerk asked, sucking a brown cigarillo that looked like it hadn't been lit in several days. He narrowed his rheumy eyes at Lauryn, giving her the once-over as if she'd just strutted in off the street instead of being a paying customer who had already given him a credit-card number and a business reference. 'This ain't no pay-by-the-hour establishment.'

Lauryn planted her fists on her hips. 'Are you suggesting that I'm a hooker?'

The clerk's lips twisted when he smiled, like a hooked worm. 'You said it, lady. I didn't.'

'Look, if I were a hooker, do you really think I'd bring my johns all the way to San Francisco just to do them in this hotel? Check our IDs. We're both from Chicago.'

Lauryn sounded a lot tougher than she felt. Living in the city had taught her how to be a bitch when she needed to be. Lauryn knew plenty of women like that; she worked with them, got drunk with them at happy hour on Fridays, attended their bridal showers and their post-divorce beer bashes. Those girls had given her yet another identity she could borrow when she needed to: the hard-edged, tough-as-nails Chicago broad.

The clerk was screwing up his mouth in preparation to make another nasty retort, when Joel stepped up to the window and spoke through the mouthpiece.

'I hope you're not going to offend the lady again,' he said in a mellow tone. Big as he was, Joel could afford to speak to nasty men in mellow tones, Lauryn figured. 'We're on our honeymoon. We've only been married for three days, so I still respect her enough to kick your ass for insulting her.'

The clerk, clearly used to being threatened but unable to do anything about it, shoved their IDs through the window with nothing more than a hound-dog stare. He pressed a buzzer behind the desk, and the door to the hotel's inner sanctum automatically unlocked.

'Classy joint,' Joel remarked, as he led Lauryn through the door.

'Can't say I didn't warn you. And what was that line about respecting me because we'd only been married for three days? That was *so* not funny. First of all, I'd never spend my honeymoon at the Landmark Hotel. Second, I'd expect any man I married to defend my honour against slimy hotel staff no matter how long we'd been together.'

Joel spread his hands in a helpless gesture. 'Hey, I think this is a great place for a honeymoon. It's cheap, by San Francisco standards, it's half a block from a bus-stop and it's conveniently located between two dive bars. What else do a couple of impoverished newlyweds need?'

Lauryn shot him a glare of disgust as she fit the key, with its dangling triangle of turquoise plastic, into the lock on her door. The room was dim, decorated in a style she could only describe as Post-Modern Hellhole, with an orange bedspread, a dejected plaid-upholstered armchair and a painting of an indeterminate landscape hanging over the bed. The only item that could qualify as an 'amenity' in the room was a box fan sitting underneath the broken air conditioner. Lauryn's spilled suitcase and discarded pantyhose didn't add anything to the room's appeal, nor did the discarded pizza box from last night's dinner. She fully expected Joel to either make a sarcastic comment, or turn around and walk out of the Landmark.

Instead, he walked inside, shut the door and pulled the chain lock. Then he took Lauryn into his arms.

'Now I can really say hello to you,' he said in a low voice that made her shiver.

Their kiss brought back memories of the times he'd touched her before – at the airport after their flight, at the bar in Fisherman's Wharf – only this time lips and tongues and lovingly exploring hands were included in the pleasure of feeling Joel's warm hard bulk. This time the pressure of his body against hers was deliberate. And this time, best of all, Lauryn could feel concrete proof that he was as excited by their closeness as she was. The contrast between his soft inquisitive lips and his erect cock was enough to make her knees buckle, but Joel's arms held her upright as his tongue wove its way into her mouth.

'How about that massage I promised you?' he asked, breaking the kiss. His broad hands rubbed the small of her back in deep circles, and Lauryn felt her muscles turn to butter.

'Sure' was all she managed to say, inarticulate with lust.

Holding her hand, Joel led her over to the bed, a cyclone of orange polyester and threadbare sheets. When he started pushing her clothes back into her suitcase, Lauryn felt queasy with embarrassment all of a sudden, as if he were looking not only into her luggage, but into her life.

'Don't do that,' she said. 'Please. I'll take care of the mess.'

'Already taken care of, madam.' He buckled the suitcase and heaved it on to the floor. 'Got any body oil or lotion? Anything that smells good will do, but it helps if it's a scent you find relaxing. No musk or anything – we'll take care of that, ourselves.'

Lauryn went to the bathroom, stumbling a bit on her weakened knees, and found a bottle of tea-tree oil in her cosmetics case. She'd started dabbling in aromatherapy a few months earlier, desperately seeking ways to reduce her stress level; her stress only seemed to be getting worse, but she still loved to dab the oil on candles and light them at night. If you couldn't have a man in your bedroom, you had to find other ways to distract your senses.

'Here you go.' She went back to the bedroom and handed the tiny flask to Joel. 'Don't use too much; it's potent stuff.'

Joel smiled. 'I know what I'm doing.'

'Oh, I'm sure you do.' She started to lie down on the bed, but Joel motioned her to the floor, where he'd arranged the hotel pillows in a nest.

'The floor? Are you kidding?' Lauryn eyed the brown carpet sceptically. The cigarette burns and dark stains in the rug were the least of her worries; who could tell what might be alive and actively crawling through that miniature jungle?

'Just lie down and close your eyes.' Joel switched on the fan beside the heap of pillows. 'Pretend this is a tropical breeze.'

'This feels crazy,' Lauryn grumbled. But she felt far from insane when Joel's fingers, dabbed with tea-tree oil, began to smooth the cynical grooves out of her forehead.

'OK,' he began, ignoring her remark. 'I'm going to tell you the best lie ever. We're on a beach in Bali, lying in a teak hut under a palm tree. No stress, no noise but the sounds of the ocean, and every once in a while a bell from a temple far away. I've got my camera with me, but the only thing I want to photograph is you. Your hair's all loose and messy, and you've got this sexy-sleepy smile on your face. You're wearing a bikini – not the top, just the bottom –'

'Hey,' Lauryn protested. 'I didn't agree to appear topless in this lie. Besides,' she added more softly, 'it's not a lie. It sounds more like a fantasy.'

'Fantasies are kinda my specialty,' Joel admitted. 'Fantasies, daydreams, lies. Whatever you want to call them. Lying is a lot like cooking; some people need the right circumstances and excuses and recipes to do it. Other people just do it naturally, by instinct, all the time. Lying is practically an art, if you think about it.'

But Lauryn stopped thinking as Joel's hands stroked her throat, then moved down to her shoulders, then lower, to places that made her flesh hum when he touched them. Skimming and stroking, his hands – along with the breeze from the fan, and the aroma of the essential oil – were taking her straight to the world he was shaping for her.

Topless, at least in Joel's fantasy, and thoughtless, Lauryn let herself go.

'You're way too good at that,' she said in a blurry voice.

'Too good at what?' he teased.

'At everything. The massage. The fantasy. Weaving a whole world for me out of nothing but some scented oil and a rotary fan. You should write a book: *The Horny Woman's Guide to Imaginary Travel: Fantasy Vacations for Nymphos Going Nowhere.*'

'I'm not much of a writer,' Joel admitted. 'That's why I fell in love with the camera, ever since I got my first point-and-click for Christmas when I was eight years old. And you know, after all that time, I still don't feel like I'm much of a photographer. I'm still learning. It's the cameras that teach me.'

'What do they teach you exactly?'

Joel was quiet for a few seconds, pressing the heels of his hands deep into the sore spot just below the middle of Lauryn's back, where all her fear and tension lived. 'Well, for one thing, photography has taught me that actions speak louder than words. Working for the papers, especially, I learned how to catch people *doing* things, not saying them. People will say all kinds of bullshit; it's what they *do* that shows what they really believe, what they're passionate about.'

'And what are *you* passionate about, Joel?' Lauryn murmured.

'Doing what I love to do. Not settling down – not settling, period. Living life as intensely as possible, whenever I can.'

'What about when you can't?' Lauryn asked. 'Live intensely, I mean? What about those times when you can't be shooting football games or riots, or trekking through the Amazon, or strolling down a beach in Bali with a goddess on your arm and a beer in your hand?'

She didn't have to see Joel's face to hear the sly grin in his voice. 'That's what lies and fantasies are for.'

'Lies and fantasies, huh?' Lauryn said, in a soft voice. 'I've made up a few of those myself.'

'So you know what I mean? Sometimes reality just doesn't meet your dreams. Or even your most humble expectations.'

'I know exactly what you mean. Better than you know.'

Lauryn forgot about the nubbly texture of the carpet underneath her, the smell of Lysol masking ancient cigarette smoke. All she smelled was the tea-tree oil, the imaginary salt wind and the clean fragrances of Joel's soap and aftershave. She didn't mind at all when he began to undo the buttons on her blouse so he could reach under the cloth to stroke her skin. His hands were artful and attentive, soothing muscles along her ribs and abdomen that she hadn't known were sore.

She also hadn't known that those places could be so responsive. When men touched her, they usually went straight for her breasts or her crotch, as if her body were a giant target board with three big red circles marking her only erogenous zones. So far, Joel's fingers had avoided any of those hot spots, concentrating instead on the softness of her waist, the planes of her belly. Even when he unzipped her jeans, it wasn't her private parts that he went for, but the indentations of her hip bones, the swell of her lower abdomen.

'Ready to turn over?' he asked. His voice was thick with desire – he seemed to find his current reality more absorbing, for once, than a daydream – but he was still simply massaging her, not yet seducing her.

Lauryn sat up and peeled off her blouse. She caught a glimpse of Joel's face before she rolled over on her stomach, and his look of barely contained lust made her own heart pump faster. She lay down with her head cradled on her crossed forearms on top of one of the hotel's thin pillows. She smiled to herself, a lazy and satisfied smirk, like a cat's. If Joel wasn't going to rush this, then neither would she.

'What happens next?'

'Huh?' Joel's hands stopped kneading her shoulder blades.

'In your Bali scenario. What do we do next?'

Joel cleared his throat. His fingers resumed their delicious work, making swimming motions as they moved down her spine. 'Well, let's see. You're topless...'

'Not yet,' Lauryn interrupted. 'But you can fix that, if you want to. Go ahead. If you're going to give me a real backrub, you need access to my whole back.'

Joel unhooked her bra. Luckily, she'd worn a new one, peach lace, instead of the old single-piece running bra that she felt most comfortable in. One by one, he slid the straps delicately over her shoulders. Funny, Lauryn thought, how men could touch a woman's body with such assurance, yet handle their lingerie as if it were made of spun glass.

'OK,' she said. 'Go on. We're on the beach, in Bali, and I'm topless. You have your camera with you, and you want to take pictures.'

'I want to, but I can't,' Joel continued. 'I'm too busy staring at you, at how beautiful you are, and thinking about how much I want you. For once I don't care what the camera sees. All I care about is my own vision, and it's filled with your smile, your skin, your hair. It's like I'm in a dream – I want to touch you more than anything in the world, but I can't wake myself up.'

Joel did stop touching Lauryn at this point. She felt the weight of his hands rise from her back, heard his breath quicken. 'I just don't know,' he said, almost to himself.

'Don't know what?'

'How I lucked into this. Bali, the ocean and especially you.'

Lauryn sat up, turning to Joel. She held his face in her hands. She could feel the twin pulses on either side of his throat working like two tiny hammers. He gulped, hard. His blue eyes, without his glasses, held an innocent half-crazy longing that reminded her of the first boy she'd kissed.

'The Landmark Hotel isn't exactly a beach shack in Bali,' she said, 'but you can touch me, Joel. However, wherever you want.'

Lauryn tossed her bra on to the bed. Then she picked up Joel's hands, which were lying on his knees as if he'd forgotten what to do with them. She guided them back to her rib cage, placing his palms against the sides of her breasts, and rotated his wrists so that his thumbs were brushing her nipples.

'How's that for a start?' she asked.

'Perfect. Absolutely perfect.'

Her breasts cupped in his hands, Joel kissed her. His mouth was tentative at first, as if they were kissing for the first time, then his lips pressed against hers with a hungry confidence that left her breathless. As they kissed, Joel clumsily stripped off his shirt, so that Lauryn could enjoy the pleasures of touching him, too. He wasn't muscle-bound, just meaty, his biceps and pecs hard and sunburned. He moaned when she combed through the blond hairs on his chest, his nipples peaking under her fingernails. She raked her nails up and down his torso, barely whisking his skin at first, then digging into his flesh with something close to cruelty. He flinched, groaned and gasped, depending on how she varied the pressure.

'You must be half feline,' he said, almost breathless. 'Because I'm starting to feel like a scratching post.'

'I didn't mean to hurt you,' Lauryn said innocently. 'How about I make up for it by doing this?'

With the flat of her hand, she rubbed the outcropping of hard flesh between Joel's thighs. Under the fly of his jeans, Lauryn could feel his erection shifting, straining. He was big, just as she'd thought. She wanted to set his cock free right now and jump on him – no more daydreams, no more teasing, just raw hot fucking. But the tiny voice inside her head, the one that always told her she wasn't good enough, was warning her to hold back.

He won't want you if thinks you're desperately horny, the voice said. *You know how men are. He's either going to assume that you're a man-eating bitch or a pathetic nymphomaniac.*

That voice was starting to grate on Lauryn's nerves.

She unzipped Joel's jeans, and as he stared down at her, slack-jawed with surprise, Lauryn bent down, pulled out his cock, and took the whole shaft into her mouth. She was all appetite – no desire to look at his cock, or fondle it, or rim the crown with her tongue. She just wanted to have him filling her mouth and her throat, stopping her breath, bringing her close to choking. Man-eater? Why not? She felt like a man-eater now, hungry enough to devour him whole.

Lauryn had always loved giving head, but she was somewhat embarrassed at how gifted she was at it. In college, she'd acquired a shady reputation as 'The BJ Queen' among the guys she'd dated, and she'd become so famous for her deep-throating talents that her roommates had begged her to give them lessons in delivering the perfect blowjob. Lauryn had obliged, teaching the other co-eds how to breathe through their noses while suppressing their gag reflexes, but she'd always felt that there was something low class about her gift, something that suggested she'd been born on the wrong side of the tracks and would never really belong anywhere else.

'God, you're good at that,' Joel moaned, as Lauryn drew her mouth up the arc of his shaft, lips creating a delicious vacuum against the satiny skin. His fingers dove into her hair, gripping handfuls of curls and using them to guide her upwards motion. All the way up to the top, till the rim of his cock head touched the back of her lips, then she focused her attentions there for a minute or two, sucking firmly as she caught her breath again. With the tip of her tongue, she flicked the strand of skin at the base of his glans. Some men were indifferent to that tiny segment of their anatomy.

Joel wasn't one of them.

His groans deepened, and his body arched backwards as he leaned back on his hands and lifted his hips, pushing deep into Lauryn's mouth again, until the tip of his penis nudged the back of her throat. Tears stung her eyes – she could hardly breathe around the thick root of his erection, and he was swelling even more – but Lauryn was in heaven. She loved this part of fellatio, when her own abandon had pushed her to the limits of tolerance, when the tension in her lover's body had hit a critical pitch, when her jaws ached and her lungs burned and a hum of anticipation filled her ears.

Gently but urgently, Joel tugged at the roots of Lauryn's

hair, pulling her up. She felt a twinge of irritation when his cock sprang free from her mouth, and her lips had to part ways with that juicy stalk. She had really wanted to make Joel come with her mouth, to literally blow him away.

'What's wrong? Weren't you enjoying it?' she asked.

'Too much. Way too much. But I don't want to come like that. Not the first time. Take your pants off. Hurry.'

Lauryn squirmed out of her jeans and peeled off her panties, while Joel lay on his back, working a condom down his shaft with an unsteady hand.

'Get on top of me,' he ordered.

Naked, Lauryn crouched over Joel. She was going to tease him – with her lower lips, this time – but he put a stop to that, taking her by the hips and pushing her on to him, spearing her with his hard-on. Lauryn yelped at the shock of being filled so quickly, so completely. His hands found her breasts again and fondled them, roughly this time, as he thrust up into her. Lauryn's hips moved to match his rhythm. He was pinching and pulling at her nipples, watching the way her face changed in response.

Lauryn was loving everything he did to her, every shift of his pelvis, every twist and tug at her sensitive breasts. The look on his face, fiercely intent, was so arousing that she could hardly stand to meet his eyes. It was as if he were looking straight through her, blue eyes piercing all the superficial layers she surrounded herself with, to see the woman inside. What was he seeing exactly? Lauryn wasn't even sure.

She closed her eyes, trying to refocus on her pleasure. The pressure of his cock against her clit was a sweetly sharp sensation; she rocked back and forth, intensifying the feeling. If she could only ride him like this, without that sense that he was staring into her soul, she could come ... she could come. But, even with her eyes closed, she knew Joel was watching her. Just a typical guy, getting off on the sight of a naked woman straddling his body, she reassured herself.

But Lauryn wasn't going to come. She felt the shimmering ball of pleasure well up in the pit of her belly, spread its glow through her lower lips, down her thighs, then fade. It wouldn't come back. Not today.

'Come for me,' Joel urged through gritted teeth. 'I want you to come on top of me.'

So Lauryn did what she had always done at times like this, when her lover's need for her to have an orgasm was so intense that it overrode Lauryn's own pleasure: she faked it. It was a bravura performance, so authentic that Lauryn actually found herself buying into the feigned moans and clenching spasms. Through Joel, she had the vicarious pleasure of seeing herself transported into a state of exquisite animal bliss.

Joel would never know that she was putting on a show. And, if he did, would he care? His own climax was so close that he was barely holding himself together while Lauryn rocked and swayed. The second she went limp, in an imitation of post-climactic joy, Joel cried out and clutched her by the waist with all his might, thrusting up and up, ending with a full-body shiver.

Lauryn rolled off of him and lay down across his chest. Joel folded her in his arms. His heart was still pounding. Sweat plastered his pale chest hairs to his skin.

'Wow,' he said. 'That's all I can say. Wow.'

'I love an articulate man.' Lauryn laughed.

She sounded happy. She *was* happy. Orgasms were overrated and, besides, how could she be absolutely positive that she hadn't had one? Coming wasn't a cookie-cutter experience; you couldn't predict from one orgasm to the next how the critical moment would feel. Sometimes the climax hit you like a tidal wave. Other times it was more like a turn of the tide, a subtle shift in your flesh, something that ebbed and receded without a lot of fanfare.

Liar, liar, pants on fire, sneered Lauryn's nasty little inner voice. *You didn't come. You're disappointed. Face it.*

'I don't think I've ever seen anything so beautiful,' Joel was saying, brushing the curls off of Lauryn's forehead. He was gazing at her as if she were a precious work of art, a rare statue that had fallen off a truck and landed, perfect and unbroken, right at his feet.

You're right, Lauryn admitted to the nasty voice. *I didn't come. But I'm not disappointed. Not even close.*

'This is better than Bali,' Joel said. 'This is better than anywhere. The Landmark Hotel is paradise, as far as I'm concerned.'

Lauryn glanced around the room, at the cigarette burns and stains on the mattress, the shiny olive-drab drapes, the pitiful landscape print on the wall. Then at Joel, his face smeared with a drowsy smile, blue eyes blinking as he drank her in.

'I never thought I'd say this,' Lauryn said, 'but I have to agree. This *is* better than Bali. Much, much better.'

They kissed again, the haze of leftover pleasure making their lips move languidly this time, slowing down the dance of their tongues. As Joel's eyelids fluttered shut, Lauryn realised that she was kissing him to sleep. Dozing with one arm wrapped around her, the other thrown across the floor at a theatrical angle, he reminded her of a sleeping kid, brave as a warrior in his dreams.

'It's not important,' Lauryn whispered.

'Huh?' Joel's eyes opened. 'What's not important?'

'Nothing. I'm very, very happy.'

Lauryn snuggled against Joel's chest, her head tucked under his chin. A half-truth was better than a whole lie, any day.

Chapter Eight

Miss Translation

During her translation seminar, Chloe tried to avoid eye contact with her professor. On any other day, the discussion of *kake kotoba*, or pivot words, would have enthralled her; Chloe loved the technique of using a single word as a hinge to connect multiple meanings in lines of Japanese poetry, especially when one of those meanings was suggestively erotic. But, this morning, guilt and pleasure gnawed at her mind, keeping her from concentrating.

Talk about double meanings – she still didn't know how to read the events of yesterday afternoon. Sex with Joel had been a total surprise; never in a thousand years would she have dreamed that she'd pick up a guy at a sushi bar. Did that mean she was changing? Becoming less mousy, more overtly sensual? Or did it just mean that she was going nuts?

Catching fragments of a debate over dual interpretations of the word 'hands' in one of the *tanka* they'd been translating, Chloe lapsed into a fantasy about the way Joel's palms had felt when they skimmed across the very tips of her nipples. Back and forth, back and forth, until the friction created an almost burning sensation in those ultra-sensitive peaks. Joel had been so in tune with her responses, observing every fluctuation in the sound of her moans, the flush of her skin, the involuntary twitch of her hips. She'd never been with a man who seemed so hungry to *watch* her; even when he was absorbed in licking the notch between her thighs, she'd seen him studying her face every time she looked down. His scrutiny had made Chloe feel like an object, an animal framed in a photographer's lens, too lost in its own appetites to be self-conscious or ashamed.

And she'd had an orgasm! Chloe never came with a lover the first time they had sex. In fact, her orgasms happened most reliably when she was lying on her futon, alone in her apartment, spinning out her fantasies about the mysterious dark-haired Japanese nobleman, and all the steamy convolutions of their forbidden love.

Change was definitely in the air. Yesterday's orgasm made her feel slightly better about missing that flight to Chicago. She couldn't wait to tell Aidan how she'd compensated for that blunder. The thought of describing her sexual encounter with Joel to Aidan was almost as arousing as her memories of the encounter itself. Warmth spread through Chloe's belly as she tried to picture Aidan's reaction. Would her therapist disapprove of her picking up a stranger at a sushi bar and taking him home for an anonymous fuck? Would he drop his mask of Buddhist composure when she told him, in luscious detail, about how her body had writhed and squirmed under the pressure of Joel's tongue?

In her mind's eye, Chloe saw Aidan's inky eyes grow darker as he listened to his meek naive client reveal all the intimate secrets of her dirty afternoon. He'd be able to control his mouth, but he wouldn't be able to do anything about those expressive eyes, or the sleek brows that rose over them. And his hands ... those long, ivory fingers wouldn't be able to stop fidgeting with a pencil, or a chopstick, or whatever stray object he happened to pick up from his desk. He'd find himself growing inappropriately, untherapeutically hard as Chloe elaborated on the pleasure she'd found in Joel's lips, hands and cock, and he'd have to cross his legs to hide his growing erection.

Aidan might have to hide something else, too, something far more disturbing to his professional equilibrium. He'd have to hide the fact that he was jealous.

Chloe had to sit on her hands to keep from wriggling in her seat. Joel must have triggered some long-suppressed appetites; she couldn't think of a time, in recent memory, when she'd been so obsessed with sexy thoughts. She glanced up at the clock (it was a ninety-minute seminar, but it felt more like ninety years), and saw Professor Tanaka watching her.

As a matter of fact, everyone in the room was watching her. The room had gone dead quiet. The five grad students sitting around the oval table were all looking at Chloe. Professor Tanaka's mouth drooped into a contemptuous scowl under his thin grey moustache; his face reminded her of the distorted expression on a *kabuki* mask.

'Ms Frost?' he said, investing the words with a brittle chill. 'Do you think you could bring your mind back to the discussion and tell us how you translated this *haiku*?'

'Um, which *haiku* would that be?' Chloe squeaked. 'I thought we were still talking about the *tanka*. The hand thing? The *kake kotoba*?'

'We've moved on from "the hand thing", Ms Frost. We are apparently making progress without you. Are you ill today? You look flushed.'

Caught with a red face and a wet pussy, Chloe wanted to sink through the floor. Maybe she was being paranoid, but she could swear she saw smirks on the other students' faces. Mind-readers, all of them, they could see every one of the lewd images that danced in her erotically awakened brain.

'See me after class, Ms Frost,' the professor said, each word clipped. 'Would one of the active participants care to read their translation?'

The remaining seventeen minutes of the seminar dragged. Chloe sat like a deflated balloon, slumped over the table, doodling in the margins of her notebook. No obscene pictures, just a lot of anxious meaningless scribbles that signified distress. When the class finally ended, Chloe waited in her seat for Professor Tanaka to gather his books, erase the chalkboard and readjust the other chairs around the table. A meticulous man, a merciless perfectionist, he wouldn't address his wayward student until he'd arranged his environment to match the equilibrium in his mind.

Chloe stayed seated through the whole obsessive-compulsive, passive-aggressive ritual. She knew better than to stand up; Professor Tanaka was self-conscious about his height and, though Chloe was no Amazon, she towered over the diminutive scholar when they were both standing. If ever there was a time to revert to her sheepish submissive persona, this was it.

'Why aren't you in Chicago, Chloe?' Professor Tanaka asked, when he was finally finished with his clockwork rotations around the classroom.

Too ashamed to formulate an intelligent reply, Chloe screwed up her face, lifted her shoulders and said, 'I dunno.'

'Are you really that indifferent to the conference? It's one of the most important opportunities that a fledgling scholar could have.'

Chloe couldn't bring herself to look up into the professor's face. She kept her eyes focused on his manicured fingernails, which were balanced on the surface of the table. 'I'm not indifferent,' she said. 'Not at all. It's just that ... I missed my flight, and had to stay home.'

'You couldn't have caught a later plane?'

Chloe shook her head. 'No. The truth is, I can't fly. I mean I can – not literally – but I'm afraid to. I've never been on a plane. Well, I tried once, but I couldn't actually board it. I got freaked out at the gate, and they had to call security.'

'Chloe, you wrote a very insightful paper about the influence of early Chinese writing on the *Manyoshu*.

Your paper was selected for presentation by a committee with extremely high standards. Your translations were intelligent, sensitive and, dare I say, passionate. Couldn't you have overcome your phobia for this opportunity?'

Miserable, Chloe hung her head. 'I guess not.'

'You guess not,' Professor Tanaka repeated in a soft tone. 'Well, then. Not only your work, but *my* work, my advocacy, went to waste.'

A few centuries ago, Chloe would have thrown herself at her professor's feet, humbling herself, begging for mercy, her long hair falling forwards to cover her brick-red face. *Forgive me, Master Tanaka, for being such an inept and timid pupil; I have the heart of a lion, the libido of an orangutan, but I am burdened by the soul of a mouse.* An intense, almost erotic scene, Chloe might have found the fantasy arousing under any other circumstances. At the moment, however, she just felt like a loser.

'I'm sorry, Professor Tanaka.'

'For what? The conference ends tomorrow. It's too late for regret.'

'I'm sorry that all your work went to waste. I'm sorry that you put yourself out for me, and I couldn't live up to your expectations. Most of all, I'm sorry that I couldn't get over all my stupid fears and get on that plane to Chicago.'

His hand came to rest on her shoulder. She still couldn't look up at him. His touch wasn't reassuring; it felt more like a dismissal, a gentle farewell.

'So am I,' he said.

The professor went back to the wooden lectern, picked up his briefcase and walked with crisp neat steps towards the door.

'Please turn off the light when you leave, Ms Frost,' were his last words to Chloe.

She wasn't sure how long she sat there, staring at the surface of the table. A student of days gone by had carved the words 'Fuck Reality' into the oak veneer. Chloe wished, for once, that she could share those sentiments. She wished she hadn't invested her whole life, her self-esteem, in academia. If she had something else to turn to now – a relationship, a hobby, even a part-time job – she wouldn't be feeling like such a big zero right now. Her identity was way too fragile, she thought, held up on props that felt sturdy, but turned out to be as rickety as toothpicks when her self-worth was tested.

Well, she did have one thing left. It wasn't much, not nearly as much she wished it could be, but it would help to get her through this crisis. She had a close trusting relationship with her therapist. Aidan would see her this afternoon. Even if he had no appointments open, he'd carve out half an hour for Chloe. Half an hour was all she needed, a thirty-minute fix.

Chloe dug her cell phone out of her backpack and speed-dialled Aidan's number. As usual, she got his voicemail, but even the sound of his voice, as smooth as the ripple of water over the stones in his fountain sculpture, soothed Chloe's ragged soul.

'Aidan, it's me. Chloe. I'm sorry for the late notice.' (Sorry, sorry, sorry, how many times could one human being apologise in the course of a lifetime?) 'It's kind of an emergency – again. Remember that flight I missed? Well, my prof had a talk with me today, and now I feel like jumping off the Golden Gate Bridge. I really need to see you. Is there any way you could make time for me this afternoon? It's almost noon now. I could be there any time you're available. I'll head over to your office now, and just hang out in your waiting room till you're free. Call me on my cell, OK?'

She left Aidan her number, then pressed several of the wrong buttons before remembering how to end a call. Of all the people on earth who should avoid portable communication technology, Chloe was probably Number

One. In Chloe's world, all communication would take place through handwritten notes delivered on horseback. It wasn't until she started therapy that she was inspired to buy a cell. With all of her emotional crises, her dramatic plunges into despair, her ups and downs and backs and forths, Chloe needed a lifeline to her therapist.

More accurately, she needed a lifeline to Aidan. Before she began therapy with him, she never felt this crazy. Anxious, yes. Depressed, sometimes. But she never used to be a victim of the kind of turmoil that required 24-hour access to a therapist's voicemail, with emergency sessions three or four times a week.

Maybe it's not my life that's driving me nuts, she thought, struck by a rare unflinching glimpse into her own heart. Maybe it's my uncontrollable lust for Aidan. With a sigh, Chloe picked up her backpack. She deliberately left her chair pushed away from the table, a small act of defiance against her obsessive-compulsive professor, and left the room. Too much of a good girl to waste electricity, she did obey the professor's instructions to turn off the light.

As she was trudging across the Quad, barely noticing the tide of students flowing around her, Chloe's cell phone went off. She scrabbled frantically through her backpack, letting books and papers fly.

'Chloe? It's Aidan.'

'Aidan?' she gasped into what she thought was the mouthpiece. 'Aidan? Aidan?' His voice was faint, distant. Chloe couldn't figure out what was wrong. Then she turned the phone right side up. 'Aidan? Sorry. Are you still there?'

'I'm here. Is that you, Chloe?'

'It's me. Can I see you today?' She pushed her hand through her hair, unconsciously grooming herself for a man who couldn't even see her.

'Sure. In fact, I was going to call you.'

'Really?'

'Yes, I was. I need to talk to you, sooner rather than later. Today would be perfect.'

Chloe's heart pounded. His voice sounded different, uncharacteristically awkward. This was it. This had to be it. Strained by the pressure of his secret desire for Chloe, Aidan had cracked. In those few words – *sooner rather than later* – Chloe heard a dammed-up flood of love and longing and sheer, hot desire. Aidan was going to tell her he wanted her, as much more than a client.

'What did you want to talk to me about?' she squeaked.

'Um, well, I think it's better we discuss it in my office. Come by at two, OK?'

'Sure. Two. Two is good. Two is great!'

Chloe's heart was pounding at an insane tempo; her head was as light as a helium balloon. Suddenly Professor Tanaka's disappointment didn't matter any more. Her phobias, her fears, her inadequacies flew away like pigeons, startled by Chloe's surge of happiness.

'I'll see you soon, then,' Aidan said, then he hung up.

Soon, soon, soon. As Chloe drifted towards the Bart station, heading for the city, the word echoed through the air along with the bell in the campus clocktower, marking her hour of triumph.

Everybody gathered around the table in the B&M conference room looked grey. Tired, bored out of their minds, and grey.

Lauryn probably looked grey, too. She sure felt that way. All of the exotic colour and explosive passion of her afternoon with Joel yesterday had given way to the sludge of preparing for yet another mass execution in Corporate America. As an 'efficiency expert', Lauryn was supposed to advise all these sludgy fish-eyed corporate honchos on how to rationalise cost-cutting layoffs. What she really wanted to be doing at eight o'clock on a

Thursday morning was spooning with Joel in bed, her bottom fitting like a curvy piece of a jigsaw puzzle into his pelvis, feeling his cock rise between her cheeks, as his body stirred in his sleep. Still half-conscious, he would reach for one of her breasts, instinctively fondling the nipple. Her moan would wake him, and with a grunt he would roll Lauryn over on to her belly, lift her ass into the air with one hand and slip into her slick wetness from behind.

After Lauryn and Joel went their separate ways, with kisses and longing glances and promises to meet again – nude – as soon as possible, Lauryn had spent the next twelve hours building a fantasy life around him. Though she knew that it wasn't unusual for women to start weaving elaborate futures with men as soon as they had swapped DNA, she felt embarrassed about how quickly she started creating a storyline for herself and Joel. She would get the job she dreamed of in Europe, and Joel would follow her there. Equipped with his digital camera and wireless laptop, he would zip off his photos to magazines and newspapers all over the world, while Lauryn busily worked on her data on a Louis XV desk in an elegant Parisian office overlooking the Seine.

On weekends, they would climb into their cool black Citroën and whiz around the French countryside, sampling wine and snapping pictures that would capture the details of their carefree life. And at night, every night, they would tear off each other's clothes and indulge in a sweet ongoing investigation of each other's body, stroking and tasting and entering and stimulating each other in every imaginable way...

'Let's face it, guys, technological advances in food processing have made a lot of your line-workers as obsolete as saturated fat, and just as dangerous to your bottom line. Check out these figures!'

Barry stood in front of a white board, illustrating his points with red and green pens as a dozen distinguished heads tried to follow his manic numbers. Lauryn had to give Barry credit: his purple-and-green paisley tie was the only spot of life in the room, and, among the men who were present, he probably had the only viable pulse.

'Now B&M has been in business for what, forty plus years? Times change. Technology changes. Hey, you guys aren't peddling Betty's Kreemy Snack-Cakes any more, you're competing with some of the leading tofu producers on the West Coast! You're health-conscious. You're cutting-edge. You've trimmed a lot of corporate fat and, though I know you folks have way too much heart to do this willingly, that's going to include trimming your workforce.'

Barry was piling on the bullshit with a forklift this morning, and the honchos didn't mind the odour one bit. Lauryn would let him do his shtick, then she would step in and crisply, calmly show them what his numbers really meant. Her part of the presentation would only last for fifteen minutes; that's how long it took before your average corporate type started nodding off, or craving a shot of Glen Livet, or fantasising about having his secretary blow him under the table. In the three years they'd been working together, Lauryn and Barry had worked out their act as precisely as a couple of professional ice-skaters.

At one point, that act used to extend into their hotel rooms, where Lauryn and Barry used to execute naked versions of their fancy manoeuvres, including the double-axle that ended with Lauryn twirling on top of Barry's face. Now, especially after yesterday with Joel, Barry's performance no longer gave Lauryn visions of his tightly gym-toned glutes, or his energetic tongue. The only response she could summon, as she watched him scribble and wave his arms and hop around like an Italian leprechaun, was a vast inner yawn.

'But that's enough of me,' Barry was saying. 'You guys are falling asleep staring at my ugly mug! Hey, nothing like a knockout blonde to wake you up, right? Let's break for ten, then Lauryn will show off her ... numbers.'

Barry's grotesque wink made the honchos chuckle. Lauryn had to bite her lip to keep from snarling at him. The broad-shouldered men in their tailored suits shoved away from the table and moved en masse to a corner of the room where herbal tea and whole-grain bagels were waiting.

After over four decades in the snack-food industry, B&M was trying to clean up its image as one of the country's leading pushers of sugar, sodium and saturated fat. In the year 2000, to commemorate their forty-year anniversary, they had christened the company 'B&M', an abbreviation of the company's original name, 'Bama Mama'. Founded in a small town in the South, 'Bama Mama had flourished during the 70s, then floundered in the 80s, only to struggle back to life after closing down their plant in Alabama and relocating to California. In Oakland, they had tapped into the health-nut market, converting their infamous Kreemy Kakes to virtuous Rice Rounds, and their insanely fattening Banana-Butter Babies to the lean-and-mean Speedee Athletic Bars.

The big-bellied 'Bama' boys, transplanted to the West Coast, looked glum as they washed down their margarine-slathered bagels with hot herbal tea. No doubt they were dreaming of the good ol' days, when black coffee and glazed doughnuts were served at every company meeting, by a 'gal' with a beehive hairdo, a hefty hillbilly butt, and a frilly Dolly Parton blouse. Instead, they were being force-fed whole grains, and the only woman in the room was a skinny blonde wearing a black Donna Karan pantsuit.

When the break was over, Lauryn switched on her laptop and launched her PowerPoint presentation. With all the zest of a humanoid cash register, she ran through the numbers displayed on the screen against the wall. She knew that she was boring the good ol' boys to tears, but she'd lost her passion for her work long ago. Maybe she'd never had any passion to begin with. Somehow she'd gone from school into workforce analysis into the head-chopping business, and suddenly she had no clue how she'd gotten here.

How ironic, Lauryn thought, that she'd ended up with a contract for a company that reminded her so painfully of her white-trash pedigree. Those plastic-wrapped Bama Mama snack cakes had been a staple of Lauryn's diet; there was always a Kreemy Kake or a Pluto Pie tucked into her lunch pail, between the peanut butter sandwich and the bag of potato chips. Lauryn's waitress mom had neither the time nor the education to make a wholesome lunch for her daughter to take to school; everything was refined, pre-packaged and thoroughly devoid of any nutritional value, with the exception of the peanut butter. If not for eating gallons of Skippy when she was growing up, Lauryn believed, she'd be four feet tall today and would have the IQ of a chimpanzee.

Her fifteen-minute presentation passed in a blur, a slow smear of spreadsheets and slack faces, then Barry took centre stage again. Lauryn knew she should go back to her seat, put up a front of camaraderie and shared zeal, but she just couldn't do it. All she could think about, when she watched Barry hurl himself into his routine again, was the fact that he'd snatched that plum contract in Belgium, while Lauryn was going to be sentenced to domestic industrial parks for the rest of her life. Instead of sitting down like a good girl and playing the faithful sidekick, Lauryn shut her laptop, picked up her purse and quietly left the room.

The hallway was deserted. Lauryn strolled down the carpeted corridor, checking out the pricey artwork on the walls. The third floor of the B&M building, where the corporate offices and conference rooms were located, reflected a blend of wealth and conservatism that was predictably showy and boring at the same time. For once,

Lauryn wished she smoked pot; this would be the perfect place to fire up a joint, filling the staid halls of B&M with the skunky aroma of weed.

Well, she didn't smoke, but there were other ways to express your disdain for corporate America. Lauryn opened her handbag and examined the contents. Yep, there it was, her loyal trusted friend, nestled against her cosmetic bag. She reached in and pulled out the little egg-shaped vibrator, which she'd thrown into her purse as she was leaving for the airport back in Chicago. She walked down the hall, a furtive skip in her step, until she found the perfect place to let the egg work its magic: right in front of a big picture window overlooking the East Bay. The marshy bay wasn't nearly as sexy as the Seine, but it would do at a pinch.

Lauryn looked to the right, then to the left. There wasn't a soul in the hallway and, judging by the pristine condition of the ochre carpet, no mortal foot had ever passed this way, except maybe the janitorial staff. Two floors below, the massive machinery of B&M was hard at work, gears grinding out the day's quota of food products. Three months from now, the staff that manned those machines would be cut by nearly a third.

Lauryn couldn't take this any more.

She unzipped her trousers, slipped her hand down her panties. As soon as her fingers reached her lower lips, reassuringly warm and softly furred, she felt her blood pressure go down. For as long as she could remember, touching herself down there had always made her feel better when she was scared, anxious or stressed. For Lauryn, masturbation wasn't just about self-induced orgasms; it was about comfort, taking herself back to that hidden world that always felt pleasurable and safe, even in the midst of an all-out shitstorm.

Lauryn flipped the switch on the little egg with the tip of her thumbnail. The vibrator came to life with a tiny purposeful drone, like an efficient insect. Lauryn felt an unexpected surge of affection for her toy, as if it were a dear old friend showing up to greet her in a hostile unfamiliar place. She slipped the vibrator under the waistband of her panties. Its buzz was muffled, though an observant bystander might have noticed its gentle whirr in that dead-quiet hallway.

Deviating from her usual tried-and-true routine, Lauryn spent some time buzzing her outer lips, feeling the accumulated stress seep out of her mind as the egg's vibration sent waves of pleasure through her flesh. She pushed the egg deep into her softest spaces, massaging the tender labia before nudging the tip of the oval into the moist inner pocket where her clit was nestled. The small bud stiffened under the egg's persistent attention. Lauryn braced herself against the picture window, left palm flat against the glass, as the ripples intensified. She didn't care if her hand left a mark on the window's pristine surface; a nice messy handprint, a sign of life, was exactly what was needed in this executive corridor from hell.

The steely coils that had gripped Lauryn's muscles while she sat in the meeting, feeling bored and trapped, were being replaced by a different kind of tension. The egg was busily bobbing its way towards her inner opening; with a gasp, Lauryn helped the vibrator find its way in. She pushed the buzzing plastic oval upwards, so deep that she could feel its vibrations shuddering through the pit of her belly, then she pressed both hands against the window and let go.

She rocked her hips back and forth, vaguely aware that her body was moving through a dance of solitary simulated sex. Half wishing that there were someone around to enjoy her performance, Lauryn arched her spine and lifted her bottom as if she were arching back to meet a lover's thrusting cock. Lauryn loved being taken from behind like an animal in heat, hard and fast and raw. She loved coming back to that primal place where the stifling structure of her life fell away, the place where her social identity, with all its holes and the affectations that randomly patched them, dissolved into a self that was purely sexual.

Lost in her fantasy of primal sex, Lauryn didn't hear the sleek Italian leather loafers striding down the hallway, or hear them come to a stop within full view of her impromptu stage. It wasn't until she was cresting the hill of her orgasm that she caught the flicker of a reflected male silhouette in the window. She didn't have the time, or the desire, to turn around before the orgasm crashed through her; at this point, Lauryn had about as much control over her body as the driver of a car without brakes hurtling down one of San Francisco's vertical hills.

A rational thought flashed across her mind as she rode out her climax: she was going to have to explain this to someone. Maybe to several someones. Coming down, she stole a moment to gather her thoughts and smooth her blouse over her erect nipples before turning around to face her audience.

Just taking a little break here, she would say. *It's a new form of stress release for women, officially sanctioned by three major talk-show hosts. The theory is that, through simulated orgasm in public locations, women can both achieve a more relaxed state and validate their inner power through a public expression of sexuality...*

'Bravo, Lauryn.' A pair of male hands began to clap. 'Great way to lose a contract! You walk out of one of our most important client meetings and sneak down the hallway for a little solo fun. But, hey, maybe I'm just pissed because you didn't ask me to join in.'

Lauryn had to close her eyes and count to five before she could turn around to face Barry. She opened her eyes to see his face set in a cocky self-satisfied smirk, his arms folded over a chest that was puffed out like a bantam rooster's. Even more pleased with himself than usual, he tapped his toe in its pricey Italian shoe and looked Lauryn up and down.

'You definitely have that post-orgasmic glow, I only wish I could have been here to help.'

'If you'd been here any sooner, I wouldn't have come at all,' Lauryn snapped. 'Did I really ever find you attractive, or was that a delusion?'

'Oh, I definitely remember a few scorching sessions in hotel rooms across the country. I was disappointed when you didn't want to share a room at the Radisson this time. Guess you'd rather order pizza from a flophouse downtown than enjoy Italian sausage in the comfort of a nice hotel. When exactly did you start slumming, Lauryn?'

'I'm not slumming, Barry. Slumming is what I did when I was attempting to find your penis so I could give you a blowjob.'

Barry clasped his hands over his heart in mock pain. 'Ow! You're not only breaking my balls here, you're breaking my heart!'

'All in a day's work,' Lauryn said.

She yanked the hem of her Donna Karan jacket into position, left her post at the window with a last regretful glance at the Bay and swept past Barry with her head held as high as possible for a professional woman who's just been caught masturbating in public on the client's turf. Out of the corner of her eye, she saw Barry shaking his head and smiling to himself.

'And you wonder why you never get those fabulous assignments in Europe.' Barry chuckled to Lauryn's back. 'What were you thinking, cutting out on our pitch like that? You could have broken that deal for us, Lauryn. Hope you have a blast playing the rebel, because it's not going to do a lot for your career.'

Holding tight to the last shreds of her dignity, Lauryn stalked back to the conference room. She could hear

Barry strolling along behind her, predictably slowing his pace so that he could watch her from behind. Knowing full well what his agenda was, Lauryn marched along with military stiffness; Barry wasn't going to catch the slightest butt-wiggle, if she could help it. As she retraced her steps down the stiflingly elegant hallway – corporate money could buy everything but fresh air, it seemed – Lauryn felt like an escaped prisoner being escorted back to her cell after a failed attempt at flight.

But those moments of flight, gazing out over the water while her flesh responded hungrily to the buzz of her vibrator, made this forced march just a little more bearable. Freedom, spontaneity and crazy-mad sex with a man she truly wanted weren't just illusions. They were real possibilities, some more distant than others, but still sweetly, achingly close to her grasp.

All a woman had to do was reach.

Chloe's knees wobbled and her breath came in short gasps as she climbed the stairs to Aidan's office. In her anxiety, she reverted to an old habit: counting. One step, two steps, three steps, and so on all the way to the top. Counting reduced her life to something she could manage, a series of objects or events that she could quantify. Otherwise, her existence made about as much sense to Chloe as one of those million-piece jigsaw puzzles, taken apart and flung out over the Pacific Ocean.

In addition to counting, Chloe had her fingers crossed so tightly that she was cutting off their circulation. How could she not have known that she wanted Aidan this much? In all of her fantasies, set in the distant world of courtly Japanese poets, Aidan had been the mysterious lover, the raven-haired ravisher, the man who was desired and anxiously awaited, but never named.

This afternoon Aidan was going to tell Chloe that he wanted her, too. There simply couldn't be any other reason why he'd called her to his office. In the months they'd been working together, Aidan had never contacted Chloe. He'd never had reason to, since Chloe's need for him put them in constant contact with each other. Today, for once, Aidan needed *her*.

'He's "Aidan" now,' Chloe puffed to herself, as she reached the top of the stairway. 'Not "my therapist", not my "sensei", but *Aidan*.'

She was already imagining the way he would greet her, drawing her into his office and closing the door before opening his arms to her and pulling her close to his lean hard torso. Chloe would feel his heartbeat under the crisp modest shield of his white cotton shirt and, below the borderline of his leather belt, she would feel a corresponding pulse in his groin, along with an unmistakable hardness that signalled better than words how much he wanted her ...

'Hey, Chloe. Thanks for seeing me on such short notice. I'm sure you must have had other plans this afternoon.'

The voice, nervous and edged with an apology, sounded so different from what Chloe was expecting that she didn't recognise the speaker at first. Then she saw Aidan standing in his doorway, arms not open, but crossed over his chest. Aidan's shirts and slacks, even his jeans when he wore them, always looked like he'd just lifted them off of an ironing board. No stray hairs ever erupted from his ponytail. He was always impeccably put together, and his perfection, all of a sudden, made him seem a thousand miles away from the dysfunctional mess that was Chloe.

'I didn't have any plans,' Chloe said. 'Can I sit down? I'm feeling kind of dizzy.'

'Sure, sure. Come on in.' Aidan stepped back neatly to let her into his office. He placed a hand on her shoulder blade – her *shoulder blade*! Could anything be less sexually suggestive? – to steer her into the chair opposite his desk. For the first time, Chloe noticed how uninviting that chair was, hard blond wood, its contemporary lines almost coldly functional. Aidan's décor, with its Zen rock sculptures and bare-bones furniture, could best be described as Buddha-meets-Ikea.

Chloe giggled.

Aidan smiled. It was his usual serenely neutral professional smile, maybe a bit wobbly at the corners. 'What's funny?'

'Your office,' Chloe said. She wasn't about to repeat the Buddha-meets-Ikea line, but she figured she might as well be as brutally honest as she could.

In any other session, Aidan would have probed at that remark, asking Chloe to tell him what, exactly, was so amusing about his office, and what had led her thoughts in the direction of his décor. Today, he took a seat, picked up a rock out of the bowl of smooth stones that sat on his desk and began to squeeze it as if he thought it might start miraculously leaking crude oil.

'I wanted you to come here so we could talk,' Aidan said.

'That's what I figured. I mean, I didn't think you'd asked me here so we could make rabid love beside your water sculpture.'

Oh, God. Why did I just say that? Chloe thought, looking frantically around the office for the nearest escape route. The open window looked inviting. Being honest was one thing; laying out your sexual fantasies like second-hand clothes at a flea market was quite another.

Unbelievably, Aidan didn't seem to have heard her. Maybe she hadn't really spoken out loud. More likely, he was used to having his female clients come on to him, and he'd learned to overlook their lapses into erotic insanity.

'Chloe,' Aidan said, with a pained expression, 'I'm trimming down my client list.'

Chloe tried to swallow the giant lump in her throat. It would have been easier to gulp down the rock Aidan was holding. 'I guess that means I'm being trimmed.'

Aidan nodded. 'Yeah.'

'"Yeah"?' Chloe laughed – a bitter sound. 'I gotta tell you, Aidan, that's not a very therapeutic explanation.'

'I know it's not. But I'm not feeling very therapeutic right now. That's part of the problem, Chloe.' Aidan took a deep breath. 'Over the past couple of months, I've felt our professional relationship . . . slipping.'

'Slipping where?'

'Into a realm that's more, um, personal. Look, to be absolutely honest with you, I feel like you're attracted to me.'

Chloe snorted. 'You're kidding, right?'

'If I've misinterpreted some of the signals you've been sending me, I apologise. Maybe I've read too much into some of the things you've said, the gestures you've made. But lately I've found myself responding to some of those signals in a way that puts me in a compromising position. So tell me, please, am I mistranslating the messages you're sending me?'

Chloe's face was on fire. She'd been caught. Next thing you know, the Therapy Police would be bursting through the door, dragging Chloe out of the office, taking her off to some sort of rehabilitation facility for patients with serious transference issues.

'No,' she whispered, staring down at her lap. 'Your translation is right on target.'

Aidan didn't say anything. Nor did Chloe. For several excruciating moments, the only sounds in the office were the rumble of traffic outside and the gurgle of Aidan's water sculpture. The sound of water falling over stones was supposed to be soothing. For Chloe, it was suddenly about as calming as the monotonous drip from a leaky pipe.

'That's what I thought,' Aidan finally said. 'Tell me, what are *you* thinking right now?'

That you're a jerk for letting me go. That you led me on by continuing to see me when you knew I felt this way. That you shouldn't have shown up in my erotic fantasies if you didn't want to be part of my dreams, Chloe thought.

'Well, I was thinking that the one good thing about this meeting is that my day can't get much worse from here,' Chloe said.

'Is there something else you want to talk about?'

'You mean like the fact that one of the professors I admire most thinks I'm a loser for missing my flight to Chicago? Or that I've developed a sudden interest in picking up guys at sushi bars? Sure, there are things I'd like to talk to you about. But what would be the point?'

Aidan looked miserable. 'I'm sorry, Chloe. Listen, I can give you the name of another therapist. You'll like her. She's a close friend of mine, a widely respected professional...'

'Whatever,' Chloe sighed. 'Give me her name. I'm definitely going to need some intensive therapy after this. I must be the first woman in history who's been kicked to the kerb by her therapist. This is a new level of rejection for me.'

'This is not rejection, Chloe. That's the last thing on earth I'd want you to think.'

'Too bad it's the *first* thing that came to my mind then, isn't it? Just give me her name, Aidan. Let's make this as painless as possible.'

Aidan was already scribbling on his notepad. He tore off the sheet and handed it to Chloe.

'Margaret Wasserman,' Chloe read out loud.

'You'll like her,' Aidan said. 'Trust me.'

'Trust me,' Chloe echoed. 'Where have I heard *that* before?'

She stood up, her knees shaking with something very different to desire, and stumbled out of Aidan's office.

Later, when she was rehashing this scene in her head at night, she'd probably wish she'd swept out of the room with an air of dignified injury. Instead, she stubbed her toe on the doorframe on her way out, and limped out whimpering.

'Chloe?' Aidan called out. 'This hurts me, too.'

Chloe looked back over her shoulder, shooting him a look that held all the pain from her freshly banged toe, along with the ghosts of her dead fantasies.

'Whatever,' she said, the only word that could effectively throw a blanket over all the disappointments of her day.

Chapter Nine

This Ain't Your Grandma's Scrapbook, Sweetie

Was it just Joel's overactive visual imagination, or did the women of the Mission District look especially lickable on this honey-gold day? Everywhere he looked, he saw a profusion of female hair and skin, hips and breasts, throats and shoulders glistening in the mellow late-afternoon sun.

Cinematographers didn't call this time the 'magic hour' for nothing; the setting sun cast everything, especially pedestrians of a feminine persuasion, in a sensual blue glow, and held them suspended for Joel's hungry gaze. He wished he could pull out his Nikon and take shots of all of them – the slim blonde bouncing by in her running shorts and Nikes; the smouldering brunette pouring out of her hip-hugging jeans; the silver-haired goddess emerging pink-cheeked from the bikhram yoga studio.

But Joel didn't photograph women. That was one of his cardinal rules, almost as hard and fast as the codes of professional ethics that had been carved in his soul during his first college internship at the *Chicago Sun-Times*. Through years of painful experience, Joel had learned that women and cameras were a match made in heaven ... for any photographer but himself. His heart was too weak, not in the way it pumped blood, but in the way it pumped lust through his veins, more potent and intoxicating than any drug.

Joel needed some kind of drug right now, even if it were nothing more mind-altering than his own fantasies of tonguing the lovely women who walked by, leaving traces of perfume and light perspiration in the air behind them. He'd just escaped the grimy warren-like offices of one of San Francisco's community weeklies, where he'd gone to meet an editor about staffing opportunities. It wasn't the kind of thing Joel was looking for – making a pittance by staying in one place, getting entrenched in neighbourhood politics, taking shots of local bands trying to make the big time and local businessmen trying to act like college frat boys at happy hour – and the editor knew it. The interview had lasted all of six minutes. No hurt feelings, no wasted time on either end.

'Face it, dude, you're not a local kind of guy,' the editor had said, before turning back to the flat-panel display attached to his gleaming new Mac. That hardware had probably cost more than anything else in the paper's office, including the editor's yearly salary.

Joel had been relieved to get out of there but, at the same time, he couldn't shake that queasy feeling that he'd just shot down another opportunity.

Joel's cell played his favourite ringtone, the opening measures of Ozzy Osbourne's 'Crazy Train'. That was the tone he assigned to women he'd met, liked and been intimate with. For women he'd been intimate with, but no longer communicated with, he'd programmed his phone to play a few ominous bars of Wagner's 'Ride of the Valkyrie'.

'Joel? Is that you?'

'Lauryn?' He was surprised at the silly lilt in his voice, the dryness in his mouth, when he said Lauryn's name. The cell phone felt slippery in his hand, and it took him a moment to realise that his palm was already moist.

'Who? Who's Laura?'

Oh, shit.

He vaguely recognised the voice; it gave him an impression of someone timid, vulnerable, maybe a touch insane.

'Sorry. Guess I spoke too soon.' Joel summoned a laugh, backpedalling as fast as he could. 'I was expecting a call from an editor. How are *you* doing?'

The woman, whose name he still couldn't recall, gave a deep sigh. 'Not good. This has probably been one of the worst days of my life.'

'Really? Talk to me.' Joel was still walking. His eyes, now distracted from the females around him, scanned the taquerias and funky salad joints for something cheap to fill his growling belly.

'Well, I went to class today, and my professor told me he's extremely disappointed that I missed that plane to Chicago. Of course, I wanted to die after that; no one lives through Professor Tanaka's wrath. Then, as if that weren't bad enough, my therapist called *me* to set up an appointment – to fire me! He cut me off his client list. You know why? Because he thought I *wanted* him in an unprofessional sense. Have you ever heard of anything like that?'

Airplane. Professor. Therapy. The pieces were coming together in Joel's girl-addled brain, forming a slender shy graduate student with light-brown hair and hidden nymphomaniac tendencies. *Chloe.*

'Damn. That's rough, Chloe,' Joel said. 'Your therapist dumped you?'

He didn't mention that he'd never actually heard of a patient getting dumped by a therapist or, worse, that he could see where the therapist was coming from. Chloe's come-ons were hard to resist; Joel himself could attest to that. A guy just couldn't see her coming; she'd sneak up on him with her sweetly tremulous voice, her curtains of mouse-silk hair and her teary grey eyes, and, before he knew it, he'd be kissing a pair of pink lips that tasted of wasabi and ginger.

'He didn't *dump* me,' Chloe said, audibly bristling.

'"Dumping" would imply that we were having a sexual relationship, and we definitely were not having one of those.'

'Then what was his problem?' Joel veered in the direction of a taco stand. He hoped that Chloe would get to the point of the conversation before he had to place his order. Women tended to get mad at him when he ordered food while carrying on a cellular conversation. Joel thought that was unfair. If you were on mile thirteen of a marathon phone call, you had to have some sort of sustenance to carry you through to the end.

'Why don't we get together and talk about it in person?' Joel suggested. 'Listen, I'm down here in the Mission, just about to order a bite to eat at Tres Hermanos. Want to come down here and join me for some tacos and cerveza?'

'Ew.' Chloe sniffed. 'You actually eat that stuff? You don't even know what's in that taco filling.'

'Hey, it's meat, right? They can't lie about something like that.'

'I'll pass. Besides, I'm not in any shape to see anyone right now. My eyes are so swollen from crying, I look like an albino rabbit with pink-eye.'

'How about tomorrow, then? We'll have dinner, anywhere you like. Sprouts R Us, the No-Meat Cafe, you name it. You can tell me all about it.'

'Really? Oh, Joel, that would make me feel so much better.'

The mixture of relief and anticipation in Chloe's voice set off an alarm bell in the primal zone of Joel's brain: WARNING: CHEAP COMPENSATORY SEX AHEAD. It wasn't so much that Joel minded being used for his body by women who'd been freshly rejected; it was just that he'd hoped he was growing past that. Maturing. Learning about what mattered in human relationships.

'I'll pick you up tomorrow at seven,' he said.

'Why don't I fix us something at my place?' Chloe

asked. That coy tone was creeping into her voice again, both unsettling and arousing.

Do you really want to do this again, buddy? Joel asked himself. One sexual encounter could be written off as a lovely accident; a second would be approaching the dangerous territory of attachment, possibly even commitment.

'Sure,' Joel said. 'Sounds great. I'll be there.'

So much for what mattered in human relationships, he thought ruefully, just before he let himself fall into the primal abyss where his desires for Mexican food, beer and sex all dwelled.

After downing a few tacos and a couple of Coronas at one of the taqueria's outdoor tables, Joel felt like he could take on the world, even a world that included multiple lovers. As he strolled down Mission, Joel kept thinking that he really should buy a gift for Chloe, something to make her feel not only special, but sexy. He thought about candy, but her contempt for taco meat suggested she was the health-nut type. A book of poetry? She already had dozens of poetry collections packing her shelves; with Joel's luck, he'd pick out a book she already had *two* copies of.

Lingerie?

Tonight, Joel felt bold enough to confront one of his biggest phobias: buying intimate apparel. Like photographing women, purchasing small slippery articles made of lace and satin took Joel to places that felt dangerously unstable. First, he had to overcome his fear of entering a business establishment that was permeated with all the sights and scents that made the feminine world so alluring and intoxicating. Second, he had to choose one sexy article from a selection of hundreds, which would require that he ask for help from a saleswoman who would probably look like she should be modelling the attire herself. Third, he would have to spend a lot of money, often breaking his meagre budget, to buy a gift that might not fit the woman he was buying it for, which would lead to resentment, self-doubt and possibly even tears on the lady's part.

Then he passed a funky little shop called Dawgs n' Kats, whose window display included an enticing arrangement of mannequins wearing scanty strings of leather that Joel would have loved to see displayed on something warmer and softer than plaster. To his shame, both Chloe and Lauryn crossed his mind as he stood outside the shop, staring up at the aloof dummies like an awestruck pilgrim afraid to approach a shrine. Each woman was gorgeous in her own way; each had a body that would knock him unconscious if he saw her wearing that get-up.

Joel took a deep breath and walked into the shop.

Dawgs n' Kats wasn't as scary as he'd expected. Loud punk rock blared from the shop's stereo, numbing his senses to a degree that allowed him to keep his head together while he browsed the racks. The girl behind the counter sported an asymmetrical green hairdo and a snarl that pretty much neutralised Joel's libido, eliminating his worries in that area. The only potential risk in Dawgs n' Kats was the customer who leaned against the counter, one bouncy hip extended as she chatted with Ms Green Hair.

The girl had black hair, tied into braids, with ruler-straight bangs. She wore black jeans, a cropped black T-shirt that read 'Idiot-Free Zone' in neon pink letters and a studded belt that made her waist look deliciously slender above the generous outcropping of her bottom. Here was a woman who'd share beer and tacos on a street corner with a guy any day, probably following up dinner with a game of pool and a few rounds of tequila shooters.

Picking up on the sonar waves of lust that Joel was sending her way, the girl lazily turned her head to check him out. Joel smiled at her. She narrowed her eyes, as if she were trying to decide whether he were worth the trouble of changing her facial expression, then she smiled back.

Joel's heart did a double-beat. The girl was cute, definitely sexy, but that smile turned her face into a valentine – a valentine with an edge. Those risky red lips held a trace of a pout, just enough to suggest that, though she was making her 'happy face', she wasn't easily pleased. Her chocolate-brown eyes returned Joel's stare evenly, holding his gaze long enough to tell him that, if she hadn't been hit by any lightning-bolts of love, she'd at least felt a zing when she looked at Joel.

'Look what just walked in, Tracy,' the girl said to Ms Green Hair. 'A grown male with no visible piercings or tattoos. He doesn't smell like an unwashed armpit, and he's wearing chinos. Your clientele is moving up the evolutionary ladder, slowly but surely. Slowly but *surely*.'

The girl's voice slowed to a honeyed drawl on the word 'surely', sending a burst of heat through his lower body. If the girl noticed any sudden physical changes in the area of Joel's trousers, she was kind enough to pretend not to notice. Ms Green Hair, on the other hand, took one look at the bulge in his chinos and sneered, as if to say, 'You may be wearing better pants than most of my customers, but you've got the same old hard-on.'

Mercifully, the black-haired sex bomb stepped in to save him from the clerk's scorn. 'I'm Veronica,' she said, holding out her hand. Joel shook it. Her grip was firm, but her skin felt like warm butter.

'Joel,' he said. It wasn't the cleverest introduction in the world, but with Veronica standing even closer, letting him smell the fragrance of baby oil that came from her skin (the combination of that innocent scent with her deadly Doc Martens was wildly arousing, for some reason), Joel felt grateful that he could remember his own name.

'Shopping for someone special?' Veronica asked.

Now, *there* was a loaded question. Joel had started this adventure on a mission to buy a gift for Chloe. Standing in front of the shop's window, he had found Lauryn joining Chloe in his lascivious thoughts. Now, if he were to be absolutely honest with himself, Joel was imagining Veronica wearing the black leather thong and matching corset that the storefront mannequin was wearing. With her hourglass figure and sugar-white skin, Veronica would look stunning in something like that. She'd look even better as Joel untied the corset's laces to see the bare sensual curves underneath.

He was trying to picture the colour of Veronica's nipples, when she grabbed his hand and led him over to one of the racks.

'So what's your girlfriend like? Let me guess – sweet and smart and shy, but, when she rips off her glasses, she turns into a raving sex maniac.'

'Wow,' Joel said, thinking that Veronica had just given a dead-on description of Chloe.

Veronica appraised him, her forefinger tapping her chin. 'Or maybe she's more the professional type. Very sleek and polished. I'm getting an image of a sophisticated blonde. But she's still a raving sex maniac.'

That was Lauryn to a T. Joel sincerely hoped that Veronica wasn't psychic; she'd kick him in the shins with those combat boots if she could read some of the thoughts that were going through his head.

Veronica rummaged through one of the racks, and finally pulled out a single strand of pink fabric, which looked more like a slingshot than anything else, for Joel's inspection.

'How about this?' she asked. 'One size fits all – yeah, right – and any girl would like it.'

'Nice,' Joel said, feeling incredibly lame, 'but does it actually cover anything?'

'Nope,' said Veronica cheerfully. 'Not anything that

you'd want to see. Trust me. She'll love it. Besides, it's on sale. You can't do better than that. Here. Take it.'

Veronica thrust the pink slingshot at Joel, eliminating his choice in the matter.

'Do you get a commission if I buy this?'

'Nah. I don't work here; I just make a few sales now and then. Tracy's so anti-social, it's a wonder anyone comes through the door. She's got a great eye for lingerie, but she hates humanity. That's a liability in the customer-service business.'

'I should say so.' Joel eyed Tracy. She eyed him back. It wasn't a pleasant exchange.

'So what do you do?'

'Photography. I'm kind of on hiatus right now.'

Veronica frowned. 'Hiatus?'

'It's a fancy Latin word for taking a break while you try to sort your life out.'

'I know what a *hiatus* is,' Veronica said, expelling a scornful puff of air from her pursed lips. 'I'm just wondering how a photographer takes one. Don't you always want to be shooting things? Isn't it, like, instinctive?'

Joel smiled. 'Yes. It is.'

Veronica looked him up and down. Her eyes alighted on the camera case hanging by a strap around his neck. 'If you're on "hiatus", why are you carrying a camera around?'

'I don't know. I guess it's just a part of me, like an extra appendage. I feel naked without it.'

'Hey.' Veronica's chocolate eyes suddenly turned a few shades lighter, as that breathtaking smile lit up her face again. 'Do you ever take pictures of women? Sexy pictures? I'm thinking of something like those glamour shots, with half the makeup and twice the imagination.'

Joel drew back, feeling like a vampire who's been splashed with holy water. 'No. No women. Never.'

'Why not?'

Because women are my weakness. Women are my personal one-way highway to insanity. Women occupy enough of my mind as it is; I need to reserve a few brain cells, and a few ethical standards, for my professional life.

'I'm bad at shooting female subjects,' Joel said stiffly.

'You're joking. How can you be "bad" at taking pictures of beautiful women? All they have to do is stand there, and you point your camera and press a button. Right?'

'Wrong. Very wrong,' Joel said. 'There are all kinds of factors to consider. Light, angle, shutter speed –'

'And you don't have to think about that stuff when you photograph other things?'

'Well, I do. But nudes, especially indoors, are different.'

'Who said anything about nudes? Listen, I need some sexy shots of women wearing clothes. You don't need to worry about the "sexy" part; the girls and the clothes will take care of that. All you have to do is point and shoot.'

'How many girls are we talking about?'

'Four. Five, if you count me.' Veronica considered this for a second. 'Yes, you should definitely include me. I might have to fill in some night, if one of the girls gets sick.'

'Fill in? As what?'

'As an escort. What do you think?'

'You want me to shoot pictures for an escort service? What do you think I am?' Joel asked, eyes darting around to see how far he was from the exit.

Veronica grinned. 'You're exactly what I'm looking for – a healthy heterosexual guy with a camera. Come on. Don't you think it would be fun?'

'Sure, for the right guy. I'm not that guy. Trust me.'

Veronica cocked her head. 'I do trust you. I'm not sure why, but I do. That's why I'm asking. Please?'

She had to know her pleading pout would kill him. Joel felt like a stag crossing the freeway in front of a speeding truck. Actually, the deer would have a better chance of avoiding the vehicle than Joel had of avoiding Veronica's request.

'At least come and meet my roommates,' Veronica suggested, long black lashes flickering prettily over her brown eyes. 'Who knows? This might open up new avenues of business for you. Think of all the referrals!'

'Ah. So you were thinking I'd do this for free.'

'Not for *free*,' Veronica replied defensively. 'Just for cheap. I can pay you.'

Cheap. Yeah, right, Joel thought, picturing a handful of grubby one-dollar bills and some spare change pulled out of a coffee can. But that mental picture couldn't overpower the enticing image of Veronica wearing something impossibly skimpy, like that thong and corset in the window. He was already thinking about how he would light her ivory skin, if she had any decent light available, or if he were the kind of photographer who knew about things like light on naked female flesh...

'Fine. I'll meet the girls. No promises, though. Just a meeting.'

'Fantastic! You won't regret this.' Veronica grabbed him by both hands and began to drag him out of Dawgs n' Kats. She pulled like a mule.

'I hope not,' Joel said, hoping that his shuddering sigh sounded more like resignation than like barely suppressed excitement. He suspected – no, he was certain – that he would regret this.

But Joel's regret couldn't compete with Veronica's monster-truck strength. Besides, Joel was on 'hiatus', whatever the hell that meant. In Hiatusville, he decided on the spot, professional standards didn't apply.

Veronica was getting that Goldilocks vibe again.

Riding the elevator upstairs to her loft, she checked out Joel from the corner of her eye. The more she looked, the more she saw to like. He was hip, but not painfully hip; mature, but not mucked down in complacency; free, but not rootless. In other words, he was just right. And, with a pang, she realised that a lot of the things that attracted her to Joel made him the opposite of Devin.

Joel fidgeted with the straps on his camera case. The old freight elevator creaked and groaned as it carried them upstairs.

'Nervous?' Veronica asked.

'Yeah, a little,' Joel admitted.

'Don't worry. No one's died in this elevator yet, at least not since I've lived here.'

'It's not the elevator.' Joel laughed. 'Trust me. When you've survived a few bus rides through the South American wilderness, complete with paramilitary pit stops, a freight elevator doesn't faze you.'

'Then what's the problem? Scared of my roommates?'

'That's more like it. Jungles I can handle. Superbowls, riots, you name it. But women are always a dangerous mystery.'

'But that's what makes us so much fun, don't you think?'

'Fun, but complicated. I've had more, um, complications in the past few days than I've had in the last six months.'

'But that's what you want from life, isn't it? Excitement, risk, adventure? Otherwise you'd be wearing a pinstripe suit and holding a briefcase, not a camera.'

'I suppose you're right.'

'Listen, Miss Vee is *always* right.'

Veronica shot Joel a sultry look from under her bangs. His edginess, and his willingness to admit it, had kicked her flirting instincts into high gear. With his restless hands and wrinkled brow, he looked like a high-school freshman on the way to pick up his first prom date. His awkwardness was refreshing; most of the guys Veronica knew were either so apathetic about women that they barely acknowledged a gender difference until you were fully naked, or so hell-bent on seeming hardcore that she felt like asking them what kind of relationship they'd had with their mothers.

Joel, on the other hand, was just a guy. A tall solid blue-eyed all-American guy, shuffling his feet and wondering what thrilling erotic risks were waiting for him at the end of this elevator ride.

The elevator stopped. The heavy door opened with an infernal grating sound.

'Abandon hope, all ye who enter here,' Veronica said, grabbing Joel's sweaty hand. 'Come on. Time to meet the girls.'

As she pulled Joel down the hallway, Veronica said a silent prayer to the goddess that her place wouldn't be too much of a wreck, that her roommates would be civil and, most of all, that there wouldn't be hostile boyfriends hanging around the loft. She didn't want some pretentious clown like Buzzsaw to scare Joel off. She could already sense resistance in his body's weight, his dragging feet.

'OK. Here we go.'

Veronica unlocked the door and shoved it open. Imogene, hearing the key in the lock, was already padding across the room like a grumpy housecat, complaining about the lack of food in the refrigerator. Veronica's pink-haired roommate wore nothing but a pair of bizarre candystriped stockings and the oversized Nine Inch Nails T-shirt that she always slept in.

'Don't lie to me, Veronica, I know you ate the last of my peanut butter. And you stole my kinky schoolgirl uniform, didn't you?'

She planted her fists on her hips and was fixing Veronica with a hostile glare, when Joel caught her eye. The metamorphosis was amazing: from being a sleepy, cranky metal-studded bitch, Imogene turned into a sweetly smirking cherub.

'Who's this?' Imogene asked.

'Imogene, meet Joel. Joel, meet my roommate Imogene. She has multiple personalities; the nice one only comes out in the presence of testosterone.'

'Screw you, Vee,' Imogene said, but her voice was a sexy purr. 'So is Joel *your* date, or do we all get to share?'

'Maybe a little of both,' Veronica said. 'Joel's a photographer. He might be willing to take the publicity photos for NaughtyChix. It all depends on whether we eat him alive first.'

Veronica hoped that Imogene wouldn't mention Buzzsaw, or his ambition of turning to nude photography after a decade spent working as a fry cook, but Imogene's smile only brightened. Apparently, Buzzsaw was a thing – literally – of the past.

'Hey, I haven't committed to anything yet,' Joel said. 'Let's take this one step at a time. What are you trying to accomplish here?'

'We're trying to fulfil every man's fantasies,' Imogene said, with a dramatic sweep of her hand.

'No, we're not,' Veronica interjected. 'That's not the point of NaughtyChix at all. My escorts are the kind that won't necessarily appeal to your average rich guy in search of a pay-by-the-hour date. My clients will be paying to meet the kinds of girls who run outside of their usual social circles. Alternative girls. Girls who know all the scariest underground nightclubs in town. Girls with tattoos and labial piercings.'

'And these men can't just meet those girls at a club or a concert?' Joel asked. 'Why do they need to pay by the hour, anyway? Dates cost enough as it is.'

Veronica sighed and shook her head. 'I knew this was going to require some education. Look, Joel, you're a guy who's living in our world already. You have what it takes to get into the underground scene: a hot body, a cute face and a camera. My clients will be wealthy workaholics who don't have time to establish a relationship by prowling through the city all night and striking up meaningful conversations. Maybe they have no relationship. Maybe they have girlfriends, or wives. Either way, they want to date someone different for a night or a weekend, someone with an edge. That's where NaughtyChix comes in.'

'I think I get it,' Joel said.

Veronica watched him carefully as he surveyed Imogene's kinky striped stockings, her NIN T-shirt, her pink hair.

'Your clients are white-bread white-collar men who want to take a walk on the wild side.'

'Exactly. And, if you think Imogene's wild, get a look at what's walking through the door.'

What was walking through the door, emerging from her bedroom for the first time that day on her way to go out for an espresso before her evening began, was Odessa. Poured into her usual costume, the black crushed-velvet gown and pointed boots of a wannabe vampire, Odessa was a vision of gothic lust. A wave of long auburn hair dipped over her eye, à la Veronica Lake, and her lips were painted the rich red of venous blood, with talons on her fingertips to match. When he saw her, Joel did a double-take, jaw dropping as if he didn't know whether to genuflect or throw garlic.

'A lot of men are into the vampire thing these days,' Veronica said. 'In case you haven't noticed.'

'Who hasn't noticed? Not me.' Odessa gave Joel a regal smile. 'Hello. Who the hell are you?'

'He's the photographer who's going to take the shots for our scrapbook. Be nice,' Veronica warned.

'Scrapbook? What scrapbook? I thought you wanted publicity shots,' Joel said. His eyes darted from Veronica to Imogene to Odessa. He looked a bit like a trapped mouse in a circle of hungry housecats.

'What we want is a collection of photos to show our potential clients all the special features that each girl offers,' Veronica explained. 'But the album has to do more than that. The way I see it, each series of shots should promise not only a hot night, but an alternate world, a taste of a different lifestyle, something spicier and more exotic than your typical fundraising dinner or five-star restaurant has to offer. This ain't your grandma's scrapbook, sweetie. We're not talking about something with pink quilted covers and little white bows. We're selling fantasies, fresh from the oven.'

'Fantasies,' Joel repeated. A light illuminated his blue eyes, as if he were finally starting to get it. 'So you're selling these guys a slice of imaginary life. A few hours of escape, to pretend they're a rock star or a twenty-five-year-old punk or a movie mogul, instead of a software engineer or a corporate attorney.'

'You got it,' Veronica said.

'Don't tell me you've never fantasised about paying an incredibly sexy woman for a night of sheer adventure,' Odessa said, giving Joel a sceptical look out of the eye that wasn't veiled with sleek hair.

'Duh, Odessa, he's a photographer. He has adventures for a living. He probably fantasises about sitting in front of the TV drinking beer and making out with his junior-high girlfriend,' Veronica said.

'Well, not really,' Joel said, shuffling his feet. 'I've done a few dangerous things here and there, travelled to some cool and dangerous places. But my biggest adventure in life is trying to balance my chequebook.'

'Still, he looks like he'll do,' said Odessa, sweeping her hair haughtily off her face so she could look Joel straight in the eye. 'If any of your pictures make me look fat, I'll tear out your jugular vein.'

'Now do you see why I don't photograph women?' Joel said to Veronica.

But his fingers were unbuckling his camera case, and he was sizing up Odessa's glamorous figure with a worshipful eye. A guy would have to be dead, or close to it, not to want to see as much as possible of Odessa's ivory skin. This auburn-haired undead-wannabe was the jewel in the NaughtyChix crown, and she knew it.

'Why don't you take a few shots now?' Odessa suggested. 'Prove to me that you won't make me look like a porker.'

Joel opened his mouth to say something, but Odessa was already reaching around to unzip the body-moulding bodice of her velvet dress. Before you could say 'holy water', Odessa was standing in the middle of the room wearing nothing but a black lace camisole and panties, a garter belt and her lace-up witchy boots. In spite of herself, Veronica felt a lurch of envy for Odessa's sumptuous body. Veronica had the ghetto booty going on, but her breasts weren't anything like Odessa's flawless twin spheres. And the extra padding that Odessa referred to as 'fat' was spread beautifully across her tall frame. On Veronica, any additional pounds only made her look stubby.

'You're such a show-off, Odessa,' Imogene whined. 'Why do you get to have your picture taken first?'

'Imogene, don't be a brat,' Veronica snapped. 'The guy already doesn't want to be here.'

'Oh, yes, he does,' Odessa said, her red lips forming a smug cupid's bow. She pushed a pile of dirty man-clothes – cast-offs of one of Imogene's dates – off the sofa and stretched out with all the grace of a white leopard. Though Joel had complained to Veronica about his lack of knowledge of light and angle when shooting the female body, he seemed pretty confident as he snapped shot after shot of Odessa. She pouted, turned, lifted her breasts by clasping her hands behind her head, striking all the classic poses in the *Playboy* repertoire.

How tacky and predictable, Veronica thought scornfully, before reminding herself that, one of these days, Odessa was going to make her Veronica a very rich shoeshine girl. Veronica breathed out slowly. This was a professional photo shoot; Joel would be paid for his time.

And, since Odessa was monopolising the camera, she could pay the lion's share of Joel's fee, at least for today. As Veronica watched Joel quickly frame and capture his shots, skilfully adjusting the lens, she realised that he was either a true pro, or doing a damn good imitation. His work was going to be pricey. Veronica hoped the shots would be worth it.

'Hey, it's my turn now. Quit "hogging" the photographer, bitch,' Imogene moaned with a sly dig at her roommate's weight.

Odessa, basking in glamorous self-awareness, didn't even hear her.

Joel lowered the camera. 'I'm not here to photograph a cat fight. If and when I decide to do this job, it's going to be on my terms. Term number one is: no bitchiness.'

'What's Term number two?' Imogene piped up again.

'I haven't figured that out yet,' Joel said. 'I don't usually do glamour shots, so I'll be making up the rules as I go.' He looked at Veronica. 'OK. Now it's your turn.'

'My turn for what?'

'To have your picture taken. You *are* one of these Nasty Chicks, right?'

Joel's frank grin, his level blue gaze, made Veronica woozy. Competency in a man always turned her on (her orgasms with Devin notwithstanding), and watching Joel's nimble fingers work the mechanisms of his camera had already revved her engine.

'Not "nasty", "naughty". There's a fine distinction,' Odessa said archly. ' "Nasty" is a lot like "naughty", only "nasty" hasn't bathed in a week and has a mystery infection.'

Veronica was glad her roommate had made the correction, because the way Joel was looking at Veronica – with a gleam in his eyes that was something between a tease and a dare – she couldn't have come back with any of her usual biting retorts. With his all-American smile, broad shoulders and polite hesitation about taking dirty pictures of naked women, Joel came dangerously close to being the classic 'nice guy'. But there was nothing 'nice' about the way he was visibly tearing off Veronica's jeans in his mind. She could feel the lust crackling around him in an electric cloud when his eyes lingered on the soft indentation where her waist curved sharply inwards before swelling into a pair of full hips.

If Joel were a 'nice guy', he'd be the type to pull out his wallet to pay for your hamburger with one hand, while discreetly unsnapping your bra with the other. Before you knew it, you'd be stark naked, legs in the air, thighs interlocked with his in the back seat of the car he'd vacuumed just for your date. And you'd be moaning and bucking and breathing like a runaway train as he moved inside you, strong and sunburned and absolutely devoted to giving you as much pleasure as he could with his all-American cock . . .

'Some other time,' Veronica said, though what she really wanted to say was, *How about right now, alone, and could we both take our clothes off and forget about the camera?*

'You sure about that?' Joel asked.

'Yeah. Go ahead and get some shots of Imogene; she's practically wetting the floor to have her picture taken.'

'Sure. But I'm going to get you. Soon,' Joel said, with a wink that filled in all the blanks in that statement.

'Hey, what kind of film do you have in that thing?' Imogene asked. 'I want to make sure the pink in my hair shows up when the pictures are developed.'

Imogene had taken Odessa's place on the leather couch. With her skinny arms and legs, Imogene was trying to imitate her roommate's cheesy pinup poses, but it wasn't really working. She looked much more like a scarecrow than a sex siren.

'This camera's digital. I can always adjust the magenta on my computer, if the colour's not intense enough.' Joel squinted at Imogene, then added tactfully, 'You know, I don't think leather's your look. How's the light in your bathroom? I was thinking we could get some shots of you in the tub, maybe sitting in a bubble bath, with your hair in pigtails. You could be playing with a rubber ducky...'

Before Joel could finish the sentence, Imogene had leaped off the sofa and was racing towards the bathroom, already pulling her T-shirt over her head, her tiny breasts bouncing. Joel smiled and followed her at a respectful distance.

Nice guy. Definitely a nice guy, Veronica thought. But with plenty of evil intentions.

Chapter Ten

Scream Therapy

Joel felt like he was escaping the loft with his life as he rode down the rickety elevator, gradually releasing air from his lungs. He'd learned a lot of breathing techniques at the monastery; being celibate for so many years, those guys had to become masters at relaxation.

The monks had also taught him to accept random twists and turns in the flow of life, and there'd been a hell of a lot of detours in his evening. A few spontaneous shots of Odessa had turned into a full-blown photo session; then Imogene had insisted on having her share of attention with a long drawn-out series in the bathroom. Fortunately, the girls had a skylight in the bathroom, so he'd managed without too much artificial light. But Imogene had primped and preened and picked at the details of the setup as if she were on the cusp of being named America's Top Model, not a skinny kid with quirky features and a shock of pink hair.

Joel hoped for the best for Veronica's enterprise, not only because she was savvy and outspoken and deserved to make it, but because he'd found himself sinking into a deep lush dangerous attraction to her. Veronica was hardly the first woman who'd ever come on strong – many were even bolder, almost military in their advances – but she was the first who'd dragged him bodily across a floor.

There was a tough boyish bite to her talk, but he suspected that, underneath all the black clothes, metal studs and combat boots, there was a woman whose soul bruised easily. Any girl with a shell like that *had* to be hiding a sweet gooey centre. The contrast between what he saw and what he sensed in that sexy bit of shrapnel had him shaking his head in dazed wonder as he walked down the street.

The night crowds were out in full force now, the streets bleeding with red traffic lights and the multi-hued neon reflected in the surfaces of the cars. Realising that he had a snowball's chance in hell of hailing a cab in this mess, Joel resigned himself to a long walk back to his hotel. Even though the Sleep-A-Ways Inn was in the Tenderloin, where there seemed to be one dive bar per capita, his room was costing him over a hundred dollars a night. If he was going to spend any serious time in San Francisco, he was going to have to find a place to rent.

But rent, with the semi-permanence it implied, made him uneasy right now. What if he got a call to go overseas again, on some tasty travel assignment? What if one of his contacts in Chicago or New York called him out of nowhere? San Francisco might be one of the most fascinating cities in the world, but there was always something more exciting, more juicy, hovering in the future.

Cities were kind of like women that way, Joel thought wryly. But what if the endless quest for more juice, more excitement, only left him dried out and overcharged, in the end?

Joel's cell phone was playing Ozzy. He had to step into the outer foyer of a cheap residential hotel to hear the caller. The doorway stank of urine and the hotel's inner door was locked up like Fort Knox. God, Joel hoped he never ended up so broke that he had to live in a place like this.

'Joel? It's Lauryn.'

Her voice rang across the ether, crisp and self-assured, but with a husky note that conjured a world of sensual delights. Joel had a vision of their last afternoon together – Lauryn stretched out on the floor, a serene smile on her face, her tight muscles giving way under his hands as her satin-smooth skin absorbed the tea-tree oil.

'Hey! It's you!' He knew he sounded as silly as a boy scout, but he couldn't help it; he had that same gut response that he'd had earlier in the afternoon, when Chloe had called and he thought it was Lauryn.

Chloe. Veronica. Lauryn. After a long drought, Joel was being flooded. Under ordinary circumstances, he would have considered this wealth of women a blessing, a reward for all the hours of itching restless meditation he'd done in Tibet. But, for some reason, this threesome of ladies – who unfortunately would probably never form a threesome in the way Joel would like to imagine them – troubled him. From the moment he met Lauryn on the plane, he'd been awestruck. She had everything he'd always wanted, but never hoped to even reach for: classical beauty, a terrific mind, a sense of humour like a dry Stoli martini and a string of achievements under her belt that any professional would be proud of. Then Chloe had come along, sneaking in with her wide grey eyes and trembling lips for a surprise attack. And, finally, Veronica had hit him like a missile today – the Vee-bomb, with her knockout figure and combat boots.

If Chloe had surprised him, and Veronica had all but assaulted him, Lauryn ... Lauryn was sinking in.

'It's me. I confess.' Lauryn laughed. She had a laugh like Kathleen Turner's, a throaty throb that left Joel weak.

'So where are you? What are you doing tonight?'

'Well, it's sort of a surprise. I'm taking someone out, and he doesn't know it yet.'

'Oh. Who's the lucky guy?'

Great. Joel was going to end up being Lauryn's buddy, the boy-next-door she slept with once, dismissed as anything serious, then forever relied upon as a friend, as if the mind-blowing sex were nothing but an introductory handshake. From now on, they'd share companionable hugs instead of four-hour sex marathons. Joel knew the drill; he'd been through it more times than he could count.

'It's you, dork. Come on, you should have seen through that like a window.' That laugh again – more of a purr, really, so sexy that Joel found himself getting hard. 'Where are you? I'll come pick you up.'

Joel looked around. With Lauryn's offer ringing like a bell in his head, the city looked brand new, transformed. Where was he, anyway? He couldn't see any street signs; all he knew was that he felt like he was in some form of heaven.

'Um, I'm somewhere in North Beach. I think.'

'Can you give me a cross street? I'm driving – I got a rental car today.'

'Sorry, I can't see anything from where I am. Everything's kind of a blur.'

'Listen, you know where Vesuvio's is, right? If you can make it there, I'll pick you up in front in about ten minutes.'

'Vesuvio's. Yeah. I can get there.' Everyone in San Francisco knew where Jack Kerouac's former hangout was, even men with love-addled brains.

'Great. I'm on my way.'

Somehow, through a combination of memory, blind instinct and instructions from homeless guys who were willing to give detailed directions in exchange for a few quarters, Joel found his way to Vesuvio's. The old bar was packed, its stained-glass windows glowing darkly. A river of tourists and locals – men with sleek women, men with edgy women, men with devastatingly sexy women – flowed in and out. Joel, standing in front with his hands shoved in his pockets and whistling under his breath, didn't envy a single one of them. He was waiting for the most beautiful woman in the city; everyone else could get stuffed.

A red two-door economy car veered up to the sidewalk at an angle, barely missing being sandwiched between a bus and a taxi. The shadowy driver waved madly, and Joel, heart in his throat, bounded for the passenger door. He opened the door and dove inside, trying his best to fold his body into the seat. He was opening his mouth to say hello, when Lauryn grabbed him and silenced him with a deep tongue-twirling kiss.

She tasted good. She smelled good. And, God, she felt good. Joel gave in to his dark side and let his hands rove all over her, groping her waist, her back, her breasts like an out-of-control fifteen-year-old. He couldn't remember the last time he'd been so happy to encounter a woman's body, not only to feel her curves, but also to remember them.

In fact, Joel couldn't remember the last time he'd kissed a woman this way more than once.

They kissed for as long as they could, until the honks and shouts from the drivers behind them got too loud to ignore. Lauryn hadn't bothered to straighten her car, and the bumper was still sticking out in the street, blocking traffic.

'Wow, you drive like a California native.' he laughed, as Lauryn pulled back into traffic with one efficient twist of her wrist.

'I *am* a native, silly. I got my training wheels in San Diego.'

'Really? That's funny, I thought you grew up on the East Coast.'

Lauryn turned her head sharply to look at him. An odd light, almost like a trapped-animal panic, flickered in her eyes, then her face resumed its usual confident expression.

'Well, I am from back East, most recently. But I was

born in California. We spent a few years moving back and forth. I just happened to be here the year I learned to drive.'

'Oh. That makes sense.'

Joel really didn't care about Lauryn's driving history; he was too busy trying to strike a balance between fondling her into an acute state of arousal and not getting her so hot that her hands slipped off the wheel.

'No,' Lauryn said with a sigh. 'It really doesn't make sense.'

She chewed her lower lip, as if she wanted to say something, but couldn't form the words.

'Is everything OK?' Joel asked. It was tough, but he forced himself to stop groping Lauryn's leg while he waited for her response.

'Terrific.' Lauryn flashed her self-assured smile. 'It's just been a long day.'

'No kidding,' Joel said. Long and complicated. Any day that included come-ons from three women, no matter how hot they might be, was too complicated for his taste. 'So now that you've kidnapped me, are you going to drag me off to some secluded place and torture me?'

'Oh, yes.'

'How are you going to do it?'

Joel went back to kneading Lauryn's inner thigh. Her flesh was warm and resilient under his hand, exactly the way he remembered it. He felt tremors run through her body as he ventured into the warm darkness between her legs and stroked the crotch of her slacks. Even through the layers of cloth, the slacks and panties, he could feel the slick promise of her excitement.

'Slowly and pleasurably,' she said, her reply so faint he almost couldn't hear it.

Joel leaned over and kissed her neck, in the corner just behind her jawbone. 'I can't wait,' he said into her ear.

She shivered. A soft pleading whimper came from her mouth. He pressed the ball of his thumb into the tender hollow between her lower lips, and the whimper became a moan.

They had left the urban gridlock behind and, at this hour of the night, most of the commuting traffic had thinned out. Lauryn rolled down her window, and a cool breeze, smelling faintly of the Bay, blew through the car.

'Where do you plan to put my body?' Joel asked.

'Right on top of mine,' Lauryn whispered. 'Or maybe under mine, if you're a really, really good hostage.'

Joel rotated his thumb, and Lauryn's hips began to squirm in the seat.

'If you keep doing that, you're taking your life into your own hands,' she warned. 'I don't drive well when I'm coming. Damn it! I almost missed the turn-off.'

Joel left his hand in its warm moist nest, but he stopped tormenting Lauryn long enough for her to guide the car off the road and on to a broad clearing, where she switched off the engine and turned off the headlights.

'Wow,' he said.

'Spectacular, isn't it?'

In the bowl of darkness that lay ahead of them, the lights of San Francisco were scattered like carelessly tossed gold coins. Overhead, a haze of white stars spread across the night sky.

'So what do you think?' Lauryn asked. 'Have you ever seen the city from up here?'

'Where are we, exactly?'

'Mill Valley. Isn't it incredible? The city looks so calm from here. So peaceful.' Lauryn unbuckled her seatbelt and nestled her head on Joel's shoulder. He could feel her chest slowly rising and falling as she breathed.

'It's spectacular. Thanks for bringing me here.'

She looked up at him, eyes glinting in the darkness. 'I can't believe I've shown a world-weary photographer something new.'

'Hey. I'm not world weary,' Joel said. He smoothed her

hair, which the wind had sent tumbling around her face. 'The world has plenty of surprises left for me.'

Like falling in love with someone like you, he wanted to add, but he didn't want to spoil the moment by sounding corny.

'This view always surprises me, no matter how many times I come up here. So many sparkly lights – I hardly know where to look.'

Joel swallowed hard. Corniness be damned. With two fingers, he tipped Lauryn's chin upwards, then kissed her on the lips. No mashing this time, no duelling tongues, just a kiss, a simple expression of an emotion he was only beginning to understand.

'I know where to look,' he said. 'There's nothing more beautiful than what I'm looking at right now.'

'You're full of it,' she said, punching him lightly in the ribs.

'No, I'm not. I'm really not. You're beautiful, Lauryn. You're everything I think is beautiful about women – you're strong and soft at the same time; you're lovely with or without your clothes on; you make me laugh, you're smart...'

'Stop it!' She laughed. 'I can't take any more.'

'And then there are the things about you that make you totally unique. Like your eyes. That laugh, like the lower octaves of a piano in a smoky bar. Your independence. Your freedom. Even that Chicago-thug attitude you pulled off in the hotel.'

'That was totally fake. I was scared to death that guy was going to call the cops and have me arrested for solicitation.'

'It doesn't matter to me whether it was fake or not. We all have to fake our way through life sometimes. It's the only way to survive.'

For a moment, Joel thought he saw that panicky gleam in Lauryn's eyes again, but it might have been a trick of the light.

'Do you really believe that?' she asked. 'That lying is a survival mechanism?'

'Believe it? I've lived it. I wouldn't be here today if I hadn't bluffed my way through some very sticky situations. Someday I'll tell you about the time I pretended to be a German tourist so I wouldn't get my balls shot off in Eastern Europe.'

Lauryn gnawed at her lower lip, exactly the way she'd done earlier. Her eyes kept darting away from Joel's. He wanted to clasp her face with both hands so that she couldn't keep avoiding him; he wanted to kiss her so hard that she wouldn't be able to keep questioning him, or herself. But he held back.

'What if it's not a matter of life or death? What if it's just a matter of making yourself seem ... I don't know ... different? Or better?'

Joel shrugged. 'You've done your time at singles' bars, haven't you? Dated guys you met on the internet? Do you think anyone's fully open about who they are?'

'Well, in those cheesy contexts, you expect people to be fake so that they can get laid. But, in day-to-day life, don't you think people should be more honest? Would you start a relationship with a woman who hadn't been completely open with you about herself?'

Joel was starting to feel like a man-kebab, twisting on a skewer over a very hot flame. 'I really don't know. I've never been in that situation.'

'You've never had a serious relationship with a woman who didn't tell you the truth about herself, then.'

Joel groaned. If he didn't stop this runaway conversation, his exasperation was going to beat his libido to a pulp. He knew there was a reason he censored his corny thoughts around women. Corny declarations of admiration, desire or love were preludes to an inquisition. He should probably just come out and confess to Lauryn that he didn't have enough experience with 'serious' relationships to answer her question in any depth. Or that the one woman he'd loved enough to commit to had crushed his heart with the heel of her hiking boot when she told him, on a camping trip in the Sierras, that he was too 'superficial' for her, and that she was in love with the sports editor at the paper where they both worked.

But, hell, Joel didn't always want to tell the truth, either. The truth was ugly. The truth hurt. So he did what John Wayne, or Genghis Khan, or any other red-blooded male would have done in this situation; he went with his gut and kissed her.

This time Joel's mouth wasn't simple or sweet, but it was sincere. To his relief, Lauryn responded eagerly, her lips meeting his without any hesitation. The tension he'd felt in her muscles dissolved as he gripped her shoulders, her upper arms, trying to show her with his hands what he didn't seem to be able to express in words: that he wanted her, no matter what she'd done, or hadn't done, or hadn't told him.

They separated long enough for Lauryn to peel off her top and Joel to unbutton his shirt, both giggling at their own urgency, then they fell together again, skin against sweet skin. Lauryn's torso was sinuous, supple; she danced in his arms with a feline intensity as he feathered her throat and shoulders with kisses. He fumbled with the back of her bra for a few moments, before Lauryn unhooked it in the front.

Half-naked, she leaned against him. Her breasts pillowed against his chest, and the stiffness of her nipples inspired an equal hardness in his groin. Joel rolled one of the pink points between his thumb and forefinger, then pinched and squeezed, making her whimper. With the other hand, he unzipped her slacks, fingers diving deep into the lush slippery softness he'd been fondling earlier. He prodded through the folds until he found the pearl at their heart, then he rubbed the very tip of her clit, trying to control himself enough not to put too much pressure on that nerve-rich nub.

The friction made Lauryn go limp all over, except for her mouth, which kept seeking Joel's lips with a greed that lifted both his heart and his cock. He hadn't been kissed with such desire since high school; in fact, this whole scene revived all the raw messy fumbling passion of his teenage makeout sessions. The scent of Lauryn's shampoo and body spray was joined by a rich musky scent that was all her own. When her hips began to grind, pushing her pussy against his hand, he quickened the pace of his fingers. The gentle rubbing turned into a more insistent vibration.

'Now, now, now,' Lauryn half-whispered, half-moaned into Joel's ear. She bit his earlobe so ferociously when she came that he was afraid she'd torn it off with her teeth. Spreading her legs as wide as the cramped front seat would allow, she surged forwards on to his hand, and he let his fingers sink into her inner lips to feel the hungry clenching of her muscles, accompanied by a scream that seemed to let out not her body's pent-up tension, but some gnawing discontent in her spirit.

When her spasms ebbed to a mild throb, Joel expected her to collapse into his arms. But Lauryn wasn't done with him yet. She yanked off her slacks, ripping one of the seams, then wiggled out of her panties. Somehow she managed to execute this three-second strip tease while unzipping Joel's fly and pulling out its fully erect contents. He gasped at the sense of release, his cock freed from its bent position. Gazing into his eyes, her face glowing with her wicked agenda, Lauryn straddled Joel. She leaned down and pulled the lever that unlocked the back of the passenger seat, and suddenly Joel found himself flat on his back, staring up at a naked triumphant wench.

'Whoa! You really know how to take control of a situation, don't you?'

'I can be very aggressive about getting what I want. And you're it, buddy.'

Lauryn slid back and forth on top of him, the silken length of her belly brushing his stomach with each stroke. She moved like a swimmer, with a graceful deliberate concentration. Each time she lowered herself, Joel thought he'd die from the slow velvet caress. Her pussy felt like a second mouth, gulping him down into a secret throat. She was gorgeous, primal, riding him that way, her upper arms sinewy as she braced herself above his body. Her breasts were hard-tipped silhouettes in the flashes of light that came from cars passing on the road; her hair was a mad mop of curls. Each time she reached the base of his prick, she applied more of her weight, and each time she gave a satisfied grunt that made Joel feel like he was more her prey than her lover.

'You're killing me,' he groaned. 'You're eating me alive.'

'You got it,' Lauryn said through clenched teeth. She drove herself on to his cock, and this time it was almost painful, her weight nearly bruising his balls. That sudden jolt was all it took to bring Joel to his peak. He'd been wound up so tight for so long – waiting for Lauryn in North Beach, feeling her up on the drive up to the hills, trying to keep his lust in check until he could give her the orgasm she deserved – that the climax crashed through him like a river bursting a dam. He couldn't see; he couldn't breathe; he could only give in and be carried away with the flood.

Lauryn's hand, stroking his cheek, brought him back to consciousness.

'Whoa,' he gasped. 'What happened?'

'You just got laid by a starving woman,' Lauryn said,

her fingers riffling through his hair. She scratched his scalp with her nails, moving across his head in light circles that made him wish they were lying in bed, so he could fall asleep in her arms.

'Starving, yeah,' he mumbled. 'I should say so.'

'I warned you, didn't I?'

'Nothing could have prepared me for this, Lauryn. Trust me.'

'There's more where that came from,' she whispered. 'Much, much more. Do you think you can survive being with a woman who wants you so much?'

Joel smiled up at Lauryn.

She smiled back.

The valley between her breasts glistened with sweat, and her ribcage was still pumping from the exertion of her ride. Her smile had the satisfied curve of a well-fed animal.

'I don't know how I ever survived being without one,' Joel said.

Chloe sat across from her new therapist. She had been facing this plump grey-haired stranger for almost half an hour, focusing her hostility into a spear of silence. Chloe longed for Aidan's office, with its minimalist blond wood and straight-backed chairs. Drowning in a wide-bodied plush red couch, so soft that it barely held her upright, Chloe wondered if this piece of furniture was supposed to resemble a womb.

'So, Chloe, tell me what brought you here.'

'The train,' Chloe said. 'I always use public transportation.'

She crossed her arms over her chest and pressed her lips into a tight line. The therapist, a woman as cushiony as her couch only more garishly dressed, sounded friendly enough. Chloe liked the sound of her voice; it reminded her of hot chocolate laced with cinnamon. And the therapist had a gradual sunrise of a smile that started with a crinkling around her eyes before spreading to her lips and lifting her rosy cheeks skywards. A semicircle of framed diplomas graced the wall above her head like a halo, announcing that Margaret Wasserman had two bachelor's degrees, a Master's in sociology, several professional certifications and a PhD in psychology.

But she wasn't Aidan.

'Chloe,' said Dr Wasserman more insistently, 'tell me. What do you want to accomplish here? Or do you want to be here at all?'

'I don't want to be here at all, Dr Wasserman,' Chloe snapped.

'Call me Maggie. Please.'

'OK, Maggie, I'm here because Aidan dumped me.'

'He didn't dump you, Chloe. He referred you for professional reasons. But that doesn't mean you don't have a right to feel rejected. Why don't you tell me about that?'

'What's to tell? I feel awful. I feel guilty. I feel like I did something wrong. Or worse, like I'm just a bad person.'

'Describe a "bad person" for me.'

Chloe twisted a strand of her hair. 'A bad person is a woman who's sexually voracious. She eroticises every human contact.'

'How so?'

'Well, first she meets a guy in a sushi bar. He's a great guy: cute, funny, compassionate, creative. He listens to her. He'd be the perfect friend, right? But, instead of saying, "Hey, let's get together for coffee sometime", this bad woman takes him home and makes mad passionate love to him.'

'Did she force this man to have sex against his will?'

'Um, no. I don't think so. He seemed to be a willing participant.'

'Did she feel like this was something she really wanted to do, or did she feel that she was manipulated into it? Maybe even coerced?'

'Hell, no,' Chloe said bitterly, tugging her hair till it hurt. 'She loved every second of it. It was the best sex she'd had in months. Maybe years.'

Maggie's plump face did its sunrise routine as she leaned back in her plush red armchair, the couch's cosy mate. 'Then why do you feel bad about it now, Chloe?'

'Because it's not something I'd normally *do*,' Chloe wailed. 'I don't run around picking up guys like some sex maniac. I don't get into risky situations. I don't take risks, period.'

'So this was an isolated incident. A detour from your usual routine. Sex was something you wanted, something you found satisfying. Both you and your partner were happy with the result. I still don't see where the "bad" part comes in.'

'I don't either, really,' Chloe admitted. 'I mean, for once, I was honest and straightforward about what I wanted. I was hot for this guy, so I asked him to come home with me. He was a terrific lover. We're going to see each other again tonight. It's just that in the beginning it was so ... impulsive. I don't do "impulsive". I'm a chicken about everything.'

'Sounds to me like that may be changing. Do you think change is necessarily bad?'

Chloe scuffed the toe of her straw flipflop along Maggie's rug, leaving a rainbow pattern in the long purple fibres. 'Bad, no. Scary, yes.'

'Could it be that what you're feeling now is fear instead of guilt?'

Chloe sighed. 'I think it's a little of both.'

Maggie shifted her large body in the armchair. 'Our time's up for today. Do you want to meet again? Feel free to refuse. No hurt feelings.'

Chloe peered out from between the curtains of her

hair. Maggie looked back, benevolent as a Buddha – a Buddha with a preference for electric-blue muumuus.

'What do you know about aviophobia?' Chloe asked. 'Can you help me get over my fear of airplanes?'

'Let's work on your fears about relationships first.' Maggie smiled. 'I prefer to start on the ground and work up.'

As Chloe left Maggie's office, the city looked cleaner, brighter. The faces of the people she passed on the sidewalks seemed to be kissed with a mild radiance; even the grimy transient who asked her for change accepted her spare quarters with a serene grace. In 45 minutes of talking to Maggie – fifteen, if you subtracted Chloe's fifteen minutes of militant silence – Chloe had started to feel more hopeful.

She hadn't confessed her raging crush on Aidan, but some things were too humiliating to mention on a first meeting. Aidan had probably given Maggie the whole ugly backstory, anyway. Chloe could imagine them together, discussing Chloe's obsessive love in hushed regretful tones.

Thinking about Aidan gave her a sharp twinge in the pit of her stomach. His office was only a few blocks from Maggie's. Chloe thought about dropping in to see him on her way home. She'd be cool, detached, as she thanked him for the professional referral. She'd assure him that she was much happier with her new therapeutic relationship, watching his graceful eyebrows sink over his inky black eyes as his mouth tightened in pain. Then Aidan would rise from his desk, lunge forwards and grab Chloe with all the suppressed passion of the past few months. He would stare at her intently, drinking in every detail of her face before he kissed her with his smooth lips. And she would finally be able to taste his mouth, caress his hair, learn the planes and angles of his body with her fingers rather than yearning with her eyes as she whispered the lines of a tenth-century Japanese love poem into his ear...

'Stop having crazy sexual fantasies, you idiot!' Chloe screamed, clutching her head with both hands.

A middle-aged couple, tourists wearing matching T-shirts from a Midwestern university, wheeled around to gawk at her. She blushed. One more San Francisco psychotic, they were probably thinking. She gave the couple a feeble smile as they bustled across the intersection, dodging traffic against the light in their haste to escape.

What would Maggie say, Chloe wondered, if she could see the steamy images that thrived like jungle flowers in Chloe's fertile brain? She would give Chloe her Zen smile, then question her artfully about her relationship with Aidan. Had Aidan ever done anything to suggest that there might be erotic currents stirring underneath their conversations? Had Chloe ever told her former therapist that she lusted after him with a passion that felt so deep it was nearly immortal?

Chloe was tired of being questioned – by therapists, and by herself. She knew what she had to do. The best way to get over being dumped by one guy was to dive head first into an affair with another one. Maggie would never recommend this approach in a thousand years, but, if the truth be told, this technique had been helping women heal their broken hearts for centuries. It would work for Chloe now.

She stopped at an empty outdoor table outside a coffee shop and pulled her cell phone out of her backpack. Since she talked to Joel yesterday afternoon, Chloe had tried to call him several times. Joel was a great guy to talk to; he knew how to listen, or to do a damn good impression of listening. In bed, he was outrageously passionate. Out of bed, he was as easygoing and reassuring as your best friend's older brother.

No answer. Still. Didn't the guy *ever* answer his

phone? Chloe thought, snapping her cell shut with an irritated click before flinging it into her backpack. How could a freelance photographer make a living if he was constantly ignoring his calls?

Or maybe he was just ignoring Chloe, guiltily glancing to the left and to the right when he saw her number on the caller ID, as if Chloe herself were lurking behind his shoulder. Then he would shove the phone back in his pocket without a second thought.

Chloe ground her teeth. Maggie had said her shy mousy client was changing, and she'd been right. Chloe could feel herself transforming, anger and frustration sweeping through her bloodstream. She could almost see her skin sprouting fur, her straight white teeth elongating into fangs, her milky grey eyes turning into gleaming ruby orbs.

Tonight, Joel was going to meet a monster. A sultry, horny, yet oh-so-subtle sex siren who would make him forget that any other woman existed. For the first time in days, Chloe knew exactly what she needed to do to make sure that *her* hungers, for once, were satisfied.

Playing hooky had never felt so good.

Wearing shorts and a jogging bra, Lauryn lay on her back on one of the Landmark Hotel's stringy towels on a sunny slope of Golden Gate Park. Every now and then, she would turn her head to peer through her sunglasses at a couple in their twenties who were noisily making out only a few feet away from her. They'd arrived only a few minutes earlier, after Lauryn had already been here for an hour. She had to assume that they'd chosen this spot because they wanted an audience; still, she felt awkward when the dread-locked girl mounted her boyfriend and began to grind away in a full-blown pantomime of copulation, her dark nipples peeking through the sheer fabric of her hippie dress.

Who are you to judge? Lauryn scolded herself. You

were screwing *your* boyfriend in a car on a public hillside last night.

Lauryn sat up abruptly on her elbows, pink stars swimming in front of her eyes after so much time baking in the sun. Since when did she think of Joel as her 'boyfriend'? She'd known the guy for less than a week; they'd had sex only twice.

But the sex had been different from her usual out-of-town flings. Most of the time, Lauryn's casual hook-ups felt like a bike ride up Mount Tamalpais: challenging, exhilarating, leaving her exhausted and pleasantly sore, but in no way transformed. In fact, a ride up Mount Tam, with its breathtaking views of the Bay, was a much more life-altering experience than any of the naked sports that Lauryn usually engaged in. Most of her lovers never called Lauryn 'beautiful', unless they were groaning it into her breasts while pumping their way towards a sweaty climax.

Joel had told her she was beautiful while she still had her clothes on. When was the last time a man (a *sober* man, no less) had looked at her the way Joel had last night, with the awestruck joy of a man who's just scratched the winning numbers off a million-dollar-prize lotto ticket?

He'd almost blown Lauryn's walls down. Caught completely off guard, she'd almost told him everything. Her mouth had been ajar, the words rising in her throat – *I'm not who I said I was; I'm a frustrated nobody who's never been anywhere but Mexico* – when Joel filled her open lips with his tongue.

Lauryn rolled over on her stomach, smiling to herself. She turned her head away from the world's horniest couple, who were so stoned on lust and some other organic substance that they'd stripped off half their clothes and were now, for all practical purposes, screwing in public. Damn punks – they were distracting her from her own lewd thoughts.

The noon sun was almost cruel in the way it bore down on Lauryn's exposed skin, but she welcomed that sensual punishment. Remembering the way it felt to straddle Joel in the car last night, taking the reins and riding him mercilessly until he almost passed out with pleasure, Lauryn began to rock her hips from side to side. The grass had already been warmed by her body; it felt moist and loamy under her mound. If she squeezed her inner muscles tight, and intensified the pressure just a bit more, she could climax secretly, right here in full view of a dozen other sunbathers and Frisbee-tossing maniacs.

I can't get over what you did to me, Joel had said, giving her one last kiss, one last dazed longing look, when she dropped him off at his hotel last night.

Those words, and the way his voice caught in his throat when he huskily spoke them, had made Lauryn shiver. She had almost asked if she could go to his room with him, so they could start the whole glorious cycle of kissing and undressing and fucking each other all over again. But Lauryn wanted to keep the night exactly as it was, the erotic memory vibrating through her flesh, for as long as she could before they made love again.

An obnoxious electronic whirr ripped Lauryn out of her reverie. She must have been cat-napping, because for a second she flashed back to her junior year of high school, being woken by her alarm clock at three a.m. for her newspaper route. The memory made her cringe. She'd had to borrow a car from her mother's grill-cook 'fiancé' to drive around the neighbourhood delivering papers at the crack of dawn so she could pay for the debating team's trip to Washington, DC that year. Her mother's scumbag boyfriend had offered to pay for Lauryn's gas, as well as throwing in a six-pack and a joint, if she'd show him her titties in the back seat.

'God, I hate my past,' Lauryn muttered, yanking her cell phone out of her canvas tote bag. A glance at the digital display gave her a lurch of nausea. 'I hate my present, too,' she added to no one in particular.

'Hi, Stan!'

Lauryn made her greeting sound far brighter than she felt, both because she had skipped out on a client meeting that morning, and because he was, after all, still her boss. She didn't have to suck his dick, but she did have to kiss his ass.

'What the hell were you *thinking*?' Stan squealed. He didn't bother with any preamble, just launched directly into a semi-coherent tirade. 'The client! You – what? Getting off in the hallway?! Barry tells me you've turned into some kind of deviant! Walking out on the presentation. Don't even bother to show up today. Look, Lauryn, do you want this job, or do you want your butt kicked out on the street?'

Lauryn took a deep breath, looking up at the sky as she exhaled. A seagull was coasting on an air current, scanning the ground for tasty garbage. What she wouldn't give to be a bird right now.

'I wasn't feeling well today, Stan. I've been fighting off this cold, and it's turned into a sinus infection. You don't want me to make our clients ill, do you?'

'Listen, you're making *me* ill, baby!' Stan's voice had lowered in pitch; now he was growling like a mobster with laryngitis. 'And don't give me this sinus infection shit; if you had a sinus infection, you'd sound nasal. You don't sound nasal to me. You sound like you're kicking back in a freakin' spa.'

'Well, as a matter of fact,' Lauryn said, 'I'm *not* sick. I'm feeling pretty damn good, in fact. I'm lying out in the park, watching the birds and working on my tan.'

Stanley's response was a sputtering silence.

'You see,' Lauryn went on, since her boss was suffering from a rare moment of mutism, 'I really *don't* want my job. I don't want to drag all over the country from one boring contract to another, waiting for the day you'll finally send me to Europe or Asia. I don't want to watch my less-qualified colleagues get the assignments I deserve simply because they happen to have a matching prick-and-balls set. Most of all, I don't want to have sex with you, Stanley. Not in this lifetime, or any other.'

'You think I'd sleep with you, ya nasty bitch?' Stanley sneered. 'I only came on to you because you wanted it, blondie. You said no because you were holding out for a nice juicy contract.'

'I said no because I'm not interested in quid pro quo sex. Not with anyone. Especially a sweaty hippopotamus who reeks of aftershave and garlic.'

Lauryn inhaled again. Her heart pounded. She didn't believe what she was about to say, but something – maybe that soaring seagull, maybe her memories of Joel last night – told her that she didn't have a choice.

'I quit, Stanley. As of right now. Let Barry finish the work at B&M; he's been longing to have the opportunity to polish your knob.'

More sputtering, followed by a stream of guttural obscenities. 'You can't quit, because I called to fire you. You're going to regret this.'

Lauryn paused thoughtfully. 'You know, you're right. I already do regret it. I regret that I'm talking to you on a cell phone and that this conversation isn't being recorded. Listen to me, Stanley. If you refuse to accept my resignation and try to fire me, I'll go to Human Resources and report you for sexual harassment. Then I'll get an attorney. I know three other women, your former employees, who are chomping at the bit to sue you. I'm sure they'd be delighted to join me.'

Lauryn had improvised the part about the three other women, but her bluff worked. Stanley wasn't saying anything. He wasn't even sputtering. For a second, Lauryn worried that he'd died of shock before she could finish stating her terms.

'What do you want?' he finally said, sounding suddenly deflated.

'Well, I want a nice healthy severance package. Even though I'm resigning, I'm sure you can arrange something. I want to take all the paid time off that I've accrued since I started working for you but haven't been able to use. And I want you to write me a beautiful, brilliant, glowing grammatically correct letter of reference.'

Last but not least, I want you to go fuck yourself. Lauryn didn't bother to state this term out loud. Her now former boss was already at breaking point; she didn't want to push him into psychosis.

'Fine,' Stanley sighed. The word was a limp white flag. 'Whatever you want. You can make all the arrangements with my secretary. I don't want to hear your tight-assed Ivy-League voice ever again.'

'Oh, one more thing. I never went to Yale, sucker,' Lauryn said. She clicked the phone off before Stanley could respond, and threw the phone across the grass.

Then Lauryn leaned back on her elbows, threw her head back, closed her eyes, and let out a wild glorious scream.

Chapter Eleven

Can A Canine Be Converted?

The hardwood floor in Chloe's studio apartment was so clean you could eat off it, which was exactly what Chloe had in mind. She had laid out two tatami mats, facing each other, separated by a black lacquer bowl filled with water, in which three white chrysanthemums floated. Her apartment was filled with the delicate aromas of steaming white rice and grilled salmon. On each mat sat a single plate. She didn't have any authentic Japanese flatware, but at least she had two thriftstore plates whose colours didn't clash. She did have a genuine sake set, a flask and two tiny cups, and the liquor was ready to be warmed as soon as Joel showed up.

If he ever showed up. He was 45 minutes late; the steamed rice was turning into wallpaper paste and the salmon was going to be shoe leather before long. Chloe wondered if he remembered their dinner plans at all. She'd called his cell phone so many times that she knew the number by muscle memory, but he never answered. Just as she was getting ready to fling the phone against the wall and swig the sake cold, she heard masculine footsteps outside her door, followed by a knock. The knock sounded heavy, resigned. Chloe half expected to see a UPS deliveryman standing in her doorway instead of the man she'd had frenzied sex with only a few days ago.

But it was Joel himself, smiling politely and holding out a cellophane-wrapped bouquet of red flowers that looked like they'd fallen off the back of a truck.

'Carnations! How ... nice.'

'Aw, it's nothing. Just something I picked up on the way over.'

Chloe took the flowers, trying to swallow her disappointment. You didn't have to be versed in several centuries of love poetry to know that carnations were a bad sign. Men bought carnations for their great-aunts or their former piano teachers, not for women they wanted to seduce. She set the flowers down on the table next to the door, on top of her stack of junk mail, then turned back to Joel. He had purple shadows under his eyes, and his hair and clothing were rumpled. Dark-blond stubble covered his jaws, making him look like a tired bear.

Chloe brushed all that off. She didn't care if Joel had just rolled out of his own bed; all she cared about was getting him back into hers.

'So tell me,' she said, stepping back and shaking her loose hair over her shoulders. 'What do you think of my kimono?'

In the spirit of the romantic Japanese dinner she was about to serve, Chloe was wearing an ivory silk kimono painted with blood-red flowers. She'd tied the belt of the kimono loosely, letting it hang open strategically over her breasts. The creamy fabric set off her pale skin and glossy light-brown hair to perfection. She'd let her hair hang free, and had dolled up her face with hints of porcelain makeup and scarlet lipstick. She'd added a touch of eyeliner, slanting upwards at the outer edges of her grey eyes to make them look almond-shaped. Her feet were bare except for a silver toe-ring on her right foot. Altogether, Chloe was pleased with the effect: a hint of innocence, a whisper of mystery, the erotic allure of the Far East, all combined to turn a geeky grad student into a modern-day geisha.

Joel's brow furrowed as he checked out Chloe's costume. Looking more puzzled than aroused, he assessed her makeup, her half-exposed breasts and thighs. His gaze stopped at her feet and lingered there for an excessive amount of time before returning to her face.

'You look great,' he said. 'Love the toe-ring. Very sexy.'

Chloe fought back the urge to slap his stubbly cheek. She bent at the waist in a ceremonial bow, looking up to give Joel a sweetly submissive smile.

'Why don't you sit down?' she said, motioning to the place settings in the centre of the room. 'Dinner's ready.'

Dinner, in fact, would be dead on arrival, but, the way things were going, Joel was likely not to notice. He walked over to one of the tatami mats and sat down obediently, wincing as he crossed his long legs.

'Is something wrong?' Chloe asked, bustling over to the stove to warm the sake. 'You look like you're in pain.'

'I'm OK. Just strained a thigh muscle last night.'

'Working out?'

'Um, sort of.'

Chloe busied herself pouring the potent rice liquor. Silence loomed in the room, large and heavy; Chloe kept having to dart around the kitchen to avoid it.

Joel cleared his throat. 'Chloe?'

She turned around. Sitting on the mat, legs crossed at an angle that looked excruciatingly uncomfortable, Joel resembled an overgrown schoolboy on the brink of a confession. Chloe sighed as she crossed the room and arranged the sake decanter and cups between the two place settings.

'Don't say it,' she cringed. 'Let's just have a drink, OK? No making out. No sex. No expectations, whatsoever.'

She sat down across from Joel, smoothing her kimono over her lap and closing it up in front. No free peeks – the show was over. She filled Joel's cup with sake, then she filled her own, thought better of it and took a deep belt straight out of the flask. The warm booze soothed her chaotic thoughts. She closed her eyes and let the liquid pour down her throat. Somewhere between her first and second swigs, she felt the weight of Joel's hand come to rest on her knee.

'Chloe, I'm sorry. You look beautiful tonight. Absolutely stunning. But I'm just ... my mind's somewhere else.'

'With *someone* else, you mean. Is that it?'

Chloe fixed Joel with a ruthless searching stare. His blue eyes shifted back and forth.

'Fine,' she said. 'You don't have to explain. I'm used to this by now. I got rejected by my therapist this week, remember? You can't fall much lower than that.'

She glanced at Joel's cup. He hadn't touched his drink. Without asking whether he intended to take a sip or not, Chloe picked up his cup and polished it off in one swallow.

'Hey, slow down!' he protested. 'Where's dinner, anyway? I'm famished. Why don't you serve the food, and we'll talk?'

'The food turned to cardboard and glue thirty minutes ago, if you want to know the truth. And I don't care if you're hungry, or if you want to talk. You're not going to get dinner or conversation from me.'

'Chloe, please. I never wanted to hurt you. Hell, I never even expected us to sleep together. It was such a big surprise – a terrific surprise – but, to be blunt, I don't think it should happen again.'

Chloe stood up, hands on her hips. She felt more like Lady Macbeth than Madame Butterfly right now: crazy-angry and out for blood.

'Why NOT?' she asked in a growl that she barely recognised. 'Don't tell me, let me guess. I'm lousy in bed. Too scrawny? Bad breath? Tacky underwear?'

Joel waved his hand. 'No. No, nothing like that. It's nothing about you.'

'Then what is it? What's the problem? You didn't have any trouble following me home the other day, or hanging out for a four-hour fuckfest. We went through a pair of sheets and three condoms. Now, all of a sudden, you're Mr Prude.'

'I'm not being a prude; I'm trying to be fair.'

'To whom? To me? I don't think so. If you were fair, you wouldn't have come over in the first place. You would have answered my phone calls and told me all this before I spent half my day preparing dinner and getting all decked out like some geisha-geek!'

Joel covered his face with his hands, as if Chloe were pelting him with rocks rather than words. 'I admit it. I'm a dog.'

Chloe stood up as straight as an arrow in her silk kimono. 'No. You're nothing like a dog, Joel. Dogs are loyal and trustworthy. They come when they're told, and they lick you when you need to be licked.'

'Does that mean you want me to go?' Joel looked up at her with guilt in his eyes, a trace of desire, a trace of relief.

'Yeah,' Chloe said. 'You should go.'

He unfolded his legs and lumbered to his feet. Then he came over to Chloe and, without asking permission, hugged her. She went rigid at first, then relaxed in the snug circle of his arms, leaning her head against the wall of his chest.

'We should have just stayed friends,' she admitted. 'That day in the sushi bar, I never should have dragged you back home and made you have sex with me.'

Joel stroked the back of her head, smoothing her long hair from the crown of her skull all the way down her back. 'I don't seem to remember being "dragged" anywhere. I was more than willing to follow you home. You're such a desirable woman, Chloe.'

Then why don't you desire me? she longed to ask, but didn't. A woman, even a woman dressed as a geisha girl, had to draw the line somewhere, to save her self-esteem.

Joel gave her a brotherly pat on the back – the ultimate male brush-off. 'I'll call you later.'

'No, you won't.'

'I will,' he promised. 'I really will. We'll meet at the sushi bar again. Start from the beginning.'

Chloe pulled away from him, a weak smile quivering on her lips. 'Sure. Call me, if you want.'

After he was gone, Chloe cleaned up the plates, the cups, the mats. She tossed out the carnations Joel had brought her, and the stack of junk mail, then set the bowl of white chrysanthemums in their place on the table beside her door. Her studio apartment seemed cleaner, brighter, without a reluctant male hogging any of her space. That's what tonight's date had been for her, she realised, as she scraped the gluey rice and dried-out fish into the trash can: a space-filler. Something to occupy her mind and heart, something to distract her horny body from the man she really wanted.

With the clean-up done, Chloe stripped off her kimono and put on her favourite manga T-shirt and comfy pink sweat pants. She scrubbed the makeup off her face, then pulled back her hair in a scrunchy. Her mind too scattered to focus on the translation that was due for her next seminar, so she switched on her computer. It had been months since she checked the online dating sites where she was registered: Cupidity.com, eVerity, Booty Buddies. She'd signed up partly out of curiosity, partly out of loneliness. Every pot had a lid, her grandmother used to say, even the scratched dented pots with holes burned in the bottom.

Cupidity.com had sent her an email with five 'meticulously screened' male profiles, swearing up and down that one of these guys was her perfect match. Yeah, right, Chloe thought. It would take more than a database to find the man who could pierce her cautious callused heart with an arrow of love.

She scrolled through the profiles listlessly. They included a 29-year-old grad student in an English-lit programme, whose interests included reading (one would hope so) and hiking (hiking boots gave Chloe corns and blisters). A 33-year-old painter seeking a 'life partner' (to hold his ladder or to pose for him nude? The profile didn't specify what he painted). A 27-year-old entomologist, who worked for a fertiliser company, who went by the username Karaoke Cowboy (pass!); a forty-year-old bisexual vegan Pilates instructor (pass again!).

When she reached the last in the list of potential mates, Chloe's eyes popped. Her hand froze on her mouse. She read the profile twice, rubbed her eyes and read it again.

> Seeking Spirit: Thirty-two-year-old therapist, dedicated to fitness and self-understanding, seeks sensitive, compassionate, creative SWF. I'm hoping to build a base of mutual respect and shared passions – music, art, poetry, spirituality – before moving on to anything physical. Eventually I want to find a woman I can grow with spiritually and emotionally, as we discover the secrets of each other's minds and bodies. I'm a sensual, gifted lover as well as a caring friend.

'You hypocritical son-of-a-bitch,' Chloe hissed, staring at the thumbnail portrait of her former therapist.

Compassionate? Caring? Who, exactly, was Aidan describing? Maybe he had an identical twin who provided all the emotional support and deep mutual understanding that Aidan wasn't able to supply. Aidan's eyes, in his profile pic, were as hopelessly seductive as Chloe remembered: a pair of dark wells that called her to dive into them naked. His forefinger rested thoughtfully against his jaw, suggesting that, in addition to being a man of resounding emotional depth, he was also an intellectual. His smooth pale lips formed a smile that was both mysterious and provocative, and the cocky lift of his black eyebrows indicated that there was more on his mind than his spiritual growth.

'I'll fix you,' Chloe said out loud. She sat with her hands poised over the keyboard for a moment before selecting Aidan's profile and hammering out a reply.

Dear Seeking Spirit: I can't tell which captivates me more, your profound insights or your alluring eyes. You can't possibly know how long I've looked for a man who wants me for more than my physical beauty, someone who sees me first as soul, second as flesh. I am a novice on the path to spiritual enlightenment, seeking a warm and wise teacher as well as a hot and horny lover. Let's meet and explore our mutual interest in banging each other's brains out!

After a couple of minor edits – changing 'hot and horny' to 'passionate and eager' and 'banging each other's brains out' to 'pursuing a relationship based on spiritual as well as physical desires' – Chloe did some plastic surgery on her own profile. From 'shy sensitive student enamoured of poetry and Japanese culture', she became a 'sensuous creative muse seeking an artist of the soul'. Absolutely perfect, utter crap.

Then she returned to her reply to Aidan's profile and hit Send.

Congratulations! read the confirmation message from Cupidity.com. *Your arrow has been sent straight to Seeking Spirit's heart!*

'Yeah. this spirit's going to get something totally different from what he was seeking,' Chloe muttered. With a disgusted grunt, she shut down her computer, turned off the lights, flopped down on her futon, and gave herself a lovely orgasm with her fingers – the only bright spot in a long miserable day.

The Bay Area was overflowing with eager investors; Veronica just couldn't figure out how to snag a salmon out of the river of money. Convincing anyone with dough to consider NaughtyChix as a viable business enterprise demanded a queasy combination of brains, balls and guts. She felt a spark of hope when she had lunch with a rich mama's boy who had inherited an impressive chunk of Marin County real estate from his wealthy mother. Veronica was halfway to giving the kid a handjob under the table before she found out all his loot was tied up in a trust fund until he got married or turned forty.

Then there was the ex-stripper who was rolling in the profits of her dead husband's dog-food empire. Veronica thought she saw some real potential there, but the former exotic dancer turned out to be a currently embittered closet feminist with a secret agenda that included extortion and castration. Veronica didn't scare easily, but that woman had her running as fast as her Doc Martens could take her.

'Why can't anyone see how lucrative this business could be?' Veronica moaned to Devin.

They were curled up together on Devin's rumpled bed, watching Ren n' Stimpy reruns on his television and eating junk food. Veronica had just come back from a coffee date with a 25-year-old entrepreneur who'd made several million dollars by turning his private list of favourite websites into a massive pornographic search engine. She'd thought for sure he was the one: randy, loaded, too young to think too hard about what he was doing with his money. But, after his third attempt to slide his geeky hand down Veronica's tight black jeans, she'd stomped on his toe then stomped out of the coffee shop.

'What does "lucrative" mean?' Devin asked, through a mouthful of Twinkie.

Veronica held up her hand, rubbing her thumb and middle finger together.

'That you could make lots of money?' he asked.

'You got it.'

Veronica didn't have the energy to give her stoned boyfriend a vocabulary lesson, but she was happy to join him as he indulged his munchies. A bag of potato chips, a couple of packs of Twinkies and three giant Snickers bars lay on the mattress between them. Devin could eat that garbage all day and never gain a pound, while Veronica could feel her ass expanding as soon as she took her first bite of chocolate.

Who cared, anyway? NaughtyChix would never get off the ground at this rate, so it wasn't as if Veronica had to worry about maintaining a sexy image. Devin never seemed to care if her weight fluctuated; even now, through the haze drifting from the bong on the floor, he was reaching for her bottom.

'Don't touch my butt,' she snapped. 'Affectionate contact could encourage it to grow even more.'

'Aw, sweetheart, you're my sex goddess. I love your big beautiful butt,' Devin murmured, nuzzling Veronica's neck. The giant bag of potato chips crackled as he rolled over on it to enfold her in his arms.

'What are you doing?' she asked irritably.

'What does it feel like? I'm snuggling my girl.'

'Well, don't! I'm too pissed off. I just want to stuff my face and be depressed.'

'OK. But can I do this?' Devin pulled up Veronica's shirt and suckled her nipple through the lace cup of her bra.

Veronica moaned and rolled over on her side, giving Devin better access to her breasts. He unhooked her bra and began to massage the twin mounds, coaxing their peaks with his thumbs and forefingers until they were as hard as cherrystones before teasing them, one after another, with his tongue. Veronica lifted her leg and let Devin insert his knee between her thighs. He knew her body so well that he didn't have to undress her all the way to make her come. No words were required any more; she could signal to him with her body, and Devin would do whatever she wanted.

Was that a good thing, or a bad thing? Veronica couldn't decide. She loved the way Devin's knee was working her now, jiggling and twisting at the same time, the point of his kneecap driving insistently into her pussy. At its best, this mute exchange of pleasure was like jamming with musicians who were also your best friends; each riff segued naturally into the next, combining into a unique arrangement of notes that built to a dazzling crescendo.

At its worst – which still wasn't all that bad – sex with Devin was a reliable efficient way for Veronica to achieve sexual release with someone other than herself. And, though she didn't mind having an ever-ready source of sex, Veronica sometimes hated the fact she could predict every motion of Devin's hands and mouth and cock.

'You're so sexy, Vee,' he mumbled into her breasts. 'You're the most awesome woman I've ever known. I don't know what I ever did to deserve you.'

In spite of herself, Veronica's heart gave way, along with her pussy, which suddenly released an ecstatic burst of heat that spread through her body like a bonfire run amok. Devin knew the pattern of her orgasms so well that he timed the pace of his knee to keep those delicious sparks going after the leaping flames had died away.

Feeling too lazily satisfied to return the favour, Veronica petted Devin's long wavy hair. Devin didn't seem to mind. Even when he didn't come, Devin was always happy to float in the aftermath of Veronica's climax and, for that, she sometimes thought she could love him.

'Hey, Dev,' she asked. 'Does it ever bother you that I'm into all this escort stuff?'

'Why should it? I think it's hot.'

'You won't be jealous when I start to have clients? Rich guys hanging around all the time, waving money in my face?'

'Nope. Doesn't bother me.'

'Even if they wanted to pay *me* to be their party toy for a night?' Veronica persisted, getting annoyed with Devin's open-mindedness.

Devin pulled away, just far enough to look into Veronica's eyes. 'Yeah, *that* might bother me,' he admitted. 'But you're an independent girl. You do what you want. That's what turns me on about you. What am I going to do, chain you up naked to my bed?'

'Might be kind of fun.'

'Nah, trust me. You'd hate it. Listen, when the other guys start to get to me, all I can do is let go. If you want me, you'll stop by again, and we'll do what we always do – make incredible love. If you don't, well, you won't.'

'And how would that make you feel, if some other guy stole me away?'

Devin rolled over and threw his arm over his face. 'Why do we have to talk about things that haven't even happened?'

'Because I'm curious. How would you feel?' Veronica pressed. She could see the tension in Devin's face as his jaw worked back and forth, as if he were chewing a very tough piece of meat. She knew her last question had crossed the border from curiosity into cruelty, but she couldn't stop.

Devin sat up, swung his legs over the mattress and jumped out of bed, exhibiting more motivation than he had all morning.

'How do you think I'd feel?' he said, his voice cracking like a teenager's as it rose to a near-shout. 'I'd want to die. I *love* you, Veronica. Don't you get that? If I lost you, I'd feel like shit.'

Which was pretty much how Veronica felt as she watched Devin walk into the bathroom and slam the door. She waited until she heard the splash of his pee, then she readjusted her bra and T-shirt and quietly left his apartment.

So her slacker boyfriend loved her.

Devin loved Veronica.

What was she supposed to do about *that*?

Wearing nothing but a hotel towel around his waist, Joel wiped the steam off the bathroom mirror and scrutinised his reflection. His hair, damp from the shower, was combed back off his forehead, making him look five years older and ten times more sophisticated. As soon as his hair dried, and he started up with his compulsive raking habit, he'd lose that slick Baldwin-boy look and, two hours from now, he might as well have been through a wind tunnel.

Not too shabby, he thought, at least from the waist up. He hadn't been back in the States long enough to pack on those extra seven or eight pounds from too many fast-food meals eaten on the run, so his waist was relatively lean. Though he only worked out sporadically these days, his pecs and deltoids still had some of the bulk he'd built playing high-school football. Even white teeth, sincere (or sincere-looking) blue eyes, and a straight sunburned nose added up to a reflection straight out of *Maxim's* advertising demographic: Caucasian male, 30–55, middle income, single but dating, perpetually horny boy-next-door.

But did your average *Maxim* reader get as much action as Joel was getting lately? Hell, Joel himself didn't get as much action as he was getting lately. So much, in fact, that for once he was turning down sweetly seductive powerfully tempting offers of sex.

He felt a surge of guilt, remembering last night with Chloe. True to form, Joel hadn't had the heart to call her to cancel their dinner plans. Instead, he'd dragged his feet going over there, stopping at a bookstore to browse the photography magazines before wandering around to find a flower stand. It wasn't until he'd paid eight bucks for a tacky bunch of carnations – he knew women hated carnations, but roses were too meaningful, lilies too funereal, and daisies too allergenic to be right for the occasion – that he remembered the pink slingshot he'd bought for Chloe at Dawgs n' Kats.

By then he was already late, too late to walk all the way back to Fillmore. The tiny strip of satin and lace still lay in its gift box in his room at the Sleep-A-Ways. It seemed like a lifetime ago that Veronica had made him buy that sexy garment for Chloe. Time passed; what could he say?

Be honest with yourself, dude, Joel thought, sternly staring down his reflection. *It's not time that makes the difference between then and now; it's Lauryn.*

Lauryn, Lauryn, Lauryn. He wished he could stop thinking about her greedy body, her sexy laugh, her mismatched eyes, long enough to cleanse his regrets about Chloe from his thoughts. Maybe cleansing wasn't an option for a diehard dog like Joel.

Ouch. Joel cringed. Even coming from his own conscience, that was a bit too harsh.

Leaving the mirror, he went to the closet in his room and picked out the clothes he was going to wear to Veronica's that afternoon. Joel usually never put any thought into what he wore, just grabbed, sniffed and checked briefly for unacceptable stains and wrinkles before climbing into whatever was available. Today, he chose a pair of charcoal slacks, a grey tweed jacket, white shirt and tie: an ensemble he saved for meeting big guns. Since Joel rarely met the big guns at any of the newspapers or magazines he worked for, the clothes were fairly clean and wrinkle-free. He wanted to look like a pro when he met Veronica today, all business, no fun. No sense misleading another woman – or, worse, falling into random spontaneous sex with her – when he already had one casualty on his conscience.

Veronica was a spicy piece, no doubt about that. But she wasn't Lauryn.

Joel had to pause for a second to let the reality of this thought sink in. Settling on one woman out of three wasn't like him at all. Could a canine be converted to a life of monogamous love? Or was that some kind of heresy?

Armed with his digital camera and his laptop computer, Joel headed out to grab a double black coffee before facing his next battle of will.

Chapter Twelve

Delusions, Illusions, Collisions, Collusions

Veronica stood behind the half-open door of her loft inspecting Joel from head to toe. He shifted his weight from one wing-tipped loafer to the other, looking itchy in his tweed jacket and clutching the handle of his laptop case like a timid door-to-door salesman confronting a hostile housewife.

Finally, Veronica spoke. 'Who are you and what have you done with my photographer?' she asked. 'You look like Ward Cleaver in that get-up. What happened to the preppy guy with the dirty mind who was here yesterday?'

'He's sweating under this tweed jacket,' Joel said with a grin that told Veronica he was exactly the same naughty boy-next-door. 'I thought I'd wear something more professional today. Show some respect for an up-and-coming businesswoman.'

'She's not coming – yet.'

Odessa stepped up behind her roommate, stealing the spotlight, as usual, in a ruby-red gown with a floor-length skirt that clung to her hips and thighs like a second skin before flaring just below the knee and pooling at her feet. Cut to the navel, the décolletage left nothing to the imagination. From the look on Joel's face, wavering between agony and ecstasy, as he got an eyeful of Odessa's sumptuous curves, Veronica could tell that the dress had had its desired impact.

'OK, Joel,' Veronica said briskly, 'once you've picked your jaw up off the floor, we can take a look at those shots.'

'I can't wait to see them,' Odessa purred. 'Especially the ones of me.'

'Where are the rest of your roommates?' Joel asked, glancing around the loft as if it might be filled with hidden women.

'Working, playing, fucking. The usual,' Odessa said. She sauntered over to the kitchen, which Veronica had decorated lovingly in a vintage 50s theme, pulled up a chair and patted the vinyl seat. 'Step into our office. Show us why we should hire you.'

'Odessa,' Veronica said with deadly sweetness, 'let's not forget that Joel is a pro. We're amateurs. He's doing us a favour here. A paid favour, but still a favour.'

'And we have favours we can do for *him*, Veronica,' Odessa shot back, delivering an equal measure of saccharine.

'I didn't know this was going to be a bartering arrangement,' Joel said. He laughed uneasily, tugging at his tie. He cleared his throat a couple of times, then sat down at the table and unpacked his laptop. Veronica noted the splash of colour in his cheeks. Just like the first time they'd met, his awkwardness excited her, ignited something predatory in her libido.

'Well, it's not. But that doesn't mean we can't have a little fun along the way. I think Odessa and I can agree on that.'

Veronica came up behind Joel. Under the pretence of looking over his shoulder at the photos on the laptop monitor, she leaned against his chair so that her breasts were brushing his tweed-covered back. She exhaled softly against the nape of his neck, smiling to herself when her warm breath brought visible goosebumps to his skin.

'Hey, bitch! I wanna see too!'

Odessa bumped Veronica's hip with her own. This was going to be a lusty battle, Veronica thought: two big-assed alpha females duelling for the attentions of an unsuspecting male. They ought to have a film crew from *Animal Planet* to capture the event. Veronica planted her feet into the linoleum floor, standing her ground. Odessa didn't back off, but she stopped shoving. However, she did place a proprietary hand on Joel's shoulder, her crimson-tipped fingers arching like claws.

'Calm down, ladies. They're only pictures,' Joel said, though he didn't sound very calm himself, as he watched the slideshow of his own photos. Odessa, in all her half-nude glory, lay stretched along the couch like a concubine in a seraglio. The chocolate sheen of the leather cast rich dark-brown shadows on her ivory skin; Joel had tinted some of the photos sepia to heighten this effect, turning all the darker hues to copper and gold. There was Odessa looking seductively introspective, with her hair falling over one eye; Odessa toying with an exposed nipple as she peeled down the strap of her bra; Odessa with her head thrown back, eyes half-closed, a hand dipping between her thighs to explore herself below.

Joel loosened his tie and unbuttoned his collar, and was shifting around in his chair as if he were wearing a hair shirt.

'Why don't you take off that jacket?' Odessa suggested, scratching Joel's shoulder with her nails. 'It's already too warm in here.'

'Maybe it wouldn't be so warm if the kitchen weren't so *crowded*,' Veronica said, shooting her roommate a meaningful look.

'There's nothing wrong with a crowd, if everyone's getting along, ladies. Remember what I said last time? I don't do catfights.'

Joel slid his arms out of his jacket, took off his tie and unbuttoned his collar. A light sheen of sweat glistened on his forehead. Veronica was surprised that his glasses weren't steamed up at this point; the shots of Odessa were so sultry that they'd left Veronica feeling a bit moist and light-headed herself. Living with Odessa on a daily basis, dealing with her diva syndrome and her unquenchable thirst for attention, Veronica often lost sight of her roommate's hard-hitting beauty.

'Oh, we could get along just fine, if Vee would play nice.'

Odessa wrapped her arm around Veronica's waist, drawing Veronica into the warm plushy valley of her deeply curved torso. Veronica felt more than a hint in the pressure of Odessa's lush breast and firm hip against her own. Her roommate had something very naughty up her tight red sleeve and, the way Veronica's body was responding, she knew she was going to be pulled into Odessa's little drama, like it or not.

'You know, I've been thinking, Joel,' Odessa went on, 'that I'd like to show another side of myself in these photos.'

'Really? What do you mean?' Joel asked, rising to the bait.

'Well ... I don't know why I should limit my clientele to men. We're trying to offer a very open service here, right? To people of all different tastes and predilections? That would include women as well as men.'

Silence fell, vibrating with unspoken possibilities. Another trait that Veronica often forgot, in her daily wrangles with Odessa, was her roommate's ardent bisexuality. Odessa adored other women, and she had apparently decided that Joel needed a visual demonstration of her Sapphic gifts. Taking Veronica by the hand, Odessa led her back to the leather couch, the starting point of this whole adventure.

'What are you waiting for?' Odessa said to Joel, just before giving Veronica a push that sent her sprawling on the couch. 'Get over here and bring your camera.'

'Odessa, no! Are you kidding?' Veronica squealed. Veronica wasn't a squealer by nature, but with a stunning redhead bearing down on her, she felt very intimidated all of a sudden.

'Vee, think about it. This could be the best thing that ever happened to our business. Not only will I attract more clients if people know I like women; I'll attract more men. Think of the possibilities! Think of the *money.*'

Veronica was aware of Joel standing somewhere in the background like a dumbstruck lottery winner. He hadn't taken any shots of the two roommates yet, but he had his camera at the ready, his anticipation so strong that Veronica could feel it sizzling in the air.

'It's not the money I'm worried about.'

'Then what is it, Vee?' Odessa demanded.

'It's *you!* You're going to eat me alive!'

Lying on her back, about to be devoured by a giant, auburn haired vixen, Veronica felt like a hapless human in a lesbian version of a Godzilla movie.

'That's right, sweet thing. And you're going to love every second of it.'

Odessa's cushiony lips silenced Veronica's protests as she worked at Veronica's belt buckle with her nimble fingers. Veronica's experience with other girls was limited to a few makeout sessions in college, the details largely lost in a haze of Peach Schnapps and keg beer. Now Odessa was bringing those blurry memories back to vivid life, reminding Veronica how her pulse used to skyrocket when she touched another girl's breasts or kissed her lips, the softness familiar and exotic at the same time.

While she was kissing Veronica, Odessa manipulated her roommate's body so that Veronica was lying lengthwise along the couch. Then she unbuttoned Veronica's jeans, and tried to ease them down over her hips.

Veronica burst into crazed laughter. She couldn't help it. Odessa was tickling her, and she knew the redhead would never get her jeans worked down past her butt.

Odessa frowned. 'Stop giggling, Veronica. This is supposed to be a serious sex scene.'

'No, no. The giggling is great. You're both perfect,' Joel said, camera whirring away.

'I'm sorry, Odessa,' Veronica gasped. 'It's just that you're never going to separate me from my Levis that way. They might as well be glued to my hips and ass. Let me do it.'

Veronica sat up, kicked off her Doc Martens, pulled off her top and bra, and squirmed out of her pants. She left her red nylon thong in place so that Odessa could peel it off with her teeth, which she proceeded to do without any instruction, shaking her head and growling. This sent Veronica into another helpless giggle-fit, but she didn't try to hold back this time – she was having too much fun.

Her laughter died away, as did her self-consciousness about being photographed during her first sober lesbian experience, when Odessa got serious about exploring Veronica's pussy. She parted Veronica's thighs and arranged her splendid body between them, making appreciative murmuring noises as she opened Veronica's pink moist inner folds.

'My, my. What a pretty pussy you have,' Odessa said huskily.

Veronica looked down at her roommate. The desire that glowed in her sherry-brown eyes was so genuine, so arousing, that Veronica thought she could have come on the spot if she didn't know that Odessa had more surprises in store for her. Odessa's fingertips were circling the pale-pink outer edges of Veronica's nipples, turning the sensitive areolae into crinkly pink ridges surrounding the darker-pink stems. She kept up this torture until the pleasure got so excruciating that

Veronica almost begged her to stop, then she began to pinch and squeeze the buds themselves as her lovely auburn head sank into the softness between Veronica's thighs.

Veronica's last lucid thought, before she let herself get lost in the delectable waves that Odessa's tongue was sending through her body, was that these photos were going to be way too racy for her business. For internet porn, maybe, but not for a professional escort service, where any sexual encounters were supposed to be a matter of personal choice, rewarded only by 'gifts'.

Then Odessa began to lap at Veronica's clit, while caressing her torso from nipples to belly-button in alternating catlike strokes, and Veronica's brain stopped spinning. The room around her filled with an ecstatic pink haze as Odessa's tongue flickered faster, lashing at the swollen button between her wet folds. The redhead's long nails sank into Veronica's soft belly, kneading her flesh, digging deep as she felt Veronica's muscles tremble and grow taut.

Veronica's spine arched. She stopped breathing. Her whole body hummed, from head to toe, just before the first wave struck. Clenching, writhing, whimpering, she dissolved into a honey tide. The pleasure was so exquisite that it brought delicious tears to her eyes.

'Again!' she gasped. 'I want it again.'

'Not yet, you greedy girl,' Odessa's throaty voice scolded. 'It's my turn.'

The auburn-haired goddess sat astride Veronica's upper thigh and rode her, back and forth, her warm dampness coating Veronica's skin with each slippery glide, until she bucked to her own orgasm, breasts shivering, beautiful head thrown back.

'Lovely,' Odessa sighed, collapsing on to her roommate with a contented moan. Veronica could feel Odessa's heart hammering through the velvet depth of her breasts.

Veronica peeked over Odessa's round white shoulder. 'What happened to Joel?'

'Oh, he headed for the bathroom as soon as you came. What do you expect? There's only so much lesbian passion a guy can tolerate before he has to take care of business.'

'You know, I never used to think you and I got along,' Veronica murmured, curling a long strand of Odessa's hair around her finger.

'That's only because we always had our clothes on,' Odessa replied, nuzzling Veronica's neck.

After leaving Veronica's apartment, which he would forever remember as the Loft of Sapphic Love, Joel had some trouble readjusting to reality. It wasn't every day, or even every lifetime, that you saw one of your oldest fantasies fulfilled. How often did a guy get so aroused that he was beyond the point of being able to jerk off? When Joel had ducked into the bathroom, it was only to recover from the shock of the incredibly erotic scene he'd just witnessed. He leaned his forehead against the cool tile, then went over to the sink to splash his face with cold water; his pulse had finally slowed, and some of the moisture had returned to his mouth.

Now he was grateful, so very grateful, that he had Veronica to guide him through the streets of North Beach; stumbling down the street by himself, he could have been hit by a delivery truck or mugged by a teenage junkie, and would never know what happened.

Veronica herself didn't seem dazed at all. Bouncing along in her thug boots, she had all the springy energy of a puppy discovering a new neighbourhood. She kept pointing to everything – cars cruising down the street, concert posters on telephone poles, homeless men sleeping in doorways, empty syringes in the gutters – and nattering to Joel about how 'cool' and 'awesome', or 'sad' or 'tragic' it all was. All of her responses seemed to have been heightened, intensified.

No big surprise there, Joel thought, grinning to himself and shaking his head. After that earth-shaking orgasm Odessa had delivered, it was no wonder Veronica's vision of the world had shot to a whole new dimension.

'You're not going to believe the coffee at this place,' Veronica was saying, tugging at Joel's elbow. 'Or the pastries! Have you ever had kolache? It's like a Czech danish – heavenly. Oh, and listen, you won't believe how awesome this street is! Check it out. Doesn't it look just like Eastern Europe? Not that I'd know, I've never been there, but, of course, *you* have. What do you think?'

'Yes. Yes, it does.'

Veronica glanced up at him, brown eyes sparkling. 'I told you. Isn't this the coolest place in the world?'

Joel nodded and smiled. With Veronica leading him down the tree-lined block, Odessa's scent still lingering in her hair, he was willing to agree to anything, to accept any surprise that came along.

Except for one thing.

'Holy shit,' Joel whispered.

As soon as they rounded the corner, he spotted a slim blonde walking towards them, her wavy hair whipped into pretty chaos by a brisk breeze. She wore a knee-length sea-foam cotton skirt that revealed the outlines of her inner thighs in silhouette, and her breasts nudged each other gently under a lace camisole. A pair of huge tortoiseshell sunglasses hid half her face, but Joel knew in his gut who the woman was – that graceful stride, the sideways tilt of her chin, the curious smile could only belong to Lauryn.

But it wasn't the sight of Lauryn that shocked Joel the most. What hit him in the gut was his response to her, seeing her in this unplanned unexpected moment, as a woman who might have been a stranger. The moment he recognised her, the world suddenly separated itself into two kinds of women: women who were Lauryn, and women who were not. And for the first time in recent memory, or possibly *any* memory, Joel knew without a doubt which kind of woman he wanted.

The only thing spoiling this epiphany was the very sexy material reality of Veronica, standing next to Joel and clinging to his hand.

For a few seconds, Joel tried to convince himself that this blonde vision was too tall, or too short, or too something, to be the woman who'd given him the ride of his life on a hilltop overlooking San Francisco. Besides, today was a work day. Shouldn't Lauryn be at her job across the Bay, instead of cruising along a San Francisco street, wearing summer clothes and carrying a Nordstrom's shopping bag?

'Joel! Hey!' Lauryn lifted a slender arm, waving.

She was far enough away that Joel could have made a run for it, but Veronica still had an iron grip on his hand. Instead of fleeing, he stopped dead in his tracks, Veronica still forging ahead like a freight train after its caboose has plunged off a cliff. And Joel just stood there, watching Lauryn get closer and closer.

Closer and closer.

Behind those sunglasses, her eyes were invisible, so Joel couldn't read her response to Veronica. He could only stand there dumbly and wait for the inevitable collision.

'What a surprise to see you here. So what are you up to?' The blonde lifted her sunglasses, pushing them back to hold her curls in place, eliminating the last possibility that she was anyone but Lauryn.

'Not much. Just taking care of some business this morning.' Joel lifted his laptop in a half-hearted attempt to prove that he'd been doing anything like business that day.

'Hi. I'm Veronica.'

Veronica stepped between them, holding out her hand. Time stopped as Joel watched the two women, waiting to read his fate in their exchange.

'I'm Lauryn. Good to meet you.'

They shook hands, looking for all the world like two executives meeting at a corporate luncheon. Joel, still waiting for the catfight to erupt, hadn't stopped shaking.

'So how do you know Joel?' Veronica asked.

Lauryn laughed. 'Long story. It started on a plane, about a week ago. The plot's been thickening ever since.'

Thickening, not unlike Joel's tongue. The two women were both looking at him now, wearing the same expectant expression. He knew he was supposed to say something, preferably in English, but the only words that came to mind were the instructions on what to do in case of an airline disaster. He kept waiting for the oxygen mask to fall down over his face so he could breathe.

'Joel and I ran into each other in the neighbourhood a couple of days ago. He's shooting some pictures for my business.'

'Oh, really? What do you do?'

'That's a long story, too. But the short version is, I'm starting an escort service.'

'How fascinating! And profitable, I would think. Especially in a city like this.'

'Totally. I don't expect anything less than a fabulous success. Joel's doing the spreads for my portfolio, to advertise the girls who are going to work for me.'

'Hmm. Not your typical gig, is it, Joel?'

For the first time, Joel caught a flicker of suspicion in Lauryn's eyes. It was almost a relief to see that she was catching on; for a moment, Joel had felt that he was in the nightmare equivalent of a Tupperware party, where all of his lovers, past and present, would show up to chat about everything but him.

'Yeah, it's not his usual line of work,' Veronica continued, 'but he's already done some eye-popping stuff. You should see it. These pics are going to make me rich.'

'Always nice to meet an enterprising woman,' Lauryn said. She was addressing Veronica, but her eyes hadn't left Joel's face.

'I thought you'd be at work today,' Joel said lamely.

'Actually, I don't work for Kramer & Associates any more. I had to resign. Now I'm just another vagrant, hanging out in San Francisco,' Lauryn said. A light laugh punctuated her statement, but Joel wasn't fooled. He could see the puzzle pieces coming together in her brain as she sized up Veronica's knockout figure, her grip on Joel's hand.

'That sucks,' Veronica said. 'What are you gonna do next?'

'I have no idea. Just taking some time off, for now. I'd like to get on with some hot new startup company. Put my MBA to good use, for once. But, in the meantime, I'm just thinking about a few things, making a few changes in my plans.'

Joel wasn't sure, but he thought those last words probably included him. His heart felt like it was sitting directly on his diaphragm, heavy as a boulder. He tried to let go of Veronica's hand, but she only tightened her grasp and moved in closer. Any stranger passing by would assume that Joel and Veronica were either lovers, or Siamese twins. Joel had no doubt which conclusion Lauryn would draw.

Joel was getting some action from a punk girl from North Beach. What else was Lauryn supposed to think?

'Anyway, it was a pleasure to meet you, Victoria.'

'Veronica.'

'Right. And Joel, nice to see you again. I've got to go – I'm late for a massage.'

'Not such a bad thing, being late for a massage,' Veronica remarked, with a sly grin.

'No, it's not. Especially when it's given by a six-foot-three Norwegian stud,' Lauryn replied. She winked at Veronica, but didn't even glance at Joel as she strode away with her shopping bag.

Veronica watched Lauryn until she turned the corner. Then she let Joel have his hand back, almost throwing it at him in her indignation.

'What was that all about?' Veronica demanded, her brown eyes burning holes through Joel's skull. 'You're fucking her, aren't you?'

Joel hung his head, wondering how a day that had started so blissfully could go to hell in less than ten minutes. 'Veronica, listen. I'm a single guy. I see different women ... you didn't think that you and I had anything serious going on, did you?'

'Are you joking?' Veronica scoffed. 'I thought you were cute, that's the beginning and end of that whole story. I'm not pissed off on my behalf, Joel, I'm pissed off on *hers*. That's a woman who thinks you're exclusive with her. I can tell. Oh, she probably knows that you're a freewheeling dude who dogs around like any other guy, but, in her heart, she's got this fantasy that the two of you are going to live happily ever after.'

'How do you know all that?'

Veronica rolled her eyes. 'It's in her body language, idiot. And, believe it or not, it's in yours, too. You want her. You just don't know if you want to give up all the other women on the planet for her. Am I right? Or am I wrong?'

Joel nodded, mute. Women bonded at the strangest times, and often those times seemed to occur when Joel happened to be in the same place at the same moment with two women who had no idea they'd been sharing a lover. He never wanted to be in this position. He hated being fought over, like a mouse between two cats, but, more than that, he hated being *bonded* over.

'Give me her phone number,' Veronica demanded, holding out her hand.

'What?'

'Lauryn's phone number. Give it to me. *Now.*'

'Why?'

'Why do you think? Because I'm going to call her, and we're going to meet.'

'Where?'

'I have no clue. Judging by her outfit and the Nordstrom's bag, she probably won't want to hang out at Dykester's Leather Bar. I'm thinking more along the lines of a champagne brunch, but the champagne had better be free, 'cause I'm broke as a joke till I can get my business off the ground.'

'When?'

'No clue. That depends on when Miz Blondie can fit me in between massages and shopping. Just give me the number, Joel. I've got people to do, places to see.'

Joel pulled his cell phone out of his jacket pocket, along with a pen and a crumpled fast-food receipt. He flipped open the phone, found Lauryn's number, and copied it out for Veronica. Whatever the two women discussed, whatever verdict they reached, Joel deserved the sentence. Unlike Veronica, he hadn't been able to watch Lauryn walk away. That would have been too painful, would have felt too much like a loss.

'Don't be too hard on me, when you talk to her,' Joel said, trying very hard not to beg. 'If there's any possibility that I still have a chance, I need to hang on to it. I love her, Veronica. I'm just starting to see it. For the first time in years, I'm in love with one woman. I know it sounds insane, because I'm still attracted to other girls. That, um, thing with you and Odessa today – God, I've never seen anything so exciting in my life. I'll go to my grave remembering that. But I love Lauryn. I *love* her.'

Veronica gave him a quizzical stare. 'That's her problem, not mine. Who said we were going to talk about you, anyway? What, do you think you're the only topic of conversation in the world?'

Joel stared back. 'Then what are you going to talk about?'

'I want to find out if she might be interested in working with me. She's out of a job, looking for a hot new startup, has an MBA. I need someone who knows how to run a business. I figure I'll give her a call, find out if she's open-minded enough to take on Naughty-Chix. The worst she can say is no.'

'Yeah. The worst she can say is no,' Joel repeated. He felt very light all of a sudden, not quite dizzy, but almost weak with hope. Whatever Lauryn had read into this three-way collision today, there might still be a chance that he'd come out of it unscathed.

Coffee and kolache forgotten, Veronica pocketed the scrap of paper with Lauryn's phone number on it, then she kissed Joel on the cheek and slapped his butt – hard – at the same time.

'Ow! What was that for?' Joel asked.

'Well, the kiss was for taking some great pictures. The slap was for being a dog,' Veronica said. 'I need those shots in print, by the way, for the NaughtyChix scrapbook. I'll use the digital versions for our website. And we still need to do some spreads with the other girls. Give me a call later on. We'll talk.'

She gave Joel a final wave before skipping away, to the best of her ability, in her chunky, ass-kicking boots.

At eight on a weekday morning, the 24-hour diner was packed with a combination of cops having breakfast after a long night shift, yuppies slumming for a greasy-spoon breakfast and ravers who hadn't been to bed. Waitresses who appeared to be hungover were rushing around to serve pancakes and omelets to customers who were definitely hungover. Chloe surveyed the chaos with satisfaction. The venue was so *not* Aidan; if he actually showed up to meet the mystery woman who had contacted him through Cupidity.com, she would know beyond a doubt that he was desperate.

'There aren't any tables left. You can take a seat at the bar, if you can find one,' the hostess said to Chloe. She pointed to a row of tall stools. Most of the seats were already overflowing with the hefty bodies of truckers and postal workers.

'I'm looking for a man,' Chloe said. 'I just can't find him yet.'

'Aren't we all? Good luck with that.' The frazzled hostess elbowed Chloe aside to seat the next group of customers.

Chloe stood on tiptoe, scanning the restaurant for Aidan's black ponytail, his composed smile. At first she didn't see her former therapist. Then she did a double-take. The pale thin man with drooping shoulders and grey smudges under his eyes couldn't possibly be her poised serene exotically handsome Aidan. He sat alone at a table for two near the window, chin propped on his hand as he looked out of the window, searching the stream of pedestrians that passed by. Every now and then, his dark eyes would light up before returning to dull hooded introspection.

Suddenly he turned away from the window and stared straight at Chloe. She yelped and ducked behind the broad back of a man who was reading a *Chronicle* as he waited for a booth. Peeking around the edge of the man's newspaper, Chloe saw that Aidan was staring out of the window again.

The guy with the newspaper glanced back over his shoulder. 'Are you a private investigator or something?' he asked.

'No. I'm just waiting for my breakfast date,' Chloe said meekly. She hadn't been aware that she was clutching the stranger's beefy arm. 'Sorry. I'm a little on edge this morning. I thought I saw someone I knew.'

'I'm not used to being used as a human shield,' the

man grumbled. 'Maybe you ought to sit down. You look like you just saw a ghost.'

'I think maybe I did.'

Chloe didn't know what to do. She hadn't counted on Aidan showing up this morning, and she certainly hadn't expected him to look like a man who'd lost several days of sleep, his job, his house and his best friend. After her initial response to his profile, they'd exchanged a flurry of short emails, arranging a time and place to meet. Chloe had been careful to keep her messages as generic as possible, leaving no clues to her true identity. Her plan had been to spy on Aidan for a while, from a distance, before strolling over casually and acting as if they were meeting by accident. She would act surprised and appalled when he told her he'd been stood up, while secretly enjoying his status as the duped and rejected male.

Now that she saw him gazing forlornly out of the window, Chloe felt sick with guilt. She couldn't remember why she'd set this up in the first place. Part of her, the small vindictive part, had wanted to wound him. But, from the looks of him, pushing his silverware around the table in dejected patterns, someone had beaten her to it.

'Aidan!' she called, pushing through the crowd. 'Aidan! It's me!'

She waved like a maniac.

A smile spread across Aidan's face when he recognised Chloe, growing as he watched her hurry down the aisle. By the time she reached his table, his face was illuminated with something close to joy. He half-stood, banging into the table and sending his silverware clattering to the floor. Chloe crouched to pick it up, blood filling her head, staining her cheeks. She stood up and collided with Aidan, who had bent down at the same time. Their eyes met and, in an instant of mad confusion, Chloe thought she read desire in his face. Or maybe he was just hungry.

This little drama lasted only a matter of seconds, but to Chloe it felt like an eternity passed before she scuttled to the opposite side of the table and sat down.

'What are you doing here?' Aidan asked, scooting his chair back to the table. 'This is the last place I'd expect to see a vegetarian introvert.'

'Oh, they make a decent veggie omelet,' Chloe said. She tried to sound casual, as if she came here all the time, but it was hard to sound breezy when you were breathless. 'Have you ordered yet?'

'Just coffee. At least I think it's supposed to be coffee.' Aidan made a sour face at the barely touched cup in front of him.

'Do you want to go somewhere else?' *Like my apartment?* Chloe thought. She had lost all sense of where this scenario was going. All she knew was that seeing Aidan again had revived all her longing, her lust. Even in his haggard state, he was the most beautiful man she'd ever seen.

'Well . . . I'd love to. But I'm sort of meeting someone.'

'Really? Who?'

Aidan hunched his shoulders and gave her a feeble smile. 'Sounds silly, but I made a date to meet a woman I met online.'

'Wow. I've never done that. Dated anyone I met online, I mean,' Chloe lied. 'Does it ever work out?'

'I don't know. This is the first time I've tried it. I posted a profile on a singles' site a few months ago, got a few replies. I was never interested enough to follow up, and I let it go for a while. Then, the other day, I get this email, and there was something about it that spoke to me. I can't quite put my finger on it. She seemed like the sort of woman I'd like to talk to, if nothing else. And, to be honest, I needed to talk to someone – to anyone, about anything. I'm not very good at reaching out at times like this.'

'Strange, coming from a therapist.'

'It is strange, isn't it?' Aidan said wryly.

'What's going on?'

Aidan sighed. He drummed his fingers on the table. 'I'm having a hard time with a few things.'

'Like what?'

A waitress butted in to take their order. Chloe asked for an omelette and iced tea; Aidan pondered the menu while the waitress tapped her sneakered toe.

'Oatmeal,' he said at last.

The waitress rolled her eyes, as if she couldn't believe she'd waited forty seconds to hear the word 'oatmeal', then she huffed away.

'What are you having a hard time with?' Chloe asked, when the waitress was gone.

'It's hard to explain. I probably shouldn't try.'

The conversation had veered off track, and now Aidan didn't seem to want to steer it back on course. Without giving herself time to think about what she was doing, Chloe reached across the table and squeezed his hand. His skin was smooth, cool, the bones resilient under her fingers. She'd never touched his hands before, though in her sweltering fantasies those hands had touched her most intimate places, bringing her more pleasure by proxy than she'd experienced with most lovers in reality.

'Tell me. Please?' she asked. 'I'm not your client any more.'

'That's right. You're not, are you?'

'Yeah. You dumped me, remember?' Chloe let go of his hand.

'Chloe, I didn't dump you. That's the last thing I wanted to do.'

Chloe picked at her napkin, tearing it into tiny flakes. 'Then why did you do it? I mean, Maggie's great, but she's not you.'

'After a while, I realised that it was the only thing I *could* do. I couldn't see you professionally any more. It wasn't ethical. And now, I can't seem to get back to where I was before you left. I'm taking some time off. Planning a trip to Japan.'

'Japan? You're kidding! That's always been *my* dream!' Chloe cried, almost dizzy with envy and longing. 'If it weren't for the flying thing, I'd be in Tokyo right now. Or Kyoto. Or anywhere.'

'I know.' Aidan smiled. 'It's something I've wanted to do for a long time. Look into some family history, absorb some of the culture first-hand, dig into some of my spiritual roots. I'm leaving in a couple of weeks. Meanwhile, I'm hanging out here, trying to get my head together.'

'How's that been working out?'

'Not so well,' Aidan said. 'Not well at all.'

'Why not?'

Aidan hesitated. 'Do you want to know the truth?'

'Is it going to hurt?'

'I don't know, Chloe. It might.'

'OK. Go ahead and give it to me.' Pushing the shreds of napkin into a small mound, Chloe avoided Aidan's eyes. The space between herself and Aidan was electrified with unspoken thoughts.

'I've always prided myself on my professional standards. I've always thought of myself as a therapist who could be compassionate and emotionally detached at the same time,' Aidan continued. He spoke with painful hesitation, as if every word cost him a shred of his soul. 'Chloe, from the first time you came to my office, all that was gone. And I felt like shit, because I kept seeing you anyway. I kept thinking that my feelings would change, or go away. I hoped it was just loneliness, or good old lust, or something I could deal with in other ways. But it wasn't any of those things. It was you.'

Chloe's ears were ringing. She opened her mouth, but she couldn't speak through the wads of cotton that seemed to fill it. The waitress stepped in, dropping their food and the cheque in front of them without ceremony. Chloe took a sip of her iced tea, wetting her mouth's parched tissues.

'Why?' she was finally able to ask.

'Why what?'

'Why did you, um, want me? I was a mess. I still am.'

'Chloe, you're beautiful. You're sensitive, caring, romantic. The first time we met, you read me a poem that you'd translated. And there was something in your voice, in the way you read ... you'd spent so much time with every word; you turned each line into a world of its own. You had this quiet passion that I fell in love with.'

'Jeez. I wish I'd known,' Chloe squeaked.

'That's the problem. You *couldn't* know. I couldn't have told you. I should have referred you to someone else immediately, but I didn't. Like I said, I thought I could be a professional about it. But I'm human. I fucked up.'

So did I, Chloe almost said, thinking about how she'd deceived Seeking Spirit. But she didn't.

'You didn't fuck up, Aidan. I'm here, aren't I? I survived.'

'Yes.' Aidan nodded. 'You certainly did. Only to be more lovely and intriguing than ever.'

'Who, me? Intriguing? You must have me mixed up with another one of your female clients. Maybe that drama queen – Dawna.'

'No, Chloe. You're the one who's always fascinated me. Only you.'

He beamed, and suddenly the pale fatigued stranger that Chloe had seen when she first walked into the diner turned back into her handsome dark-eyed nobleman.

'You don't really want that nasty oatmeal, do you? They probably found a way to put animal fat in it.'

'Food is the last thing in the world I want right now,' Aidan said.

Chloe felt a pressure on her knee. It took her a moment

to realise that it was Aidan's hand, warm and insistent, requesting everything that he'd never been able to ask for. She looked up and saw him watching her.

'So where do you want to go, Chloe?'

'Everywhere,' she said.

Chapter Thirteen

Up in the Air

Massage was the answer to so many of her problems. As Lauryn lay on the table under Kurt's capable hands, feeling a delicious soreness spreading through her trapezoids as he worked out the knots between her shoulder blades, she wondered why she'd ever thought she needed any other balm for her frustrations. Here was a man – a Scandinavian god with chlorine-bleached hair and aquamarine eyes – who could soothe her tensions, while making her feel sexy, adored and utterly worthwhile. Without knowing anything about her, he had drawn her into a world of acceptance and trust; she could give herself up to him, mind and body, knowing that he would leave her deeply satisfied.

It didn't matter that she had to pay Kurt to reach this state of Zen-like calm. Everyone paid, in one way or another, for acceptance. Better to pay with cash than with a chunk of your integrity.

Exiting the day spa with a lighter wallet and a lighter heart, Lauryn congratulated herself. Her muscles were humming, her skin was glowing – all the physical benefits of sex, without having to fake anything. With Joel, she'd had to fake a past, a professional identity, even an orgasm, to get a massage that wasn't half as good as the one Kurt had just delivered.

After a lot of walking and a lot of soul-searching yesterday afternoon, followed by a solitary orgy of pinot grigiot and Ghirardelli bars in her hotel room, Lauryn had made up her mind. Drunk on wine and chocolate, she had decided that men were like helium balloons. Fun, colourful, you inevitably wanted to hold on to them. But, the second you relaxed your grip, they'd be sailing skywards, only to find their way in another woman's grasp.

Best to just willingly deliberately let them go.

Strolling through the Market District, Lauryn knew she was attracting a lot of glances from well-toned well-heeled men in executive suits. This city was full of men: grounded, sophisticated, charming men. Why should she settle for one shiftless sexy charming photographer, who had no money and no taste in clothes? Sure, Joel was well travelled, but he bounded around the world like an overgrown kid, chasing anything that snagged his curiosity, whether it be a city, a work of art, a football game or a woman. It was all the same to a guy like Joel; life was a giant playground, filled with all kinds of pretty playmates.

Here was another one of them right now: Veronica, striding up to Lauryn with a self-assured smile in front of Janine's, the restaurant where they'd arranged to meet for brunch.

'Lauryn! You look like you just got laid,' Veronica said.

'Even better. I got massaged.' Lauryn laughed.

Veronica, dressed in skintight black from head to toe, with her nose ring, jet-black hair and heavy war paint, was the polar opposite of Lauryn's polished beauty. When they walked into the cool sedate air of Janine's, a ripple of attention greeted them. Most of the clientele were stay-at-home divorcées fuelling up for a day of shopping, or realtors meeting with clients. Lauryn was a bit too young and hip to fit in; Veronica was way off the map.

'I picked this place because they serve free champagne with brunch on weekdays, and their lox omelette is out of this world,' Veronica said, 'not because of the décor.

Beige-on-putty isn't my thing. But I thought you'd feel comfortable here.'

'Thanks,' Lauryn said dubiously.

The hostess took one look at Veronica's nose ring and boots, and led the women to a table in the far corner of the dining room, behind a potted palm.

'She's trying to stuff me out of sight,' Veronica remarked, flipping her cloth napkin on to her lap. 'Doesn't want to put the other customers off their food.'

Lauryn couldn't say she blamed the hostess. Veronica's aura was potent. Blatantly sexual, aggressively attractive, she was drawing stares even in this leafy corner. No wonder Joel liked her – that curvy body and bold attitude did crazy things to the brain.

An impossibly handsome waiter with gilded hair appeared at their table with a basket of rolls and two glasses of champagne.

'We'll both have the lox omelette,' Veronica said. 'Trust me, Lauryn. You'll love it.'

'We don't serve a lox omelette,' the waiter said with a thin smile. 'We do, however, offer a delicious smoked salmon frittata, gracefully accented with goat cheese and dill.'

'Whatever. Fish and eggs. Bring it on.' Veronica's square white teeth were already tearing into a hunk of bread. 'So what did you think when I called you?' she asked.

Lauryn took a sip of champagne. It tasted cheap, sour, but she needed a buzz to get through this mystifying meeting.

'Well, at first, I thought you were going to warn me off Joel. And I was about to tell you that you could have him, when you told me that you wanted to talk business.'

'That's right. To get straight to the point, I want you to work for me.' Veronica settled her plump forearms on the table and looked Lauryn square in the eye. 'I need someone to help me get my business up and running. You need a job. I think we can help each other.'

'Really.'

'Absolutely. Look, I know this isn't the line of work you saw yourself getting into. I don't know what you were doing before, but I doubt it had anything to do with getting people laid.'

'Closer than you might think,' Lauryn admitted. 'What I did was get people laid off.'

'I'll be straight with you – NaughtyChix isn't about selling sex, but it is about selling the *possibility* of sex. No money gets exchanged for tail, but the girls will be able to accept gifts. There'll be limits on what they can do and where, but, outside of setting a few rules, I'm leaving them on their own. The only thing the clients will pay the business for is the girls' time. Time, and the chance to live out a fantasy. That's what I'm really selling. Not flesh, but a dream.'

'Or an illusion,' Lauryn said.

Lauryn looked around at the other tables, where middle-aged women in business suits and sun dresses were talking quietly about real estate or shopping. The scene felt surreal, as if she were watching the 'normal' world play out its dramas from behind a mirror. How many of those women, she wondered, were really discussing their most recent orgasm, or their husband's sexual dysfunction, or their pool cleaner's firm buns?

'Illusion, sure. Why not? My clients won't be the type of guys who live on the edge. They'll be workaholics with depression and anxiety disorder, guys who need to take a break from reality, not have it rubbed in their faces. Does that make sense?'

'It does, Veronica. Perfect sense.'

Veronica smiled. Her teeth were brilliantly white against her red lips, and her brown eyes sparkled. Pretty girl, Lauryn thought. A very pretty, slightly scary girl.

'You can call me Vee,' Veronica offered. 'All my friends

call me that. Since we're going to be working together, that includes you.'

'Wait a second.' Lauryn held up her hand. 'I haven't agreed to do anything yet. For all you know, I might be engaged to a rich old man who's going to make sure I never have to work again.'

'Nope. You were screwing Joel. Joel isn't going to make anyone rich,' Veronica said. 'Besides, you're independent. You like to take care of yourself. You're a woman who enjoys her sexuality, and who's proud to be a hot young thang. That's why you're perfect for NaughtyChix.'

Lauryn downed the rest of her drink in a single gulp. 'Do you have any idea how it would look on my resume to say that I'd been the business consultant for an escort service?'

'Hey, the sex industry is huge here in the Bay Area. This could be a big boost for your career.'

'That's assuming that I want a career in the sex industry.'

Veronica shrugged. 'Don't think of it as the sex industry, then. You can spin it any way you want to. Call yourself an "independent consultant for an entertainment firm", or something like that.'

'I don't even know if this is legal!'

'Oh, it's legal. The way I've planned it, everything's legal. And we're going to make tons of money. This is just another startup, like thousands of others in this part of the country, only we're not selling silicon chips or a search engine.'

'Didn't you ever think about doing something different? It's great that you want to be an entrepreneur, but what about something more...'

'Tasteful?' Veronica supplied. 'Legitimate?'

'Something less risky. Where you wouldn't be constantly flirting with the possibility of getting busted for solicitation. What about catering? There are all kinds of opportunities in the service industry.'

Veronica shook her head. 'Lauryn, this is what I want to do. This is me. You know what I'm currently doing for a living? I shine shoes. I'm down there on my knees, working over guys' feet, and I know they're turned on by having a chick like me slave away over them. I get ten-dollar, twenty-dollar tips, just for rubbing away at their scuffed-up shoes with a rag and some shoe polish. NaughtyChix is going to do the same thing, only we'll be rubbing the grime off our clients' imagination, making their fantasies all shiny again. That's who I am. A girl who loves to make fantasies come true.'

Lauryn studied Veronica. 'How do you do it?'

'Do what?'

'Go through life just being who you are.'

Veronica's forehead wrinkled. 'Who else would I be?'

Lauryn looked down at her lap, pretending to smooth her napkin. She thought for a moment, then arranged her face into a professional expression. 'Do you have a prospectus? A business plan? Anything to show potential investors why NaughtyChix has a chance of breaking even in a year?'

'Nope. That's why I need you. I don't have anything yet, just a loft full of gorgeous chicks, a bunch of photos, and a great idea. I'm giving you the opportunity to get in on something fresh and exciting, for a change. You *do* want a change, don't you?'

Veronica's brown eyes had a wolfish gleam, and Lauryn was starting to feel like a lamb; the wolf, in this case, was trying to convince the lamb that being eaten alive was a wonderful experience, if only you had enough gravy.

But, in spite of all her doubts, Lauryn was starting to feel something stirring. Curiosity, maybe. Or revulsion. Or possibly a longing to do something completely different, something no one would ever expect of her. She could imagine how her mother would react, or Stanley, when they found out she was taking on this project.

That tight-assed bitch, her ex-boss would sneer. *I always knew she was holding out on me*. And her mother, whom Lauryn hadn't seen in years, would say that her daughter had always been a dream-junkie at heart, never facing reality when there was a fancy story to hide behind.

'I'll think about it,' Lauryn said.

'Don't think. Do it,' Veronica urged, her breasts spilling across her empty plate as she leaned across the table.

'I'll *think* about it,' Lauryn repeated firmly. This lamb had already made up her mind to accept Veronica's offer, but the she-wolf didn't need to know that.

The waiter, bringing two salmon frittatas and two more flutes of champagne, was a welcome interruption. Lauryn didn't usually let aggro goth girls order her breakfast for her, but she had to admit Veronica had made an excellent choice. The baked eggs, delicately laced with the smoky flavour of salmon, were light as air.

'Food's here,' Veronica said, lustily rending the frittata's golden shell with her fork. 'No more business. Let's talk about sex. Is Joel a good lay?'

Lauryn's mouthful of egg almost went flying across the table; instead, she swallowed hard and gagged. Eyes watering, she buried her face in her napkin to give herself a few seconds to think.

'I thought you would know,' Lauryn said between coughs. 'Didn't you sleep with him?'

'Nah. I would, if you weren't in the picture. He's a babe, don't you think?'

'I guess.'

Lauryn's breakfast didn't look quite so appetising any more. The eggs sagged under the weight of the oily smoked fish. The champagne, in its pretentious flute, was tepid, only a few listless bubbles working their way to the surface.

'What do you mean, you guess? I wanted a piece of Joel the first time I saw him. I love that scruffy prepster look. He's smart, but he doesn't talk down. He's arty, but not pretentious. He's got great shoulders, a firm ass. And I love to watch his hands work a camera. Yum.'

'He's not bad,' Lauryn said. 'In bed, I mean. I've had better. I've had worse.'

'Oh, come on. I saw the way you two were glomming on each other yesterday. He would have had you up against the wall in a heartbeat, if I hadn't been around.'

'I doubt that.'

'Don't doubt it, baby. The guy's crazy about you. Just before we went out for coffee, he missed out on the chance of a lifetime – he could have dived into the middle of a live girl-girl sex show. My roommate and I were getting it on, shooting some pics for our portfolio, and it got really hot and heavy. I kept expecting it to turn into a threesome, but it never did. Joel just took the pictures that we wanted. I knew he wasn't gay, so I figured he either had a head injury that affected his sexual performance, or there was another woman in the picture. When I saw you, and I saw him *see* you, I knew he wasn't damaged in any way.'

The elegant dining room was whirling. Either Lauryn had too much champagne on an empty stomach, or too much information on a closed mind.

'Want to know my opinion?' Veronica asked.

Lauryn could barely hear her through the ringing in her head. She didn't bother to reply; Veronica's question was strictly rhetorical.

'Joel is in love with you, Lauryn. Not just "love", but *luhhv*. He's got it so bad he's thinking about giving up all the tail he could be chasing – or thinks he could be chasing – so he can be with you. He's still on the fence about the whole monogamy thing, but, no matter what, he loves you. I wouldn't even be telling you this, but I owe the guy a favour for those photos. I'm not going to be able to pay him half of what he's worth.'

Lauryn shoved her chair away from the table and stood up. She fumbled in her purse for her wallet, pulled out a few bills and tossed them down.

'Lauryn? Are you OK?' Veronica asked. 'You look like you're about to throw up. Listen, I know how you feel. My boyfriend Devin told me that he loved me the other day, and it scared me shitless. A million questions flew through my head. Does he mean it, or is he just trying to get me to front him his rent money? Do I love him back, or do I just want him as a fuck-buddy? We still haven't talked about it, but someday we're going to have to. I'm going to have to tell him how I feel, and I'm not sure if I'm ready for that. I don't know if I want a commitment, at least not from Devin. It's enough to make anybody sick.'

'I have to get out of here. I need air,' Lauryn gasped. 'It was great to meet you, Veronica. We'll talk.'

'It's Vee,' Veronica reminded her. 'Call me soon, or I'll be hunting you down.'

In Lauryn's spinning brain, Veronica's words fit perfectly; as she hurried out of the restaurant, she had the distinct feeling that she was being chased.

As soon as she stepped outside and drew a few breaths of air into her lungs, the merry-go-round in Lauryn's head began to slow down. So Joel loved her. Big rumpled, disorganised, never-settle-down Joel. He had a few things going for him: the grin, the faded denim eyes, the addiction to adventure, intense kisses, gorgeous cock. But, outside of Lauryn's fantasies about the two of them travelling the world, was there anything solid about either of them?

Mind-blowing sex, travel, laughter and conversations under the stars broken by lingering kisses were great when you were in your twenties. But, after you hit thirty, all that stuff wouldn't cut it. What Lauryn needed, what she'd longed for since she was a little girl watching soap operas alone in her mother's apartment after school, was to be grounded. With Joel, her life would always, perpetually, be up in the air.

'Taxi!' Lauryn flagged a passing cab.

The battered yellow vehicle stopped, and she climbed in.

'Hey. Must be kismet, seeing such a beautiful blonde twice in a lifetime.'

The driver was the same talkative guy with the bulldog jowls who had taken her from Fisherman's Wharf to Oakland the day Lauryn arrived in San Francisco. She felt a pang for that lost afternoon: Joel; the light flirtation; the casual drinks; the long tight hug that held all the potential for passion with none of the complications.

'Where are we going today?' the driver asked, spinning the steering wheel to make the death-lurch into traffic. 'What fabulous adventures lie in store for our glamour girl?'

Lauryn grimaced at her reflection in the rearview mirror. 'Sorry. Nothing exciting. Just the Landmark Hotel.' She hesitated. 'And could you wait outside for about fifteen minutes, then drive me to the airport?'

'Whatever you want, kid. Where you heading?'

'Chicago.'

'Ah, so you lied,' the driver said, his baggy cheeks splitting into a smile. 'Chi-town. There's an adventure for you.'

Lauryn watched a young couple at the traffic light pause for a long lip-lock, as if the city around them had been built for no other purpose than to give them a romantic setting for a public french kiss.

'No adventure,' she said with a sigh. 'Just my life.'

Joel stood in line at McDonald's, waiting for his opportunity to order yet another Quarter Pounder combo. He was getting back into that lazy groove with his fast-food meals, late nights, long naps in the afternoon. One of these days, he'd have to think about working again. Gratis girl-girl photo shoots didn't count; he needed to be back on the streets again, capturing flashes of the world's swift crazy dance.

The line was taking forever. A couple of tourists – Dutch or German, Joel couldn't tell – had to know the exact metric weight of a Big Mac before they would make up their minds. A guy wearing a dusty army jacket and fatigue pants wanted to argue his way into the high-security locked restroom without buying any food. Joel was about to give up in despair and walk out, when his cell phone played a few bars of Iron Maiden.

No female ringtones this time, thank God. A work call, at last.

'Hey! Jumpin' Joel Taylor! It's me, bud!'

'Me who?' Joel asked cautiously. The caller's speech was slurred. In the background, Joel heard the monotonous chime of electronic bells.

'Me *Miles*. Who did you think? Glad I caught you. I need a favour, like, yesterday.'

Joel raked his hair with his fingers. A chat with Miles Meeker – talented travel photographer, miserable excuse for a human being – always triggered his nervous habits.

'What favour? And where are you, anyway?' Joel asked. 'Sounds like you're in a casino.'

'Dude, you are so sharp. *So* sharp. I'm in Tahoe. Just got married.'

Joel held the phone away from his face and stared at it in horror. Miles Meeker, pussyhound extraordinaire, was married? The poor woman, whoever she was, must have been drugged, gagged and bound.

'Joel? You there?' Miles's voice buzzed like mosquito.

'Yeah. I'm here. Wow, Miles, who's your victim? Did you kidnap a stripper?'

'Nah. Believe it or not, it's Shelley. Remember, that

cute little redhead who worked as a stringer for the *Sun-Times*? She's got her own byline now. The girl's gifted, in more ways than one,' Miles said with an audible leer.

'You married Shelley? Miles! How could you do that to her? Does Amnesty International know about this?'

'Joel, listen. I'm in love. Seriously, I converted. I'm not a hound dog any more. I'm coming in for a landing. Yeah, the whole wedding thing was spur-of-the-moment, but I've been dating Shelley exclusively for thirteen months. Thirteen months with one pussy! Can you believe it?'

'No. No, I don't believe it.'

'But speaking of pussy, I need you to do something for me. It's sweet, Joel. A job down in Florida, for *Skytripper*, one of those airline mags. It'll be cake. Beaches, bars, nightclubs, a few foodie shots to catch the local cuisine. And babes. Think of all those tight tan hotties, all smelling like coconut oil and sipping daiquiris with their pretty pink lips...'

'Yeah. I can see it. Why can't you do it? You need a honeymoon, right?'

'Are you feeling OK, Joel? I'm not talking about shooting a bingo tournament in Fargo in January. I'm talking about Florida. Nothing but sunshine, exotic drinks and exotic sex, in whatever order you prefer.'

'I know what you're talking about. Been there, done that, still avoiding calls from a girl named Barbie in the Keys. That's not my thing, Miles. It never was.'

'Oh, come on.' A whine was creeping into Miles's voice. 'It's all set up. I'm supposed to check in tomorrow at the Seabreeze Motel, start shooting by nine. And I can't do it, man. I'm in love, I just got married, and I'm on a roll at the Silver Nugget. Have a little pity on your old buddy here.'

'I've got someone, too,' Joel found himself saying. 'I think I'm in love with her.'

As soon as the words came out of his mouth, he looked around in a panic.

'But you're not tying the knot or anything, right? The best thing about girlfriends is you can always take a break. Or, better yet, take the lucky lady to Florida with you. Knock her socks off. Nookie on the beach has got to be better than nookie in Chicago, or wherever you are right now.'

'San Francisco. I can't be in Florida by tomorrow morning. I've got too many loose ends to tie up here.'

'Sure, you can! You've done it before. Remember your old motto? Round the world in eighty minutes; you used to live by that, buddy. Come on. You sound like my dad. At this rate, you'll be dead of a heart attack before you hit forty.'

'I'll think about it.'

'Well, you better think fast. I've got two other guys I can call. Either one of them would be on a plane by now. I'm only standing here wrangling with you because you're the best. Come on, Joel. This is eye candy. Easy money.'

'I said, I'll think about it.'

But even as he repeated those words, Joel was heading out of McDonald's, pushing through the double glass doors. By the time he nabbed a taxi, the golden arches – and the Golden Gate – were already forgotten.

Cupidity.com:
Tell Us Your Love Story!

So you've had a chance to try Cupidity – here's your chance to share your experiences with all the other curious singles. Date from hell? Match made in heaven? Lust at first sight? From ambulance sirens to wedding bells, we want to hear your love stories! Confessions, suggestions, admissions of guilt: spill 'em here!

Lauryn: Love stories? I'm still waiting for 'once upon a time'. I was woefully unimpressed with the men you matched me up with. I specified an age range of 30–45, and said (to quote my profile) that I was 'interested in meeting stable professionals with a taste for travel and fine dining, a passion for art and literature, and the occasional naked outdoor adventure'. You set me up with a 49-year-old freelance copywriter/poet who works from his studio apartment and doesn't have a car. We exchanged two or three emails before he admitted that he was agoraphobic and hadn't left his studio since the building caught fire back in January. The only positive thing I can say about Cupidity.com is that membership is free for women. I still think I should be reimbursed for the time I had to spend comforting the poor guy on the phone after I told him I didn't think we were compatible.

Veronica: OK, here's a suggestion for you: try recruiting

more human males. I'm a woman, not a weasel. Cupidity sucks.

Chloe: I have a confession. I met the love of my life on Cupidity.com, but I don't know if it counts. I'd been in love with him for months, and he'd already broken off our relationship. When you sent me his profile, I couldn't resist setting him up. I pretended to be a much more exotic woman than I really am, and lured him to a cheap diner and watched him drink vile coffee. It's very cathartic to be able to confess this here, but I'm never going to tell him. No way. It was evil. Kinda fun, but evil.

Chapter Fourteen

Three Women, Three Orgasms Redux

'Cherry blossoms. Shinto shrines. Love hotels. Cherry-blossoms-Shinto-shrines-love-hotels,' Chloe muttered.

'Good girl. Keep up the visualisation. Picture what you want.'

Aidan's breath tickled Chloe's ear. Under the thin airline blanket that covered her lap, his hand slipped under her skirt and swept up the groove between her clenched thighs.

'Open up for me,' he whispered.

'I can't,' Chloe hissed back. 'My knees are stuck together.'

Her muscles were taut, holding her legs together like the jaws of a trap. If she closed her eyes and breathed, inhaling Aidan's sandalwood scent, she could almost pretend that she wasn't on a plane. Then the flight attendant broke into her reverie with the words, 'In the event of a water landing.'

Chloe's eyelids flew open. 'Water landing? What water? Where?'

'Calm down, Chloe. We're going to be flying over the Pacific Ocean, and we're going to land safely in Tokyo. We went over this last night, remember?'

Chloe couldn't remember anything from last night, except for Aidan lying on top of her in the mellow light of the paper lantern that hung over her futon, his hips rotating in small precise circles that slowly, inevitably, drove her mad. She remembered the way his hair, freed from its ponytail, made her shiver as his mouth moved over her breasts, down her belly, up the inner curves of her thighs and into the folds between, until his tongue landed on her clit, probing with the delicacy of a hummingbird until Chloe shattered into a million ecstatic pieces.

'I think I remember something about an ocean,' she said now, struggling to breathe through the fog of panic massing in her lungs. 'I just didn't know we were going to land in one.'

'We're not. Trust me. You're safer flying on this jet than you are crossing a street in San Francisco. Now, I want you to breathe. Breathe out the fear. Concentrate on what I'm doing to you. How does this make you feel?'

Somehow Aidan had managed to pry Chloe's thighs apart. Deep inside, her body was opening up for Aidan, pussy blossoming under his touch. The flight attendant had finished going through her instructions about how to prepare for a catastrophic fiery death, and the jet was backing away from the gate. The little pill that Chloe had swallowed was starting to take effect, and the fog of terror was dissipating. Chloe leaned back against the headrest.

'Tell me where you are.' Aidan's forefinger found the twin pillows of her outer lips, his fingertip running back and forth between them.

'In a love hotel in Tokyo,' she whispered. 'I'm in a tiny sex box, waiting for you.'

'What are you doing?'

'Lying on the bed naked. Watching Japanese porn. Playing with a vibrator. Warming myself up for you. It's not midnight under a cherry tree, but I'm in Japan, with my handsome nobleman.'

'Who wants you and adores you,' Aidan added.

'Even if I'm a neurotic mess?'

'Especially because you're a neurotic mess.'

His tongue flicked the sensitive whorls of her ear in a simulation of what he'd done to her clit last night. His fingers were probing her lower lips more deeply, reviving a mild soreness that reminded her of how many hours she'd spent lost in urgent fucking over the past week. And all those hours had led up to this moment – Chloe still couldn't get over it. She was scared to open her eyes, not because she was on a plane, but because she was afraid she'd wake up from this dream to find herself sitting in Maggie's red Jungian armchair, whining to her therapist about how much her life sucked.

But she wasn't in her therapist's office. The jet taxied down the runway, engine purring into a roar as it picked up speed. She was going to Japan. With Aidan, whose lips were grazing her neck as he sank his fingers into her wetness, massaging her with his knuckles as he worked his way into the velvet tunnel.

'The flight attendant's going to catch us,' Chloe moaned. Her protest wasn't very effective; Aidan only speeded up his hand's in-and-out dance.

'So what? We're wearing our seatbelts. Let go, Chloe. You'll be flying soon.'

'Humans can't fly . . .'

'Oh, yes, they can.' Aidan's thumb found her clit and rolled the pink bead as his fingers continued to glide in and out of her pussy. It felt so deliciously nasty, being so close to an orgasm in a plane crowded with businessmen and tourists and students and families, all of them oblivious to what was going on between Chloe's legs.

The jet, against all her expectations, was rising off the ground. Chloe bit back a whimper. Her heart wasn't doing what it usually did; the muscle had stopped its pumping, waiting to see what would happen next. What happened was an explosion – not the engines, but Chloe's body sweetly exploding as the plane lifted into the air, hovered and soared.

* * *

'Whoa! There's some bitchin' glare out here.'

Devin lifted his black shades off his face, blinking like an awestruck mole.

'No kidding. They call it "sunlight",' Veronica said dryly. 'You'd be amazed at what goes on in the world outside your basement.'

She bit into her cheese sandwich and chewed it contentedly. One of these days, she'd be spooning caviar out of a silver dish in the back seat of a limo, but, for now, a homemade sandwich in Golden Gate Park tasted just fine. She'd found a secluded spot for their picnic, in the middle of a eucalyptus grove. She wanted Devin to soak up some fresh air and sunshine, but, after his months of subterranean seclusion, she didn't want his skin to burst into flame.

Devin lay on his back, arms shielding his face from the sun as he peered up through the branches of the trees. 'Look at all that blue! And the white! Amazing.'

'That's a sky, Devin. With big fluffy clouds in it.'

'It's, like, a miracle, isn't it?'

'Yeah, but don't tell anyone else. They'll think you're dropping acid.'

He rolled over on his side, propped himself up on his elbow and stared intently at Veronica. 'Vee. I have to tell you something.'

'OK. Go for it.'

Veronica braced herself. This was the part where Devin would tell her that he couldn't pay his rent this month (again), or that he needed bail money to help a buddy out of jail (again), or that he'd hooked up with a fan girl at a gaming convention and would be moving in with her (this hadn't happened yet, but Veronica lived in hope).

'Remember the other day, when I told you I love you?'

Veronica stopped chewing. She tried to swallow, but the bread wouldn't go down. 'I remember,' she said, almost choking on the sticky lump.

'I want you to know that I didn't say that because I was stoned, or because I was trying to get laid. I said it because I mean it. You're the most important thing in the world to me, Vee. I don't care if a hundred other guys chase you. I'll wait in line if I have to. I want you to succeed. I want you to have the biggest baddest whorehouse in the city – '

'Escort service,' Veronica interrupted, but the correction, for once, was gentle.

'Whatever it is, it doesn't matter,' Devin went on. 'I love you. I'm not just saying that any more; I'm *proving* it. I got a job. It's a start-up; I'll mostly be working for stock. But I'll be working. I'm giving up World of Warlocks. I killed off my characters last night. I even shut down the eBay business.'

'You did *what*?'

'I ended it. I'm off the game. I want to be with you. I'm planning on getting my own place in a couple of months, and I want you to move in with me.' Devin cleared his throat. He tore at the grass with his fingers, working at the blades as if he were trying to tear out the roots of his heart to give it to Veronica. 'I guess the most important question is, do you think you could love me, too?'

This time, it wasn't bread that held Veronica's words back. Her eyes stung. She was afraid that, if she opened her mouth, she'd either say something horribly sappy or start bawling. Neither option complemented her Cradle of Filth T-shirt.

She nodded.

Devin beamed. 'Does that mean yes?'

'In contemporary Western culture, yeah. It does.' Her eyes were moist at the corners. She wiped them with her forearm. Damn eucalyptus allergy.

Then Devin was on top of her, pushing her on to her back and lapping at Veronica's face like a puppy. The licking turned into a kiss, a meshing of tongues, a soft meeting of lips. Devin stroked the outer curve of her breast, then squeezed roughly, pinching her nipple the way she was always urging him to do, grinding against the mound between her thighs with his pubic bone. Veronica hadn't made out in the park since she was sixteen years old, hooking up with her best friend's cousin from Santa Rosa, who was pimply and had bad breath, but knew how to make a girl come with his knee.

Devin wasn't doing a bad job, himself, Veronica thought, arching up to meet him. Dry-humping was just as exciting as she remembered, only it was even better when you were in love.

Veronica loves Devin.

Someone ought to carve that into a tree, Veronica thought, because I might never think those words again.

She looked up into Devin's eyes as his rock-hard denim-covered cock hit her at just the right angle. Sweetly painful friction – the pleasure so keen she could hardly stand it – then those joyful pulsations, throbbing in time with her heart.

The Seabreeze Motel wasn't a beach hut in Bali, but there was an ocean, somewhere around here. No distant temple bells, but you could hear the occasional jubilant shout and smashing of glass from the bar next to the hotel. Instead of a salt wind, the currents from a ceiling fan above the bed stirred the sultry night air.

'I'm sorry,' Joel said, kissing the beads of sweat off the nape of Lauryn's neck. 'I should have known Miles would set us up in a dump like this.'

Lauryn smiled. 'Beats coming home to an empty apartment in Chicago. If you hadn't caught me on my way to the airport, I'd be opening up a can of chopped organ meat for my cat right now.'

'I'm amazed that I could punch your number into my phone; my hands were shaking like a junkie's.'

'I almost didn't answer my cell. I thought it was Veronica, hounding me about her business proposition. And I didn't want to tell her, for the tenth time, that I'm going to take her up on it. I'm diving into the sex industry.'

Lying on the lumpy motel mattress, Lauryn and Joel kept going over and over near-misses of the day, as if they couldn't quite believe that the story had ended the way it did. As the taxi driver had said, it all came down to kismet. If Lauryn's cab hadn't been stuck in traffic, if she hadn't stopped in the bathroom at the airport to insert her hazel contact lenses, if the line at the ticket counter hadn't been so endlessly long, she would have had a ticket to Chicago in her hand when Joel called.

Lauryn didn't want to dwell on alternate endings; spending the night in a tacky Florida motel with a sexy shiftless photographer suited her just fine.

'Don't think too much.' Joel grinned. 'That's one thing I learned in my line of work. You have to use your instincts and your reflexes to get what you want – like this.'

Lying on his back, he pulled Lauryn on top of him. Lauryn's skin was still sticky, her hair limp and matted, from the first time they'd made love that night, but she could feel herself revving up for round two. She straddled his hips and planted her palms on his chest. His body felt so warm under her hands, his pectorals meaty and firm, but she still couldn't believe he was here.

Joel had had his chance to bail, after she'd told him the true life story of Lauryn/Lauren Baxter on the long flight from San Francisco to Miami. Unabridged, unedited, nothing but the bald boring facts. She'd grown up in a shabby apartment with an overworked single mom and had never met her father. She'd spent her teenage years juggling two part-time jobs while trying to avoid her mother's leering, groping boyfriends. She'd gone to community college and a state university, had never even been to Connecticut, much less graduated from Yale. And she'd never been out of the States, except for that drunken college spree in Mexico.

Yet here Joel was, solid muscle and bone underneath her – and growing more solid by the second, as his cock stirred back to life. Lauryn shifted her weight, leaning forwards to let his erection nudge its way inside her, then slid backwards down its stiffening length. Female superior, her favourite position. She settled in for the ride, moving deliberately back and forth. Joel slid his hand into the nest of curls between her thighs, middle finger wedged against her clit. Lauryn's pussy was already primed from their first session; she hadn't come that time, but now she was ready for take-off.

Lauryn rubbed her mound against Joel's hand as she fucked him, rocking more purposefully as the tension began to build. His free hand skimmed her breasts, cupping and caressing them, tweaking their erect buds. She closed her eyes and dug in with her hips, hard as she could, faster and faster, until a skilful turn of his hand between her thighs sent her over the edge. Her climax triggered his; through the fog of pleasure, she heard Joel's groans mingle with her own, felt him thrusting hard and fast, sending her skywards one more time before they both coasted back to earth.

'Wow.' Lauryn leaned backwards, arching her spine. 'I still can't believe this is real.'

'It's real, sweetheart,' Joel said, catching his breath. 'You're in paradise.'

She looked up into the fan, its blades spinning lazily. A dark mass, the size of a deck of cards, suddenly sprouted legs and scuttled across the water-stained ceiling.

'Joel? What was *that*?'

Joel glanced up, his eyes following Lauryn's pointing finger. 'You've never met a Florida cockroach?'

'No.' Lauryn shuddered. 'Can't say that I have.'
'Baby, you haven't lived.' He laughed.
He reached over to the bedside table and switched off the lamp. In the darkness, Joel drew Lauryn down on to his chest and held her tight.
'No, I haven't,' she said. 'Not yet.'

Printed by Libri Plureos GmbH in Hamburg, Germany